WRITTEN IN

Dilys Xavier

IBSN: 0232-14562-2-1

Dilys Xavier has asserted her rights under the Copyright, Design and Patents Act, 1988, to be identified as the author of this work.

Published in 2015 by Underwing Press Ltd.

Printed and bound in Great Britain by Clays Ltd, St Ives plc.

ISBN: 978-1-911445-08-1

Published in 2016 by Endeavour Press Ltd.

Printed and bound in Great Britain by Clays Ltd, St Ives plc.

Endeavour Press is the UK's leading independent publisher.

We publish a wide range of genres including history, crime, romance, historical fiction and thrillers.

Every week, we give away free e-books.

For more information about our titles, go to our website:
www.endeavourpress.com/our-books/

Or sign up for our newsletter at:
www.endeavourpress.com

Also by Dilys Xavier published by Endeavour Press:

The Shadow of Langley Hall

Chance of a Lifetime

Roses For Katie

The Legacy of Hope House

I am indebted to my husband, Francis Xavier, for his contribution to this story. He also writes under the name of Donnie Hughes.

Table of Contents

Chapter One

Suzi Lysle Spencer swung her Honda into the curb outside the red brick office building and stared hard at the gold letters on the front window: 'Duncan and Associates, Solicitors'. She stepped out of the car, locked it, and took a few measured breaths to calm her racing pulse. Having composed herself, she walked into the cool interior of the solicitor's outer office and gave her name to the receptionist at the desk. The woman used the intercom to say that Suzi had arrived, and nodded as she switched off the instrument.

'Mr Duncan will see you now, Miss Spencer,' she said, getting to her feet. 'Please come this way.' She knocked on a door and pushed it open, at the same time giving Suzi's name to the heavily jowled man sitting behind an enormous oak desk. He struggled to his feet and held out a podgy hand.

'Miss Spencer, aah...' He stopped and gestured with a sweep of his arm at the vacant chair opposite his own. 'Do sit down.' He picked up a beige folder, and withdrew the contents. 'Now, you are here for...'

'About the estate of the late Bartholomew Armitage,' Suzi said, as if he needed reminding of the purpose of her visit. 'Uncle Bart died intestate.' She paused, and for some reason, suddenly felt intensely awkward.

The solicitor tapped on the document in front of him in silence, so she continued, hesitantly. 'As Uncle Bart's sole surviving descendant, I believe I have a claim to Caxton Manor estate. He was my late mother's uncle, but I always regarded him as my uncle too.'

'Yes, of course.' Mr Duncan peered at her from beneath his bushy eyebrows. 'However, Miss Spencer, I have to inform you that you may not be the only surviving descendant. You see, I have received another claim to the estate.'

Suzi felt the blood drain from her face as she stared at the solicitor in disbelief. 'But, Mother always told me...' She stopped as the man held up a restraining hand.

'Whatever your mother told you, your connection to Mr Bartholomew Armitage is through cousins way back, some generations ago, Miss Spencer, but you are not closely related to each other.' Mr Duncan gave a little cough before continuing. 'Mr Armitage did not leave a will, so we were obliged by law to place a notice in the national newspapers here and abroad, so that anyone who might have reason to make a claim to the estate, could do so.'

'Oh? I had no idea about this,' Suzi said, almost whispering.

Mr Duncan went on. 'It would appear that the deceased's very much younger brother emigrated to New Zealand, where his wife gave birth to a child. Shortly afterwards, they were both killed in a road accident, but the baby survived.'

'I see,' Suzi said, quietly. 'We were unaware that Uncle Bart had a younger brother, let alone that there was a child. None of us knew of this orphan.'

Mr Duncan stopped talking for a minute to assess whether Suzi was taking it all in. 'Yes, it was a disaster, but the child was subsequently adopted.' He looked over his glasses at her. 'Are you following me? Now then... it is that orphaned child who is making the claim, but with a different surname through adoption.' He stopped for a few moments to get his breath back. 'It's complicated, and of course, the person will have to prove eligibility to realise the claim. We will see what transpires.'

'Exactly who is making the claim?' Suzi asked, in a clipped voice, unwilling to allow the solicitor to side-track her.

'I'm not at liberty to divulge that information, Miss Spencer.'

'So what happens now?'

'I'll check the other person's credentials, then I'll know what to do.' Mr Duncan shuffled the papers into a neat pile, and slid them back into the folder. 'You must realise that this means you may have to share the inheritance if the other claim is proven. Then it will probably be necessary to sell Caxton Manor.'

'Sell Caxton Manor?' Suzi looked taken aback. 'I wouldn't want to sell that lovely old house—it's a piece of local history.' Suzi ignored his outstretched hand as he climbed ponderously to his feet. 'And you can tell this person that I'll challenge any other claim to the estate.' She glared at the solicitor as if he were responsible for the way things had turned out. Then, without giving him a chance to say more, she gave a curt, 'Good morning, Mr Duncan,' turned on her heel, and stalked out of the office.

*

Slipping in behind the wheel of her bright yellow Honda, she clenched the steering wheel tightly as she recalled the times she had visited the manor when Uncle Bart was alive; walked through its spacious rooms, traced her fingers over the fabric of the splendid old building and inhaled its essence. On the understanding that she was Uncle Bart's only surviving relative, she had been convinced that it was only a matter of time before the manor was hers. But now it seemed she might have to share it with a stranger.

'Damn and blast,' she muttered, and switched on the ignition. Without making a conscious decision of where to go, she crunched the car into gear and accelerated down the road in the direction of Caxton Manor. Just as she was about to swing into the entrance, a large, white van burst out through the driveway of the old house and headed straight towards her. In a desperate effort to avoid a collision, she swung the wheel hard to the left and braked. It was too little, too late. The van hit the rear end of her car, pushing it sideways across the road into a ditch. She was uninjured, but by the time she clambered out of the Honda, the van had disappeared.

Suzi stared at the crushed mudguard of her car as she punched in the emergency number on her mobile, and, while she waited, she noticed that the heavy chain and lock that normally secured the gates to the estate were lying on the ground across the road; she concluded that the place had been broken into.

Feeling quite shaken and with her heart pounding, she crunched her way up the gravel drive, quickly spotting a blue Ford nose down in a flower bed with the driver's door wide open. A shaft of sunlight peeping through the overhanging trees highlighted shattered window glass that littered the driveway.

'Oh my God,' she muttered, as she reached the slightly open front door of the house and peered inside. Her stomach knotted as she heard a groan, and with that, a man staggered towards her and reached out. Before she could react, he sank to the floor with blood trickling down his neck. Suzi called the emergency service again and quickly explained what had happened.

Within minutes the paramedics were there, sliding the man onto a stretcher, but as she watched the ambulance leave for the hospital, a police car pulled up and two officers climbed out. When she identified herself, and outlined her link to the manor, the policewoman offered to escort her around the property to see if anything was missing. After checking the ground floor, they made their way upstairs and searched each room, but it was only when they reached Uncle Bart's bedroom that Suzi realised what the thieves had taken.

'The four-poster's gone,' she cried, and spun around to face the policewoman. 'Please find the thieves before they get rid of it.'

'If we had a description of the man driving the van, or the registration number, it would help some,' the policewoman said, 'but I expect the van was stolen as well.'

When they returned to the ground floor the policeman turned to Suzi. 'Nothing else missing?' When she shook her head, he nodded. 'Just as well—they must have made off quickly when they were disturbed.'

'Can you describe the four-poster bed?' his colleague asked.

'Yes, it's carved in oak. I know exactly where there's a photo of it. I'll fetch it.' She returned in a few minutes clutching a sepia print. 'The family crest is carved on the bedhead. Please circulate a photocopy of this around the auction houses.'

While they were talking, someone collected Suzi's car for repair and pointed out that the sticker on the rear window of the victim's Ford Mondeo indicated it belonged to a car rental company, and suggested that it should be towed away as well. When all the formalities had been completed, the police officers put away their notebooks and turned to Suzi.

'You're minus your vehicle now, so can we give you a lift somewhere?'

'Oh, please. I need to get to town.'

*

It was late morning before a subdued Suzi arrived at the Stow Restaurant she operated with the aid of her business partner, Mark Brinstead. He stopped what he was doing immediately she walked into the kitchen.

'Are you okay? You've been ages with that solicitor.' He moved quickly to her side when she let out a sigh. 'Hey, you look shattered. What's up?'

'Everything.'

'What? Is there a problem with the solicitor?'

'Yes,' Suzi replied wearily, 'and a whole lot more.' She went on to relate what had happened, and sighed again. 'I suppose I should be grateful that they didn't clean the place out.'

'It seems the man you found at the house interrupted them.'

'No doubt about that.' She snapped her fingers and then reached for the phone. 'I should find out if he's okay. I'm also curious to know why he was there.'

Suzi listened as the police officer explained they had identified the man as Steve Pardoe, apparently visiting this country and sightseeing places of interest. Finding the gate open, he had made his way in and discovered the house was unsecured, when he was attacked.

'He's given us a reasonable description of the men and the registration number of the van,' the detective said. 'Of course, as we suspected the vehicle had been stolen, but we've got something to go on, so maybe we can trace them and hopefully locate the stolen property.' Then the line went dead.

5

'What did they say?' Mark inquired, as Suzi replaced the phone.

'Oh, the usual spin, that they'll do everything possible, and so on.'

'And what about the man you found in the house?'

'He's in hospital. It seems he had stopped to take a look at the manor at the precise time that burglars were looting the house. I'll look in to see how he is.'

'Until you get a temp vehicle you can borrow my car,' Mark said, digging his keys out of his pocket. 'I won't need it until I've finished here tonight.'

Suzi was soon at the hospital and quickly found the ward Steve was in. He seemed to be asleep, but as she approached his bed, he opened his eyes and smiled wanly.

'Hello,' she said, quietly. 'I'm Suzi Spencer. I found you in Caxton Manor this morning.' She watched his eyes focus on her face. 'How are you feeling?'

'Oh, you're the little angel who rescued me,' he said. 'Thank you for being there.' He gave a weak laugh. 'I'm okay, apart from a whopping headache.' Steve struggled to a sitting position. 'They said I have a hairline fracture, but apparently it's not serious. I should be out soon.' He grasped her hand. 'What did you say your name was?'

'Suzi Lysle Spencer.'

'Well, Suzi Lysle Spencer, thank you for coming along at the right time.' Steve grimaced as pushed himself further up in the bed. 'If you hadn't come by I could have lain there for hours, bleeding—they damaged my vehicle. Anyway, what made you turn in to look at an old empty house?'

Without answering, Suzi tried to imagine what he would look like without the white swathe around his head. He seemed all right to her; able to think clearly, and quickly gave the impression he was impatient at having to stay there. Suzi continued to study his face and felt surprised at the feelings he generated in her, for not only was there a natural concern for his well-being, there was an underlying attraction as well. When he peered expectantly at her, Suzi jerked her mind back to answer him.

She shrugged. 'Oh, it's special, historical,' she replied, hastily. 'But I wondered why you were there too.'

'Just having a sticky beak.'

'A what?'

'A nosey around. I'm looking at everything of interest in this old country of yours.' Steve laughed and went on to explain that he had driven past the property the day before and had noticed the beautiful wrought iron gates. 'They were secured with a huge chain and padlock. Next time I passed, the gates were open, and the chain was lying on the ground. That made me suspicious, so I thought I'd go into the grounds and look around, y'know, just investigate. I knew something was up the minute I saw the van with the motor still running.'

'You should have called the police.'

'I just didn't stop to think—you don't do you? Then everything happened so quickly,' Steve said. 'As I walked into the hall I saw two men hauling a bed down the staircase. Next thing, someone hit me on the head.' He gave a small laugh. 'Serves me right for not minding my own business.'

'But the police said you were able to describe the men.'

'Well, it was hazy, but I wrote the van's registration number in the dust on my car roof before I went into the house, so I got that right.'

'That was clever.' Suzi's remark brought a smile to his face. She gave him a quizzical look. 'I'm trying to place your accent, but I'm reluctant to ask if you're Australian.'

'I'm a Kiwi. Born and bred in New Zealand, the land of the long white cloud.'

'A Kiwi. I'll remember that.' Suzi reached out and touched his hand. 'Well, Steve, I must go now. I've a restaurant to run, you see.' She paused and then smiled warmly. 'You're welcome to be my guest for dinner at our place while you're in the area. Here's the phone number,' she said, handing him a business card.

'I'd like that, and thanks for taking the trouble to look in on me.' He laid his hand over hers. 'I'll give you a bell when I'm out of here.'

As she drove away, Suzi hummed a tune and wondered why she was so pleased at seeing a total stranger again. Try as she might, she could not get Steve Pardoe off her mind for the rest of the day.

*

As she slipped into bed that night, she realised meeting Steve Pardoe had taken the edge off the disappointment over her inheritance. It had given her something else to think on. Then the verse of scripture that Uncle Bart had loved to quote popped into her mind. He had always solemnly intoned the words whenever she had complained about life's injustices.

She wanted to find it right now, so she jumped out of bed and padded into the sitting room to fetch the old family bible. She quickly leafed through the pages until she found what she was looking for, in the book of Ecclesiastes. Old Uncle Bart's voice seemed to echo in her head as she read the timeless words aloud.

'"To everything there is a season, and a time for every purpose under the heaven."'

As she closed the book, Suzi recalled her maternal grandmother's admonition. The old lady was adamant there's a reason for everything. 'We must fulfil our destiny,' she would state emphatically. And then again, there was Jennie, with whom she had worked years ago; she always claimed that everything was preordained. 'Chance is a fine thing,' she would say, 'it brings whatever is written in the stars for us'. If that was so, had her spontaneous trip to Caxton Manor been predetermined? She smiled. Was she meant to meet Steve Pardoe? Surely they could have met under more favourable circumstances. But did it matter? A smile played around her lips as she fell asleep.

She woke early, recalling having stirred in the night, and now, in a state of half-sleep, a dream tugged at her memory. The more she tried to remember it, the more it eluded her. Then she opened her eyes and thought of Steve, feeling sure he had been part of the dream. Maybe she should file it under pleasant memories and not concern herself whether the chance meeting was written in the stars or not. But, as she drifted off to sleep again, she recalled that dreams sometimes come true.

Chapter Two

'Okay, okay,' Suzi muttered, as she rushed from the bathroom to snatch up the phone. A man's voice wafted down the line before she could speak.

'Hello, is that Suzi Lysle Spencer?'

'Yes,' she replied, unsure who was calling.

'It's Steve Pardoe.'

'Steve? Ah, I should have recognised your accent.' Suzi smiled as she recalled their conversation at the hospital. 'Where are you? More importantly, how are you? Have you made a full recovery?' The questions tripped off her tongue.

'I'm fine, thanks.' He laughed softly. 'Hey, you suggested dinner at your place, and I'd like to take you up on the offer.'

Suzi hesitated. She had intended the invitation to show an appreciation of his effort to stop the thieves at Caxton Manor, but that was before he had stirred up those feelings within her. She thought quickly. Proud as she was of Stow Restaurant, she was reluctant to spend an evening with him in a place where she would be unable to relax and enjoy his company. It would be better to go somewhere else, somewhere private, somewhere away from Mark's questioning gaze and the prying eyes of the staff.

'I can't stop to talk now,' Suzi said. 'Give me your number and I'll ring you back to make arrangements. You've caught me at a bad moment—I've just popped out of the shower.'

She made a note of Steve's number as he continued to talk. 'I'm leaving for Belgium pretty soon, and I'd hate to miss out on a free meal, so I'll look forward to hearing from you.'

She replaced the phone, delighted he had phoned, and thrilled at the thought of seeing him again. Ahead was a busy day at the restaurant, but her thoughts were on Steve Pardoe more than on anything else.

When she arrived, the first thing she did was to forewarn Mark that Narelle, the senior waitress, was to be hostess for the following evening. He gave her an inquisitive look. 'Sorry, Mark, but I'd forgotten an arrangement I'd made for tomorrow evening. I can't cancel it at this stage, and anyway it's important.'

Mark nodded, and curled the corner of his mouth, a habit that usually indicated he did not believe what he was hearing. However, he made no enquiry as to what it was about or whom she was meeting. 'How about we discuss the menu for that large dinner party we're having on Sunday?' he went on, drumming his fingers on the kitchen surface. 'I keep telling you we should think seriously about new premises. We've outgrown this place, so you'd better put your thinking cap on.'

'Too soon, and too risky. We should concentrate on weddings and parties and not try to compete with the big boys.' Suzi stabbed the table with her finger. 'You're too stubborn to listen to me.' She turned away, knowing he did not realise her objections were centred on the necessity to consolidate before expanding.

She gazed out onto the busy street, nodding as sensible thoughts ran through her mind. *After all, we've only been in business for just over a year. The restaurant is well patronised and provides the bulk of our income, but it's early days yet, and we must use common sense.*

'Trying to do things the way we are means setting up in a hall every time we book something big,' Mark complained, following her around and interrupting her thoughts. 'It's messy, it's time consuming. If our premises were bigger, we could have everything under one roof.'

Suzi took a deep breath and stared straight at him, wondering was he so thick he couldn't see the folly of what he was suggesting? She was about to lay into him with the whys and wherefores once again when the early arrival of a party for lunch brought their disagreement to an end. She knew it was inevitable that Mark would demand that they discuss it again. He seemed determined to have his way, even though he knew she could ill afford to take the risk, with her house fully mortgaged, plus the personal loan to finance her share of the business.

She recalled discussing that very same situation with her friend, Charlize, when Mark had first suggested their buying a restaurant. At the time, she and Charlize had met for coffee in the Old Forge Inn shortly after Suzi's mother, Annabelle, had died following a long illness. Her mother had never come to terms with her husband's abrupt departure for Scotland when he had been made redundant. She had never been very outgoing, but after he left she had become even more introvert and difficult to live with. Few people mourned her passing; even fewer attended her funeral.

Judith Brinstead, an old school friend and former neighbour, had driven down with her brother, Mark, to pay their respects and attend Annabelle's funeral. Although their paths had diverged over the years Suzi had kept in touch, and had visited Judith in Leicester for a weekend when Mark happened to be there. When he learned that Suzi was in charge of catering at The Lodge, he had laughingly suggested, 'How about we go into business together? I've finished my training as a chef, so we could open a restaurant. With our combined talents we should do very well.'

When Suzi returned home she forgot all about the idea, but, to her surprise, a few days later she received a letter from Mark, saying he had given considerable thought to the idea, and wanted to know if she would be seriously interested in his proposal.

As they had a second cup of coffee Charlize had asked how Suzi really felt about the idea.

'I don't know. Mark said he's tired of working for others and wants to branch out on his own. He says meeting me at the right time was fortuitous and could be a heaven sent opportunity for both of us.'

'But you don't?'

'A heaven sent opportunity? No, not really. According to Judith he's a brilliant chef, but not very good with the finer details of running a business. He needs someone to take care of that side of things.' Suzi sighed. 'I wouldn't consider it under normal conditions, but I may take him up on the idea. Anyway, I feel I can trust him.'

'And nothing else?'

'What do you mean?' Suzi looked quizzically at her friend, and then laughed. 'You mean a personal relationship? Oh, no way, not with Mark. First of all I don't think it's wise to become involved with a work colleague, and secondly, he doesn't appeal to me. No spark there.'

Charlize had warned her at the time that Mark might not see that as an obstacle, but Suzi had dismissed that out of hand. She and Mark had spent months looking for suitable premises and were just about to give up when the Stow Restaurant came on the market. Somewhat against her better judgement, Suzi had gone ahead with the plan, and had invited local media personnel to a complimentary meal before the restaurant was officially opened. It had paid off, and since then the restaurant had done well.

They had capitalised on the influx of tourists that thronged the picturesque village a few weeks later. By the time the winter set in they were nicely established and well patronised by the local community, catering for weddings and all kinds of parties.

When Uncle Bart died, she had turned immediately to Charlize for comfort. 'I was so fond of Uncle Bart,' she had said. 'I imagined he'd go on forever. Just shows, doesn't it?' From there on, with Uncle Bart having no other living relatives, Suzi did not envisage any problems about inheriting Caxton Manor. The thought of using Caxton Manor as a venue for what Mark was proposing had never occurred previously, but now she thought differently. It provided the means to expand the business without a huge financial outlay. Of course they would have to make some alterations to the place, but that did not concern her too much. Charlize had listened patiently while she talked, and had counselled her not to borrow any more money.

'You're up to your neck in debt now with the Stow, Suzi,' she reminded her at the time. 'If you took out a mortgage on the manor and things went pear shaped you'd risk losing everything.'

'There's always that possibility,' Suzi agreed, 'But you know me. I've a habit of making dreams come true.'

But Charlize had the last word. 'Just remember, dreams can turn into nightmares.'

And now, as Suzi dismissed her reverie, she said goodbye to the last customer and prepared to close the restaurant. It was only then that she remembered her promise to ring Steve Pardoe. She picked up the phone and dialled his hotel.

'Suzi.' Steve sounded pleased to hear her voice. 'I was hoping you wouldn't forget.'

'How could... ?'She stopped and gave a self-conscious laugh. It wouldn't do to let him know he had been on her mind for days. 'If you're free tomorrow night we could meet for dinner, but I would prefer somewhere more private than my own restaurant, if that's all right with you.'

'That's a good idea. Best not to give the natives too much to talk about, eh?'

'You've hit the nail on the head. Too many wagging tongues in this place.'

'And no doubt a jealous boyfriend lurking in the background?'

'I won't answer that. Shall I pick you up at the hotel?'

He agreed readily. 'Until seven tomorrow then.'

As she replaced the receiver, Suzi wondered why he had made the remark about a jealous boyfriend, but then her thoughts settled on Mark. Although he was a likeable person, and nothing was too much trouble for him, his attitude towards her had changed over the last few months. She had made it clear from the outset that she was happy to be a business partner, but he was becoming persistent in wanting it to be something more.

*

The following day her mind was mainly preoccupied with the thought of meeting Steve; the hours dragged. The luncheon bookings were light and there were few walk-in diners to take her mind off him. Suzi kept looking at her watch, willing time to pass, and, as soon as everything was set up for the evening meals, she closed the doors and hurried home. It was only as she pulled into her driveway that she began to have second thoughts about things. After all, she knew nothing about the man; he could be married, on the make, or… She stopped and raised her brows. 'What *is* the matter with me thinking like this?' she murmured, consoling herself that they were meant to spend this time together, because *chance is a fine thing*.

However, the niggling fears returned as she looked into her wardrobe. She wanted to look attractive, but without giving the impression she had taken too much trouble. Finally, she settled on a navy and white pinstripe suit, matching it with a long-sleeved blouse of pure white silk and a navy tie. She swept up her hair into a chignon, balancing the coiffure with a pair of exquisite blue lapis lazuli long-drop earrings. Then she smiled at her reflection, convinced she would have Steve's undivided attention.

He was waiting in the foyer when she arrived. Obviously impressed, his eyes ranged over her shapely figure and back to her hazel eyes before uttering a word. 'Suzi Lysle Spencer,' Steve muttered in a low pitched voice, 'you look stunning.'

Suzi coloured slightly as she murmured a thank you, but she was pleased with the compliment. 'My car's outside.' Then she glanced sideways at Steve as he slipped into the car beside her, immaculately dressed in dove-grey trousers and a pale grey shirt with a tastefully patterned tie.

'We'll go to the Old Forge Inn,' Suzi said, letting out the clutch. 'It's my favourite place.' She glanced at him again. 'Oh, by the way most people call me Suzi.'

'I'll bear it in mind. But I like the sound of your full name. I find it both attractive and intriguing.' He held up his hands as if fending off a question. 'Don't ask me why.'

Within a very short while she nosed the car into a parking space outside the quaint little sixteenth century coaching house situated just off the busy road that ran through the tiny hamlet of Penhow. The manager greeted Suzi by name as they entered the beamed dining room, and ushered them to a small intimate bar. As Steve read the menu, Suzi silently studied his face. He had an air of confidence about him as if he were accustomed to making decisions and getting things done. He caught her eye in the bar mirror and raised his glass.

'To an enjoyable evening.' She returned the toast, then Steve gestured to the tiny windows that caught the last rays of the setting sun. 'Now tell me all about this interesting little place. I guess it has quite a history.'

Suzi had just finished answering his questions when the manager informed them that their dinner was ready. When the waiter asked if they would like a bottle of wine with the meal, Suzi deferred to Steve. He chose a merlot from a Hunter Valley vineyard. There was little conversation while they ate, and, as the waitress cleared away the dessert plates, she asked if they would like their coffee and liqueurs served beside the fire.

'That would be lovely,' Suzi said, and they made their way to the fireside. After an hour or more of conversation, they were reluctant to tear themselves away from the cosy warmth and bring the evening to an end, but when a member of the staff pointedly asked them if they wanted more coffee, Suzi knew it was time to leave.

When they reached his hotel, Steve grasped her hand and raised it to his lips. 'It's been a delightful evening, Suzi Lysle Spencer,' he said, softly. 'You are a not only a very beautiful woman, but a charming companion, as well.'

'Thank you. I've enjoyed your company, too, Steve.'

'It's a pity I won't see you again before I leave.'

'Yes,' she agreed, and then suddenly blurted out. 'If you're free tomorrow I can show you some of the local sights. A mini tour of the area?'

'I'd like that,' he said, eagerly. 'What time will you call?'

They arranged a suitable time, and Steve said goodnight again. Then just as he was about to get out of the car he leant across and gently brushed his lips against her cheek. She smiled happily as she drove away.

Yes, she thought, I've got every reason to smile.

*

When Suzi edged her car into the kerb the following morning, Steve jumped in beside her and looked at her with a twinkle in his eyes. 'Suzi Lysle Spencer, you look more gorgeous every time we meet.'

'Enough of your blarney,' Suzi laughed, but the compliment delighted her. 'You look most presentable yourself.'

'I try to please.' He grinned broadly. 'So where are we going?'

'The Wye Valley. It's really picturesque at this time of the year. We'll start there, have a look at Tintern Abbey and then head towards Trellech.'

Suzi groaned inwardly as she saw two tourist buses disgorging their passengers in front of the famous abbey ruins. Steve seemed unconcerned about the seething crowd of people ahead of him, but it was obvious he was not keenly interested in the ruins. He bought a few postcards to send to his family in Auckland and then they made their way back to the car. When they reached the top of the hill, he asked her to stop so that he could take a few photographs.

'I'll show you a better spot,' she said, swinging the car down a narrow lane. She drove head on towards a closed gate and then backed up a narrower track to a clearing next to a stile. The vista was breathtaking; a small herd of cattle grazed the undulating land, and in the distance a plume of smoke issued lazily from the chimney of a small cottage nestling in a green basin beneath a grove of trees. It was like a picture postcard.

'I want a shot of this,' Steve said, clicking the shutter several times. 'What happens when you meet someone coming the other way?'

'You stop, and search for a space to pass,' Suzi said, offhandedly. 'It's easy when you know the roads. I grew up driving around these lanes, so it's second nature to me.' Minutes later she drew into the forecourt of the local pub.

'What's up there?' Steve asked.

'I'll show you,' she said, taking his hand as they walked along a pleasant tree-lined path leading to a well-kept cemetery of an ancient church. There, a raised stone dais topped by a large Celtic cross stood proud. Unable to enter the locked church, they made their way towards a stile set in the boundary fence. Beyond it lay the site of an early Norman fort.

Suzi pointed to a huge circular mound. 'It's all that remains of the fort. It was standard practice for William the Conquer to erect wooden structures. He placed them in key positions, intending to assert his authority over the rebellious local Celtic tribes.'

'You certainly know your Welsh history,' Steve said, as they strolled leisurely back to the little pub. 'Shall we have a coffee inside?' In a matter of minutes, he placed a coffee before her on the table, and smiled. 'You're a delight to be with. I'm really enjoying our time together.'

'You said that last night.'

'Did I? I must be paying you too many compliments.' He laughed softly. 'But seriously, I appreciate your kindness. I'd never have found these places on my own.'

'My pleasure.' Suzi murmured as she glanced at her watch and made a face. 'I must get back to open up for lunch, so I'm afraid we have to go now.' When they reached the restaurant Suzi introduced him to Mark. As the first guests arrived she sat Steve at a table looking out on the square, while she greeted the customers one by one. It wasn't until after the last person had left that she brought two chicken salads to the table and sat down beside Steve. By the time they had finished the meal, Mark and the waitress had gone and they were alone.

'We re-open later for the evening,' she explained. 'And now, I suppose I'd better take you back to the hotel.' Suzi fiddled with her napkin, then laid a hand on his arm. 'I'm reluctant to let you spend the afternoon propping up a bar, so why don't I drive you past a few Welsh castles? There won't be enough time to go around them, but at least you'll have seen them?'

'That sounds great, if you can fit it in.'

When she finally dropped him off at the hotel later in the day, Suzi had barely enough time to change for the evening. As she combed her hair, she thought about their time together, and wondered what would have happened if he had decided to stay in Britain for the remainder of his visit; it would have been pleasant to have spent more time with him.

She smiled as she recalled how their chance meeting at Caxton Hall had seemed preordained. For her, the meeting had been an exciting interlude, and now she was wondering what might have happened if he didn't have to return to New Zealand. She sighed softly at her wishful thinking.

She had just finished breakfast the next morning when Steve rang. 'I couldn't resist the chance to thank you again for the past few days.' His voice sounded a trifle husky. 'I enjoyed your company more than I can say—you made my stay so enjoyable. I'd like to have spent more time with you, but...'

'I've enjoyed it too, Steve,' Suzi replied, with a catch in her throat. It was hard to think she wouldn't see him again, but she resisted the temptation to ask for his address in Auckland. She breathed in deeply to control her emotions. 'Take care, and have a pleasant trip home when the time comes,' she said, as brightly as she could manage, considering the sinking feeling in the pit of her stomach.

Chapter Three

It was only as he took his seat on the plane for Amsterdam that Steve realised he might still have the opportunity to see Suzi again before he returned to New Zealand. Because of the incident at Caxton Manor he had been unable to keep his appointment with the solicitor to discuss what had bought him to the country in the first place. He had phoned from the hospital to apologise and make another appointment, but the receptionist said that Mr Duncan was unwell and would be unavailable for the rest of the week.

Steve had then decided to continue on to Europe and return to see the man at a later date. It had been his intention to fly home from Frankfurt after visiting his friend in the Netherlands, but now he had return to Britain for another appointment with Duncan. As he thought about the situation, he wondered why Suzi had been interested in the house. It was obvious she had a love of ruins and other old buildings in the area but, in his opinion, there was nothing very special about Caxton Manor.

Although she had been very friendly and charming, she had not divulged much about her personal life, so he knew no more than what he had gleaned during their time together. He felt sure that if he decided to spend more time in the UK their relationship might deepen. But did he want that? Moreover, did she?

After all he had commitments at home to be considered, but even so, Suzi had made quite an impression on him and captured his thoughts rather more than was comfortable. As he quietly mused over the involvement, he admitted to being strongly attracted to her; he felt as if something was pulling him towards her against his better judgement. His thoughts were interrupted by the stewardess announcing they were about to land.

Steve searched the sea of faces in the main reception area and quickly spotted Pieter Boersma. The Dutchman clapped him on the back as they shook hands.

'Hello, Steve, it's good to see you again. Did you have a good trip?'

The two men had been friends for a number of years, but although Pieter had adjusted easily to the New Zealand way of life, he had always retained a love of his native country. When his father hinted he might retire and sell his thriving antique business in Holland, Pieter decided to return home and step into the breach. And now, two years later, he was convinced it had been the right decision.

'I still miss some of the things about New Zealand,' he confided to Steve, as they drove towards a suburb of Amsterdam. 'But I'm pleased I came back home.'

'And now you're happily married?'

'Oh, yes. Gina's a wonderful wife. She has a good eye for a bargain, too.' Pieter chuckled. 'If I under-price an item, or pay too much for one, she soon lets me know.' He paused before climbing out of the car and turned to Steve. 'We're going to an auction this afternoon to see what's on offer. Maybe you'd like to come along?'

Pieter introduced Steve to his wife, who immediately made their guest feel completely at home. As soon as their lunch was over, Gina insisted the two men should go to the auction together so that they could enjoy a man-to-man afternoon, but asked her husband to be conservative about his choice of purchases.

*

As Pieter inspected a collection of fine bone chinaware, Steve wandered around and eventually found himself in the furniture section. An ornate four-poster bed caught his attention and reminded him of the burglary at Caxton Hall. The police had shown him a photocopy of the old sepia photo of the bed and now, as he looked closely at the headpiece, the ornate carving convinced him this was the one that had been stolen.

He hurried to search for his friend and found him conversing with another dealer, and when he realised their conversation could continue for some time, he interrupted them. 'Pieter, please excuse me for butting in, but I think I've found something that was stolen from a property in Wales. Can you have a word with someone in authority here about it?'

'You'd better show me first.' Pieter excused himself and followed Steve into the furniture section.

'I saw a photo of it,' Steven said, pointing out the various identifying marks on the piece of furniture. 'I'm positive this is the same bed.'

The two men returned to the main section of the building and notified the auctioneer's secretary, who phoned the police immediately. The detectives were reluctant to accept Steve's word, because he had not actually seen the bed, but when Pieter invoked the name of a cousin who was in charge of the CID section in Leeuwarden they took notice. Eventually, a fax arrived from the Welsh constabulary confirming the break-in and attaching a picture of the bed.

By the time they left the police station, Steve felt exhausted. He gestured to a nearby bar. 'Come on, I'll buy you a drink.' They were waiting to be served when Steve gave a deep sigh. 'What a waste of an afternoon.' Then he brightened up. 'I must ring Suzi and tell her the bed's been located.'

'Who's Suzi? Tell her what?'

'Just someone I met in the UK She's got something to do with...' He stopped, and gazed at his friend almost absentmindedly. 'Wait a minute, she never did tell me how she knew so much about Caxton Manor.'

'Isn't that the place you hope to inherit?'

'Yes it is.'

'So where does this Suzi woman fit into the picture?'

Over the next fifteen minutes Steve related the events preceding the assault and his consequent conversation with Suzi in hospital. He went on to tell his friend about their time together and how much he had enjoyed her company.

'I never gave much thought as to how she knew about the bed, or how she obtained the photograph of it,' he concluded. 'She must have known where that photo was, but if she knew the previous owner of the place, that could explain it.' He shrugged and gazed thoughtfully ahead.

'This Suzi, she turned you on?'

Pieter's remark jolted him. 'Yes, she most certainly did.' He gave a small laugh. 'And I think she fancied me, but, you know the old saying, ships that pass…' He left the sentence unfinished.

'And how's things with Kirsty?' Pieter asked, deliberately changing the subject. 'It's obvious you haven't tied the knot yet?'

'No, we make plans, and then change our minds.' He shrugged his shoulders. 'I always manage to find an excuse at the last moment.'

'Is there someone else?'

Steve shrugged. 'No, not really.' He laughed. 'It's just that it's an obligation thing with Kirsty, if you know what I mean. I'm not seeing anyone else or playing around… it's…' He stopped again and sighed. 'Well, it's an odd arrangement, but I have to abide by it.'

'But what if this Suzi woman lived in New Zealand?'

'Well, that might be a different matter, but she doesn't, so that's that.'

'And you're not concerned if Kirsty finds out about it?' Pieter asked, quietly.

'I hope she doesn't, but it doesn't matter really—got nothing to hide, done nothing wrong.'

When they returned to the house, Pieter pointed to the phone. 'Feel free to use it.'

After dinner that evening Steve phoned Suzi's number, but all he got was an answering machine. Rather than try again later he left a message to say the police had taken possession of the stolen bed and would hold it until it could be returned to the UK. He sat nursing the phone in one hand as he thought about the break-in at Caxton Manor. Strangely enough he had not been over concerned about it at the time and yet he should have been, because it was likely that he could soon inherit the place. It was now too late in the day to check with Duncan's office about his rescheduled appointment.

When he returned to the sitting room, Pieter looked up. 'Everything okay?'

Steve gave a little laugh. 'She wasn't there so I left a message.'

The next few days were taken up in sightseeing. The Boersmas went out of their way to show him all the famous buildings within a fifty-mile radius, and when he finally said goodbye he felt drained; it had been too much to assimilate in such a short time.

Steve booked a seat on an early morning flight to London and then rang Suzi's number. He waited impatiently for her to pick up, but it continued to ring until the answer machine clicked in. Rather than leave a message he hung up. Maybe it wasn't a good idea anyway because she had obviously not expected to see him again. The remark he made to Pieter about ships that pass in the night popped into his head and with that, he made up his mind to see the solicitor and then catch the first available plane back home.

By the time Steve landed at Heathrow Airport, he had decided to try Suzi's number one more time. As he walked towards the phone, for some reason he reminded himself that he was still a free man, and a long way from Auckland. The coins dropped as the connection was made.

*

It continually surprised Suzi how often Steve's name popped into her mind. She still felt peeved she had been out when he phoned to say he had located the stolen bed. She wished he had phoned again; better still, she wished he'd turn up on her doorstep again just one more time. She dropped into her favourite chair, her thoughts dwelling heavily on him. It annoyed her; it wasn't like her to go gaga so quickly over a stranger, however handsome. Besides, she reminded herself, what if he has a wife tucked away in Auckland? But maybe... maybe what? She jumped out of the chair, determined to push all thoughts of him out of her mind. She had taken a few hours off from work, so, as a distraction from her current thoughts, she gave the house a good clean, then hurried off to open up the restaurant for lunch. She stepped inside just in time to grab the shrilling phone.

'Suzi Lysle Spencer?'

'Steve? Oh—Steve Pardoe,' she cried, unable to conceal her excitement. 'It's great to hear your voice again. Where are you?'

'Heathrow Airport.'

'En route to New Zealand?'

'Not yet, I'm just back from Holland. I have to see to unfinished business here before I go back.' He hesitated momentarily. 'I was kind of hoping we might touch base again before I fly home.'

'That would be lovely. I'll look forward to seeing you.'

'Okay, I'll book a room where I stayed last time.'

Suzi hesitated and then blurted out. 'No need for that—stay with me. There's plenty of room here and you're most welcome.' She giggled. 'And, as the Irish say, oceans of hot water.'

'Okay, thanks, I'll take you up on that offer.'

'Come to the restaurant and I'll give you a house key.'

It was only as she replaced the receiver that Suzi realised the implications of her invitation, but it was too late now, the man was on his way. Then she recalled Charlize's words: 'What if there's a wife tucked away in New Zealand?'

'Don't care,' she muttered. 'It's all innocent, and I'll probably never see him again, so I'll enjoy our time together while I can.' She escorted the last guest to the door just as Steve drew up to the kerb outside.

'Hi there,' she breathed, huskily. As he kissed her cheek, she sensed he was resisting an impulse to take her in his arms, so in an effort to defuse an almost electric situation, she pulled him into the restaurant and led him to a seat by the window.

'What would you like to drink?'

'Coffee will be fine. Will you join me?'

'I'll be with you in a few minutes.' The young waitress who brought his coffee to the table gave him a long look before moving away to continue resetting the tables. Suzi bustled over a few minutes later and

25

sat down beside him. 'Now, tell me about your trip. I suppose you did all the touristy things, canal trips, cycling, and so on?'

'All that, and more,' Steve said, relating some of his experiences.

'Hey, I forgot to thank you for finding the bed and phoning to tell me. That was a stroke of luck. Sorry I wasn't here to take your call.'

At her insistence Steve filled her in on all the details and was about to ask her where she had found the photo of the four-poster, and how she knew so much about Caxton Manor, when the telephone rang. Suzi answered it and, by the time she put the phone down, the waitress had finished setting up the tables for the evening and left.

Suzi joined Steve again. 'I've a few jobs to do before going home, so rather than sit and wait for me here, take my front door key, let yourself into my house and make yourself comfortable. It's barely a mile from here.' She drew a sketch to help him find it, and promised to join him as soon as she could.

*

An hour later she knocked on the door. Steve opened it and immediately gathered her into his arms. Their lips met and held as she pressed herself into his firm body. Then he suddenly but gently eased out of the embrace. She felt unwilling to end this intimacy, but sensed there was something holding him back. Her eyes searched his face in an endeavour to understand his actions. 'What is it, Steve?'

'Nothing. No, that's not true.' He sighed. 'I'd be the first to admit I want make love to you, but…'

'But?'

'But only when the time is right… for us both.'

Suzi felt a thrill of delight. She had not expected Steve to be so attuned to her thoughts and feelings, but this meant something, moreover, she was pleased he was sensitive about it. Rather than reveal the emotions she had battled with from the moment she had walked into the house, she nodded, and silently led him by the hand to the kitchen. 'A coffee will perk us up.'

As they drank, Suzi explained how busy she was going to be over the next few days. 'I'm sorry that means I won't be able to spend as much time with you as I'd like.'

He shrugged. 'Can't be helped, you didn't know I was coming.'

She watched him closely as she spoke; saw a shadow of disappointment cross his brow as she outlined her busy workload, but he had not allowed it to etch itself into his face. So he's not possessive, she thought, and that's good.

'The good news is I've arranged for someone to take care of things tonight so we can have some time together.'

'Good, shall we go out to dinner, or would you like an exhibition of my culinary expertise? I picked up a couple of steaks on the way here, and found the makings of a salad in your fridge.'

'And dessert?'

'I'll surprise you.'

'That sounds fine.'

The steaks were done to perfection and the salad was prettily arranged. A touch of class was added to the meal by a bottle of New Zealand wine Steve had also bought. They finished the meal and sat back for a couple of minutes, but when Suzi made a move to clear the table he stopped her.

'There's more yet.' A few minutes later he placed a covered dish on the table and then whisked the lid off with a flourish. 'I hope it's up to your standard.'

'Crêpes Suzette!' She gave a cry of delight. 'Hey, you're a super cook.'

After they had cleared away the remains of their dinner Suzi produced a bottle of Armagnac that she kept for special occasions and poured them both a generous portion.

As they sipped the liqueur, Steve began to relate some of his past. 'I was an orphan—I never knew my parents. Vince Pardoe and his wife, a wonderful couple, adopted me and raised me as their own.' He went on to explain that he had a degree in engineering and was involved in the family business. 'You see, my adoptive father had been the manager of an American agency specialising in the manufacture of pumping equipment, and when the company decided to concentrate their efforts on larger projects, Dad was offered the existing business at a knock down price. He went for it, and set up his own company and branched out into other areas as well.' He smiled broadly as he thought about it. 'We've been very successful, and now we're looking for new markets.'

'So, you're not just a good-looking guy who can cook, but a prosperous businessman as well?' Suzi leant over and brushed her lips against his cheek. 'Thank you for sharing with me.'

Steve stood up and stretched. 'It's been a long day.'

'Yes, and a lovely evening.' She gently pushed him towards the spare room. 'Sleep well.'

*

Suzi had not surfaced the following morning by the time Steve set out to keep his rescheduled appointment. The receptionist was most apologetic when she informed him that the principal he was to have seen had been called away on an urgent matter.

'It's unlikely he'll be back today, and he's attending a board meeting on Monday,' she explained. Rather than vent his frustration on the harried woman he asked her to make sure he could see the man on Tuesday.

'That's my last chance to see him,' Steve said. 'I fly home the day after.' He spent the remainder of the day driving around the countryside, and once or twice considered calling into the Stow Restaurant, but resisted in case it embarrassed Suzi. Having seen all he wanted for one day, Steve went back to the house and relaxed in the lounge.

He was half asleep when Suzi finally arrived home at the end of the day. She looked exhausted. Steve made coffee, but when she began to drift off to sleep even while he was talking to her, he gently pulled her to her feet. 'Bed for you, Suzi. You're done in.'

Suzi slept late and staggered into the kitchen rubbing her eyes. After a leisurely brunch, they climbed into her car and headed for the Gower Peninsular, spending the afternoon poking along the coast. They stopped for a drink at a friendly little pub on the way home, and the appetizing aroma wafting from the kitchen reminded them that they hadn't eaten much all day so they ordered a meal.

Neither of them said much as they drove home, and Suzi was acutely aware that these had been their last few days together. Soon, Steve would walk out of her life and she would never see him again. He had made it abundantly clear how deeply he was attracted to her, and she felt that under normal circumstances he would have taken advantage of the situation. After all, she had invited him into her home, and their close proximity had been conducive to further intimacy, but he had resisted any temptation he might have had.

'You okay?' His question cut across her thoughts. 'You're rather quiet.'

'Yes, I'm all right.' But as she closed the front door behind them she slipped easily into his arms. 'Hold me close, Steve.' They remained locked together in silence for a few minutes then Suzi broke free. 'I'll get us a drink.' While they sipped their liqueur, she sat as close to him as she could on the sofa, trying not to allow her emotions get the upper hand, but eventually she climbed to her feet. 'You have to be up early tomorrow, so I should let you go to bed now.'

Steve showered and made his way into the bedroom, and was about to slide under the duvet when he heard a noise by the door. He looked up, surprised to see Suzi standing there, a beam of light from the hall shining through her wispy wrap, outlining every curve of her shapely legs, the soft roundness of her hips and the pouting breasts. All were silhouetted in sharp contrast to the dim surroundings of the room.

'I hope you've been comfortable here,' she said, in a voice barely above a whisper. 'If there's anything you...' She stopped and looked at him, with a beseeching smile on her lips. In a flash, she knew that Steve was unable to resist his desire for her any longer. He moved quickly across the room and gathered her into his arms. Then, all restraint gone, she led him to her own room and pulled him down onto her bed, with a small cry of delight as their lips met.

Steve groaned softly. She sensed his arousal, and realised his control was holding him in check, but knew now that his longing for her had completely enveloped him.

'It's all right, Steve. I want you,' she said, lifting his head to look into his eyes. As if they had been lovers for years, time seemed to stand still as they moved together. Sated and spent, they clung to each other long after, and then love's slumber claimed them. As the first rays of the false dawn lit up the sky, they disentangled. Steve raised himself up on his elbow to look at her.

'You have touched something deep inside me, Suzi Lysle Spencer,' he said, softly, tracing his finger gently across her brow.

'Same for me,' she murmured. 'I wish you were staying. I wish you never had to…' When he remained silent, she sat up and continued. 'Steve, I feel there's someone special in your life, someone waiting for you back in New Zealand, someone to whom you are committed.' When he began to speak, Suzi placed a finger against his lips. 'I'd like to be able to say I don't care, but I do.'

'It's a complicated situation and I don't know how to explain it to you, Suzi.'

'Then don't try. And don't make any promises you can't keep.' A soft smile lit up her face. 'I was determined to share that wonderful night of love with you, regardless of the outcome. It was even better than ever I could have imagined.' She gazed deep into his eyes. 'Now, I'll be able to cherish the memory of it when you're no longer here.' Steve was about to say something, but Suzi stopped him again. 'Hold me again, kiss me again, and love me one last time.'

There seemed little to say afterwards, and then they both showered and dressed in comparative silence. Steve packed his bags while Suzi prepared breakfast. An air of disbelief hung over them as they ate, as if neither was willing to accept the depth of feeling they had for each other. As Suzi watched Steve battle with his feelings, she had a brief moment of remorse. Maybe she should have resisted the temptation to seduce him. Then she pushed the thought from her mind, because she knew that they would both look back on their night of love with a great deal of joy. She had never felt so sure about anyone or anything in her life before. She had been able to open her heart to him without any reservation, and nothing could mar that experience; it would stay with her for ever.

Steve held her close for a long time as they said their farewells, and then he kissed her gently before whispering goodbye. He hesitated as he climbed into the car, then ran back up the steps to where she stood watching him. He tugged at a dress ring he wore on his little finger and pressed it into her hand. 'A token,' he said, and then kissed her cheek again.

Tears welled up as he drove away and she sniffed noisily. Clutching the token, she made her way indoors and sat down in an easy chair to savour the memory of their precious hours together. She placed the ring on one of her fingers, but then decided to put it away for a while. Wanting to take her mind off their parting, she stripped the two beds, tidied up the rooms, then cleaned away the breakfast things and made more coffee. She was idly toying with the spoon half an hour later, and still mulling over the events of the past few days, when the ringing telephone pulled her out of her daydreams. It was Charlize.

Chapter Four

The receptionist looked up as Steve approached her desk and for a moment he was afraid that she was about to tell him there was another problem. Then she smiled and reached for the intercom machine.

'Mr Pardoe is here, Mr Duncan.' She listened to the garbled reply and then stood up. 'Please come this way.'

With some difficulty, the paunchy solicitor struggled to his feet and extended his hand when Steve entered the room.

'Please have a seat, Mr Pardoe.' He gestured at a chair. 'Now, let me see. Ah, it's about Caxton Manor.' He peered at Steve from beneath bushy eyebrows. 'You replied to our advertisement.'

Steve looked at him in disbelief. They had been corresponding for weeks; he had phoned from New Zealand to say he was coming to the UK specifically to address the matter, and now he was being treated as if he had just walked in off the street. He cleared his throat noisily and glared at the older man.

'I sent you photocopies of my birth certificate along with those of my deceased parents and their marriage certificate, which you have acknowledged.' He paused in an effort to keep his voice under control. 'The purpose of this visit was to look at the property, and to show you the original documents in order to verify them and set the wheels in motion.'

'Yes, of course, Mr Pardoe.'

'I believe that I am the only relative of the late Bartholomew Armitage. My adoptive parents assure me that he never had any children, legitimate or otherwise and that, as far as they knew, there are no other living relatives.' He paused again. 'It would appear that I am the sole beneficiary.'

Mr Duncan looked over the top of his steepled fingers. 'Yes, but your adoptive parents are probably not fully conversant with the situation, and evidently unaware that he had another relative from way back.'

'What are you saying, sir?'

'I am saying that there is another claimant to the estate.'

'Another claimant?'

'Yes, indeed, and it would appear the claim is as valid as your own.'

Steve stared him as if he couldn't believe what the man was saying.

'And you have kept me waiting for three weeks, and dragged me halfway around the world to tell me this?' When the solicitor remained silent, he continued in an abrasive tone of voice. 'So who is this other person?'

'I'm sorry, Mr Pardoe, but I am unable to divulge the identity of the other claimant. All I am prepared to say is that this person resides in this country. Now, let me get on with the matter, Mr Pardoe. I have another client waiting.' The solicitor sighed and looked annoyed as Steve continued to glare at him. He placed his pen on the desk, clasped his hands together, and leaned back in his chair as he returned Steve's glare. 'Mr Pardoe… please. I really must ask you to stop pressing me to divulge the identity of the other claimant. You will discover who it is all in good time, and not before.' His tone of voice had sharpened now. 'I would remind you that it is your claim to the estate that we are discussing, and no one else's. So please, let us proceed.'

It was as though Steve had not heard the man. 'Does this other person have a greater claim than I do?'

The solicitor totally ignored the question. 'Now then, Mr Pardoe, this is as far as we go today. I have all your documents and the name of your solicitors in Auckland, and I shall notify them immediately when the matter is resolved.'

Steve climbed to his feet and walked out of the office without saying another word. He shook his head in disbelief as he climbed into the hire car and headed for the M4. As he sped up the motorway, a thousand thoughts chased through his mind, each one seeming more ridiculous than the last. He was almost tempted to turn back, to drive to Suzi's and confide in her. He took a deep breath, deciding to leave things as they were for the moment, accepting that he had to think things through. He was smarting with indignation as his thoughts surfaced; had he known someone else was involved he'd never have bothered to come all this way. *Why should I?* he thought. *I'm content with my life; I enjoy my work, and I get on famously with my adoptive parents.* As far as he was concerned, what he had already was far more important than half an old building of dubious worth. He shrugged impatiently and concentrated on the road.

It was only after he had checked the car in at the airport that he remembered how his adopted granny would always counsel him that everything happened for a reason. Her words echoed in his brain. 'Your destiny is written, Stevie… nothing happens by chance.'

*

The long flight back to New Zealand enabled Steve to put things in perspective. His bitter remark to the solicitor about wasting his time had been uncalled for really, but it had felt good to get if off his chest. However, the trip had not been without some compensation. It had been good to meet up with Pieter Boersma once again, and he had enjoyed his visit to Wales. And of course there was Suzi Lysle Spencer. He smiled as he recalled their time together. She had touched a part of his heart that no other woman had ever reached before, and, although he did not like using that overrated word, love, it was appropriate. It was the only expression that truly described his feelings for her.

Of course it was natural to dwell on the pleasurable side of their time together. However, his conscience had been pricked when she told him of her intuitive feelings the morning after they had slept together. He recalled her words as they nestled in each other's arms: 'I feel that there is someone else in your life, someone to whom you are committed in one way or another.'

Steve knew he should have told her about Kirsty; should have explained their unusual relationship and the obligations it imposed on him. He could have explained that he felt trapped by the circumstances surrounding their union. However, he had not wanted to spoil the closeness they had just experienced in each other's arms. And telling her would have achieved nothing, anyway.

His mind slipped back to the day his mother told him they were going to foster a girl. A playmate for you, she had said at the time. He recalled how the gap in their ages had been a barrier as they grew up, but when he returned home after university, that had changed; he found the gawky, adolescent girl had become an attractive young woman.

Steve had accompanied her to a party one night where both of them had too much to drink. When he woke up the next morning, Kirsty was by his side. Still slightly hung-over and only half awake, he had turned over in bed and pulled her into his arms. Almost immediately she had grasped his manhood and coaxed it to full erection. His eyes had snapped open and he realised with a shock who it was as she pushed him onto his back and straddled his thighs. But by then it was too late.

He had never been able to analyse his feelings at that time. The sight of her naked body astride him seemed to limit his ability to think clearly. He should have stopped it right then, but her gentle rhythm was so hypnotic that he could only gaze up into her deep brown eyes and sigh contentedly. As they lay together afterwards, Steve realised that he had wanted to bed Kirsty ever since he had accidentally surprised her one morning when stepped naked out of the shower, shortly after he returned home from university. They had laughed about it at the time, but it had ignited a slow-burning fuse of desire.

Unable to resist the allure of her nubile body, Steve sneaked into her room the next night, and the night after, following that first time. Because they were not related in any way neither felt there was any stigma attached to their actions. But their nightly dalliances had not gone unnoticed. Vince had called them into his study one evening and expressed his displeasure in no uncertain terms.

'I'm having difficulty to know how to begin,' he said, looking from one to the other. 'Your mother and I are not too old to know what's going on when we hear the noise that you two are making in the middle of the night.' He had paused to let his words sink in. 'I turned a blind eye to it the first few times because I felt sure it was just a flash in the pan. But it's become a regular occurrence, hasn't it?'

When neither of them answered he rounded on Steve. 'You do realise your mother is responsible for Kirsty, don't you? And that it's our responsibility to see that she comes to no harm.' He glowered as they both listened in silence. 'I expected better from you, Steve. You should know better.'

'We didn't…' Kirsty's voice broke as tears filled her eyes.

Vince looked at her with a mixture of censure and pity and then turned to Steve. 'Right, this is the score. If you want to continue to sleep together on a permanent basis, you'd both better think about the consequences.' He had held up a hand to stop Kirsty's protest. 'I don't think either of you would have any trouble finding someone to bed, so this… this…' He stopped and glared at them as he pummelled his fist on the desk.

'It's a bit more than just a roll in the hay now,' Steve said, quietly.

Vince did not let him continue. 'Whatever, let me make one thing clear, I want no illegitimate offspring running around this house.' He had glared at them again. 'If you both feel so strongly about each other then you'd better get married. Make it legal, and then no one can point a finger at either of you.'

'But nobody else knows.'

'Oh, but they will,' Vince said, brusquely. 'Oh, yes they'll know, in due course. Somehow or other someone will twig what's going on… you mark my words. Now just you both think about what I have just said.' He had then dismissed them with a swift wave of his hand.

Steve had been extremely upset by Vince's tirade. He could never remember his father speaking to him in that tone of voice before, or being so angry. He was still upset when his mother confronted him.

'I want you to know that your father and I hoped that the pair of you would come to your senses after the first week.' Norah bit her lip before continuing. 'We were loath to make an issue of it, because we didn't want either of you leaving home at this stage.' She grasped Steve's hand.

'You know how much he depends on you now.'

'Is that the only reason?'

'No, of course not. We love you both and we don't want to lose either of you,' Norah had replied. 'However, you know we're concerned about Kirsty. She has a dark side to her nature. We guessed she'd been sleeping around before you returned home, but we could do nothing about it.'

'But that's pretty normal behaviour these days.'

'Yes, but it's the company she has been keeping. Some of them are... well, shall we just say they're not law abiding?'

'Do you think she'll stop associating with them because of me?'

Norah bit her lip again before answering.

'Some of the people she's mixing with have criminal records.' She grasped his hand. 'If you make a commitment to her, it might change things. You'll help keep everything under the one roof, and no one will be able to destroy the family unit.'

Steve had been stunned by his mother's remarks, but when he thought about it later, he understood better. However, it had put him in an awkward position. Although his relationship with Kirsty had developed into something akin to love, he did not want to commit himself to marriage. However, he did care enough about her to want to protect her from her own foolishness and wayward actions. He had to do the right thing by her; he owed that to his parents as well.

Although he and Kirsty agreed not to sleep together until they had resolved the situation, two nights later she slipped into his room, shrugged off her nightie and snuggled down beside him. As she lay sleeping in his arms he decided he had to accept his parents' conditions. After all, it was the right thing to do. That was nearly two years ago and they still hadn't set a date. However, most of their acquaintances acted as if the event had already taken place, and so did their parents. There seemed no way out of it now.

His thoughts were interrupted by a voice at his side. He turned to see a flight attendant bending over him.

'We're about to land, sir. Would you please put the seat in an upright position and fasten your seat belt.'

*

Kirsty waved frantically at him as he cleared customs and walked out into the main concourse. She clung to him for a long time after they kissed. 'I've missed you something terrible, Steve,' she murmured, into his hair. 'I'm never going to let you go off again like that... never. You belong here, with me.'

Vince Pardoe almost echoed her words that evening. 'Next time you go gallivanting around on the other side of the world you must take Kirsty with you. We're not going to put up with her shenanigans while you're away.'

They had all questioned him at length about the trip and, when he told them there was another claimant to the manor, they were both surprised and upset. When Vince asked if he had met the person in question he explained that he could not be told who it was, and went on to talk about the break-in and the burglary. His mind dwelled on Suzi for a while, but he was careful not to mention her by name; he simply referred to her as the woman who had found him in the house and called an ambulance.

Kirsty was extremely loving that night and by the time they went to sleep, Steve was exhausted. She slid into his arms again the next morning, but when he reached over to touch her face she grasped his hand and held it up.

'Your ring. Where's your ring? You promised never to take it off.'

'Maybe it slipped off when I washed my hands somewhere,' Steve replied in a deliberate off-hand way. 'You know how easy it is to lose something that way.'

'It has never slipped off before.'

Her look made it clear that she didn't believe him. After all, she had made him promise faithfully it would remain on his finger no matter what happened.

*

Charlize phoned and wanted to catch up on all the news, but soon seemed to realise that Suzi wasn't ready to talk yet, so they arranged to meet soon and have coffee together.

Mark gave her a long hard look when she arrived at the restaurant later that morning. It was as if he had also been affected by her liaison with Steve. Soon, the pressure of work filled her mind, and it was mid-afternoon before she had a chance to sit quietly and think about things. Steve's on his way home, she thought, and I must do what Charlize said, namely file the episode under pleasant memories and get on with my life.

Two days later, as they were about to close for the afternoon, a man burst into the restaurant and insisted on seeing the manager. When Suzi asked if she could help, he demanded to know why he had been turned away from the restaurant the previous Sunday.

'What do you mean—turned away?'

'I rang up and made a booking. I wanted to give my wife a surprise, but when we got here we weren't allowed in.'

'On Sunday there was a private function going on, that's why.' Suzi took a step back to get out of range of his alcohol-laden breath. 'The restaurant wasn't open to the general public.'

'You didn't say that when I phoned up,' the man protested.

'Let's have a look in the book, shall we?' Suzi reached for the reservations book. 'What did you say your name was?'

'Smithers.' He continued to talk as she turned the pages. 'I booked a table for Sunday and I wasn't allowed into the place. My wife was very upset. I promised to take her out for dinner and… ' He stopped as she laid the open book in front of him.

'See here, Mr Smithers, your booking is for next Sunday. You arrived a week early.'

'Don't you be telling me what I did.' He pushed the book away. 'It's your fault. You wrote down the wrong date.' As the irate man continued to berate her in a loud voice, Mark came out of the kitchen. He had been cutting up some meat and still carried the carving knife.

'What's the problem?' he asked, as they looked in his direction. 'Is this creep threatening you Suzi?'

The man paled visibly as Mark advanced towards them, still with the knife in his hand. 'It's not fair,' he gulped, 'I just wanted to know why I was turned away on Sunday, that's all. I wasn't going to hurt her. There's no reason for you to threaten me with a knife.'

Mark dropped the knife on the floor, and grabbed him by the shirtfront.

'I don't need a knife to sort you out, mister. If you come in here and distress Ms Spencer again, you'll be in more trouble than you can handle.' He marched the man backwards to the door. 'Get out and stay out, you drunken bum.'

As the door closed Mark turned to Suzi.

'Are you all right?'

'Yes, yes, I'm okay.' But as she spoke tears ran down her cheeks. It was as if the incident had unleashed all the feelings she had bottled up since she had met Steve. As she began to sob, Mark placed a protective arm around her shoulders.

'It's okay, Suzi,' he murmured, holding her close. 'I'm here to look after you. I'll see you come to no harm.'

Without thinking, Suzi nodded her head. It was only later that she realised the implication behind his words.

Chapter Five

Suzi lay awake for a long time that night, thinking about the events of the past few weeks. Steve had come into her life like a whirlwind, but he was out of it just as quickly. It wasn't likely she would ever see him again—he had no reason to return to Wales. Then she thought of Mark and began making comparisons. Although he might not have the charm or charisma to set her heart aflame, he was genuine, and they got on well together.

She had been both amazed and delighted with the way he had rushed to defend her that afternoon. The incident with the drunken man had been unsettling, but thanks to Mark's timely intervention it had come to nothing. The man had obviously drunk too much and probably wouldn't remember anything about it when he sobered up. Nevertheless it could have been nasty.

She wondered if had been the natural outcome of Mark's concern for her well-being, an attempt to gain her affections, or simply an automatic response to protect her. Then she reminded herself that it was unlikely he'd had enough time to weigh pros and cons. No, it was not his style to be analytical—he was just a nice guy. And now, as she reviewed their relationship, Suzi realised she had come to depend on him far more than she had ever expected. And, for some reason, that troubled her.

Charlize had repeatedly counselled her to find a new boyfriend, but that was easier said than done. Because of her involvement with the Stow Restaurant, she wasn't as free as she once was because the work was not conducive to a normal active social life. Mark had made it clear he would like them to spend time together on a social basis, but they never managed to make it happen. And yet she liked him as a person, and trusted him enough to form a partnership. 'That must be worth something,' she murmured into her pillow, moments before she fell asleep.

*

It was business as usual the next day and neither of them mentioned the inebriated man's intrusion. Mark seemed chirpier than usual and Suzi assumed he was pleased that he had been there to defend her. That evening he came out of the kitchen as she was saying goodnight to the last customer, and beckoned her. She thought he wanted to tell her he was going home as he usually did, but he pointed to a table by the window.

'I'll wait over there for you.' He sat fiddling with the cutlery until she joined him a few minutes later.

She looked at him quizzically. 'Everything all right?'

'Fine.' His voice was a little husky. 'I just thought I'd wait until you've finished.'

'Want a coffee?'

'No thanks. I want a few words, that's all.' He cleared his throat. 'Do you realise that we never see each other outside of the restaurant these days? We spent a lot of time together when we were starting up the business, and I enjoyed that.'

When Suzi hesitated, he continued. 'Why don't we go somewhere for a drink together?'

'Right now?'

'Why not?' He pointed to the clock behind the reception desk. 'It's not late. The Royal Oak will be open for hours yet.'

'Okay, that's a good idea.' Then she held up a hand as if in protest. 'On one condition—we don't talk shop.'

It seemed as if they had only just sat down in the corner of the village inn when they were told it was closing time. Suzi looked at her watch and realised that they had spent two hours over a few drinks. It had been pleasant and, true to his word, Mark hadn't mentioned the Stow Restaurant or any aspect of their business relationship.

'Shall we do this again soon?' He jiggled his car keys as they walked out of the pub. 'I'd like to take you somewhere nice for dinner one evening.'

'Fine by me.' Suzi paused before opening the door of her car, laid a hand on his arm, and then brushed her lips against his cheek. 'Coming here was a great idea.' She slipped in behind the wheel. 'See you tomorrow,' she called out as she drove off.

Mark smiled and saluted her as he climbed into his own vehicle, and drove off in the opposite direction.

The following week they dined at the Lockkeeper's Arms, a small picturesque inn situated on a nearby canal. Their window table gave them an unsurpassed view of the waterway and the tree-lined former towpath that now attracted energetic cyclists. A few boats were tied up to a pontoon immediately in front of the inn, and beyond them lay the lock that gave the place its name. The walls of the bar were festooned with boating paraphernalia and numerous old photographs of the days when the waterway was vital to the nation's economy. A montage of scenes depicting its former glory, the work of a local artist, graced a wall near their table. They studied the lifelike portraits of Irish navvies knee deep in slush, two horse drawn barges, and a woman hanging out washing on a narrowboat.

They both ordered the host's recommended dish of the day, which was surprisingly well presented. The atmosphere was subdued, but pleasant, and Mark seemed pleased that she approved his choice of venue. When he began talking to the publican in an Irish accent she almost laughed aloud. She had forgotten his wicked sense of humour, and that he could mimic almost anyone. She looked at him over the top of her wineglass and smiled in response to the gleam in his eyes; the gleam that had been missing for a long time—too long.

'Penny for them,' she said, as he caught her gaze.

'And to be sure 'tis a lovely evening, oim thinking,' he replied, in the vernacular.

'I'll drink to that, and here's to more of them.'

'You'll not forget the penny now, will ye?'

She shook her head. 'I owe you.'

Suzi slipped out of the car when Mark slid to a halt outside her bungalow. She would invite him in for a coffee another time, when maybe the memory of the handsome New Zealander had waned a bit. She leaned over and kissed him lightly on the cheek. 'Sweet dreams. See you tomorrow.'

The next day was busy, but she made time to ring Duncan's office to enquire about her inheritance. She was kept holding the line for an inordinately long time but at least, when the receptionist came back to her, she apologised for the delay. When she was finally put through, the solicitor told her that he had seen the other claimant, but he still had to evaluate their respective claims.

'Rest assured, Miss Spencer, I'll notify you both immediately I have something to tell.'

She banged down the receiver in disgust. 'Stupid old codger,' she muttered. 'That old man is much too full of his own importance.' The she picked it up again and phoned Charlize. They had not spent much time together over the past few weeks, and she had missed her.

*

They agreed to meet the following day at the local inn. And now as they faced each other across the table, Charlize wanted to know why Suzi had changed her mind about Mark.

'I seem to recall you saying, no way, so what's happened since then?'

Suzi toyed with her spoon for a minute, and then laid it down and looked directly into her friend's eyes. 'I've thought a lot about things since my encounter with Steve,' she said, quietly. 'I'll never see him again, so it's a hopeless situation, but I can't pretend. I'm pretty certain that what I feel for him is love, love at first sight, if there is such a thing. There's a danger that maybe it'll cloud every other aspect of my life if I'm not careful.'

'But, Mark? Are you sure? Do you honestly think he's the right one to help you through this?'

'I don't know. I'm feeling rather vulnerable at the moment, and he really is so considerate.'

'That's hardly a reason to become romantically involved with him, is it?'

Suzi was just about to answer when the publican approached and asked if they wanted coffee or something stronger. As they looked enquiringly at each other he placed some new cardboard beer coasters on the table.

'How about a Fourex? You might get lucky,' he said.

'What? Drinking Fourex? Ha… you must be joking,' Charlize added.

'I'm serious. You could win a holiday for two in Queensland. Look here.' He turned over the nearest bright yellow beer mat. 'It tells you what to do on the back.'

Charlize took the coaster from him and then read aloud the competition rules printed on the reverse side. 'Find the missing X, and finish the following sentence in twelve words or less. The Sunshine State is really great… blah… blah… blah.' She looked at Suzi. 'Come on, you're good at rhymes. Think of something.'

'Oh, I can't be bothered. You do it.'

Charlize scribbled a few lines on a paper napkin and laughed. 'There we are—a sure-fire winner. Listen to this.

The Sunshine State is really great,
The sun, the surf and sex can wait,
Just lead me to a Fourex, mate.'

She handed it to the publican when he came back with fresh coffee.

'Here, you can put your name to it if you like,' Charlize said, flippantly.

'Won't do me any good, it's not open to anyone associated with the company.' He handed it back to her. 'Fill out the coupon and I'll give it to the rep next time he comes.'

'What will you do if it wins?' Suzi asked, laughingly, as the man walked away.

'We'll both go on the first available plane, that's what.'

'And buy all the Fourex we can drink?'

'No way, I'll stick to the sun, surf and sex.'

After they had said goodbye, Suzi headed back to the Stow Restaurant to prepare for the evening guests. Mark stopped, cleaver mid-air, when she poked her head into the kitchen, and smiled as she walked over to where he stood. 'I think it would be a good idea if we took a break before the Christmas rush.'

'Do we deserve it? More importantly, can we afford it?' he replied.

'Yes. We've been hard at it for a year, so we could afford to close for a few days.'

'And face the seasonal onslaught with renewed vigour?' Mark grinned. 'All right—sounds a good idea. Let's look at the bookings for next month first.'

As soon as they decided on a suitable date, Mark arranged to have some maintenance work carried out while the restaurant was closed. They went out to dinner again the following Monday, but, when Mark suggested it should become a regular event, Suzi held up her hand. 'I'd prefer to do something different.'

'Okay,' Mark agreed, wholeheartedly. 'I'll take you to a bowling alley on our next evening out.'

The following week they went to dinner at a new up-market restaurant, and two weeks later spent a day at the races. Much to Mark's delight Suzi seemed to have an uncanny knack of picking winners and insisted on paying for everything. But she argued against his suggestion to go to a local point-to-point meeting, because she didn't fancy watching elderly horses coping with the rough ground and badly made hurdles on a farmer's field.

By the end of the month the vivid memory of her intimate relationship with Steve was fading. Although she thought of him from time to time, her deepening association with Mark made it harder to recall those tender moments. Suzi had accepted Mark's tentative kiss on their second date, and now it had become a natural part of their evening together. But that was as far as she wanted it to go at this stage.

Two days later Mark laid some travel brochures on the desk in front of her.

'I thought we could go to Malta, or maybe Cyprus,' he said, brightly.
She looked at him in surprise.

'Together?'

'Well yes—how else?' Mark replied, as if it was a stupid question.
'When you suggested we should take time off before Christmas I
naturally assumed you meant together.' Mark grasped her hand. 'We've
enjoyed all the outings we've had so far, so there's no reason why we
can't enjoy a holiday together.'

'Let me think about it for a little while, okay?'

She wrestled with the idea for a few days, unsure whether to agree
or not. If the holiday was a success it could mean the start of a
more intimate relationship. On the other hand, if it turned out to be
disappointing it could seriously affect their business association. She
would suffer the greater loss if things went pear shaped. Her savings
had been invested in the restaurant, and there was the bank loan too.

She wavered for a couple of days, then finally agreed, both agreeing
on a trip to Cyprus. Mark made the bookings, and then placed an
advertisement in the local paper to notify the public that the restaurant
would be closed for a few days. Finally, he placed an identical sign in the
window.

The day after their decision, Suzi received a cursory note from the
solicitor's secretary in reply to her letter asking to be brought up to
date on the proceedings. Apparently Mr Duncan was on holiday, but
she would bring it to his attention as soon as he returned. There was
nothing else to do but wait.

She was still waiting when they closed the restaurant doors a week
later. They drove up to Gatwick in Mark's car and booked into a nearby
hotel for the night so that they would have plenty of time to catch the
morning flight to Cyprus.

*

Now back in the swing of things in New Zealand, Steve had little
time to think about Suzi over next few days as he caught up on the
backlog of work. Vince had been asked to submit a tender to supply

pumping equipment for a company in Rotorua, and he wanted Steve to have a look at the layout of the factory first.

'Why not take Kirsty with you?' he suggested. 'After you've seen Murray, you could spend a bit of time sightseeing.'

Kirsty was delighted with the idea.

'Hey, I've never been to Rotorua,' she exclaimed excitedly. 'I'll get some brochures, eh?'

That evening she ignored her favourite soap on the television and spent the time deciding which attractions in the famous tourist town were the best. Steve pointed out that they wouldn't be able to visit everything she had circled, but promised to take her out to the Maori village. The idea really excited her, and they left early Friday morning arriving in Rotorua in time for lunch.

While Steve inspected the premises and discussed the layout with Tim Murray, Kirsty went looking for a place that still featured a natural hot-pool. Underground streams ran beneath most of the hotels in the area, but access to them had recently been rescinded to conserve the resources, so she was delighted to find one that had not been affected by the closures.

They dined at the Chevron Hotel that evening, where part of the entertainment package included a group of Maoris who performed some of the traditional dances and songs. When they had finished performing, some of them approached the diners and gave them leaflets advertising a hangi.

'A hangi... wow.' Kirsty's face lit up as she read the pamphlet. 'Let's go, eh? There'll be lots of food and lots of booze, and then we'll go back to the hotel for a night of sex.'

'Is that what you get up to with your Maori friends?'

'Yeah, it's great fun. No holds barred, everyone whooping it up. Yeah, we have some good times. I went to lots of them.'

'We are talking past tense, aren't we?' Steve watched her face as he spoke.

'Of course.' Kirsty's forced laugh seemed to mock her words. 'You know I love you, don't you? And we're going to be properly married, one day.' She grabbed his arm and pulled him around to face her. 'We are going to have a proper wedding, aren't we? In a church, with all the trimmings?'

Steve nodded, but he couldn't bring himself to utter the word 'yes'.

After one more drink they got ready for the hangi.

By the time the kitchen staff had laid out the food on the long benches at the far end of the room, Kirsty was almost beside herself with excitement. She heaped her plate high and headed for the nearest vacant table. As Steve sat down beside her, she signalled to the waitress.

'Can we have some wine?'

'Would you like to look at the wine list?'

'No, just bring us a house wine.'

'Red or white.'

'One of each, eh?'

Kirsty ate quickly, went back to the buffet and heaped her plate high again, and replenished Steve's more than once. By the time they got up to go Steve staggered away from the table; he had eaten far too much for comfort. When they returned to the hotel he flopped onto the bed with a groan, while Kirsty disappeared into the bathroom. Two minutes later she came back into the bedroom, pulled her dress over her head and threw it on the chair.

'Come on Steve, it's time we got it all together.'

Steve made a half-hearted excuse about being too full, but she would not take no for an answer. When they finally rolled apart, he wondered whether any man had ever fully satisfied her. Maybe those Maoris she used to date had more staying power than me, he thought, as she snuggled into his back. Something she had said about them earlier tugged at his mind, but he couldn't recall what it was.

I'll ask her tomorrow, he promised himself, before drifting off to sleep.

Chapter Six

It was mid-morning before Steve felt well enough to face the day, but Kirsty seemed to have suffered no ill effects from the mountain of food and excess of wine she had consumed the night before. She watched him drain another cup of coffee, and laughed.

'You need a hair of the dog,' she said, picking up the phone. 'I'll order a double brandy with a dash of bitters to fix you up.'

Whether it did him any good was debatable, but Steve had to admit it cut through the bilious haze, and gave him the strength to drive out to Whakarewarewa.

The inhabitants of the authentic Maori village still cooked their food in the traditional way, but there was no sign of activity this morning. A collection of empty pots dangled on bits of wire into the boiling water.

'Maybe they're feeling under the weather, too,' Steve muttered, as they made their way back towards the mud pools. A group of tourists had already gathered around a geyser reputed to erupt at regular intervals. After waiting for about five minutes the guide explained that if the water level was depleted it wouldn't blow.

'I'd better give it a bit of hurry up,' he grinned, upending a container of soap powder into the hole.

The geyser gurgled and spluttered for a few minutes and then, to everyone's delight, spouted a frothy mixture of steam and soapsuds high into the air.

'Had enough of this now,' Kirsty said. 'Let's have a bite at that café over there, and then go somewhere else.'

They left the complex and as they headed north away from the invasive sulphurous fumes Steve sighed with relief; he'd never been able to get used the smell that permeated the area.

Kirsty glanced sideways at him as he wound down the window and

50

muttered, 'Thank goodness we don't have to put up with that anymore.'

'Just as well you're not a Maori, then?' she chided.

Steve didn't bother to reply and turned off the main road, following the signs to Waitomo Caves. The seemingly bored guide there gave a potted dissertation about the natural phenomena and then led the way into the bowels of the earth.

It took a while to become accustomed to the darkness as they descended to the underground cavern where the boat waited. But by the time the guide slipped off the mooring ropes and pushed the craft out into the middle of the underground lake, Steve's eyes had adjusted to the gloom. Everyone on the boat seemed to hold their breath as they gazed at millions of glow-worms clinging to the cavern roof. Those tiny lights created a spectacle beyond description. It was truly magical.

'That was really something, wasn't it?' Kirsty exclaimed, as they emerged into the sunlight again. 'I'd have sat there for hours, just watching the changing pattern of lights.'

The trip back home was an anti-climax after what they had seen, and neither of them talked very much until they reached the outskirts of Auckland.

'When are you going to find out if you've inherited that fellow's house in the UK?' Kirsty asked. 'What's the hold-up, do you know?'

'No idea,' Steve replied. 'These things take time. I expect I'll get a letter from the solicitor in due course.' He stopped the car and reached out for her hand. 'It's been nice having a weekend away together… again,' he said, quietly. 'And, apart from eating too much at the hangi, I enjoyed it.'

'Me too. Let's go to Wellington next time, eh?' Kirsty wriggled her body and waggled her outstretched hands to imitate an aeroplane. 'We could fly. Easier than driving, eh?'

Later that evening Vince asked about the outcome of their trip to Rotorua and was highly amused at how much Kirsty had eaten at the hangi.

'You should have known better than try to keep up with her,' he said, shaking his head. 'She always ate more than you, even as a little girl. Most of the indigenous natives are the same and although she's only half Maori, she seems to have inherited their hearty appetite.' Then he became more serious and posed his question quietly. 'How are things between you? Okay?'

'I guess so,' Steve replied. 'Why do you ask?'

'Your mother seems to think something's amiss. Is there someone else? She says you were a bit guarded when you talked about your trip to Europe.'

The earnest expression on his father's face made Steve hesitate before answering. 'I'm not going to let you and Mum down, if that's what you're thinking. I promised to marry Kirsty, and I'll honour that commitment.'

'When?'

'As soon as...' Steve stopped, and gave a hollow laugh. 'It's always been as soon as something or other, hasn't it? Something stops me, Vince. I don't know what it is, but I can always justify a delay.'

'She's been complaining to your mother since you came home.'

'What about?'

'She's convinced you found someone else there and you don't love her the same anymore... you know, the usual things women imagine.' Vince grasped his son's hand. 'It's normal for that initial all-consuming lust to abate. Everyone goes through the stage of "can't get enough", and then finds out it isn't the be all and end all of a relationship after all. But Kirsty still thinks it is, or that's what she implied to Norah.'

'What am I to construe from that, Vince?'

'She's always going to be demanding, son, so it might be better to tie the knot as soon as you can.' Vince paused to let his words sink in. 'If she's married she'll be less likely to go looking elsewhere for a bit of you-know-what. Marriage will be a deterrent.' He wrapped an arm around Steve's shoulders. 'Sometimes I wish I hadn't suggested that you accept that responsibility, but it's a bit late now; you should have thought carefully before jumping into bed with her.'

'I know.' Steve gazed into the older man's eyes as he continued. 'But I can understand why you did it, and I don't hold it against either of you.'

'Thanks, son, that means a lot to me. Don't worry, it'll work out all right.'

At his parents' suggestion, he agreed to discuss a date for the wedding. Then he reminded them that Kirsty wanted to honeymoon in America, for some seemingly illogical reason, and that meant being away for a least a couple of weeks. He was also concerned about the increasing pressure on Vince to cope without him. The third consideration was just as important, to Kirsty anyway: she wouldn't get married unless he agreed to leave for the States straight after the ceremony.

*

Over the next couple of days, Steve thought about his conversation with Vince several times. Had his encounter with Suzi Lysle Spencer altered his relationship with Kirsty? Why should it, he questioned? But deep down he knew it definitely had. Did he love the auburn-haired Welsh beauty? He was reluctant to use the word love, but she had touched something deep inside him, and it was a constant reminder of their rapport. He had considered phoning her a couple of times, but checked the urge when he reminded himself that he had no right to expect her to feel the same way about him.

The pressing workload focused his mind to the exclusion of everything else for the next week, and he stayed late at the factory after Vince had left on several occasions. He had just come home one evening when he heard Kirsty answering the phone. He had no intention to eavesdrop, but it was hard to ignore the excited tone in her voice.

'Iritana,' she squealed. 'Hey, you, when did you get out? Yesterday? Hey, we must get together real soon.'

Steve peeked around the doorway and saw Kirsty nodding her head excitedly. So Iritana had been released from prison? It seemed only yesterday that she was arrested and sentenced. I wonder if her companion is still inside, he thought. What was her name? Then as if in answer to the unspoken question Kirsty squealed again.

'And Hepora could be home before the end of the month? Oh, that's great news.' Her high-pitched laugh made him wince. 'We'll celebrate—have a party, eh?'

Not wanting to hear more, Steve walked into the kitchen and poured himself a beer. What did it mean? Was she going to pick up where she left off with her wayward Maori girlfriends again? Would she go missing for whole weekends, as she had done in the past, when their boozy parties spilled over from a Friday night to encompass the next few days as well? This is what Vince and Norah feared would happen if they didn't get married. But he reasoned that there was no guarantee that marriage would change her.

Kirsty said nothing about the phone call, but Steve was convinced she was aware he had overheard the conversation. The wariness hung over them like a dark cloud, so that when a letter arrived from Mr Duncan a few days later, she eyed him suspiciously. It was as if she thought he was hiding something from her. To allay her fears he handed her the letter.

'Who's this Suzi Lysle Spencer he mentions?' she demanded.

'It seems she is the other claimant,' Steve explained. 'He wouldn't tell me at the time, kept it a big secret, but it appears we have equal claim to the inheritance.'

'What does that mean?'

'We have to share it.'

'You mean sell the house and split the proceeds?'

'I don't know. It has to be resolved,' Steve replied. 'When I saw Duncan, he casually suggested that maybe I should approach the other claimant about buying my share of the place. However, I doubt she could afford that.' Even as he spoke, Steve knew it had been a big mistake to admit that he knew that much about Suzi's financial situation.'

'How d'y'know she can't afford it? Is this the Suzi you mumble about in your sleep?'

'That I what?'

'I just want to know if it's the same one?' Kirsty glared at him. 'Did you take her to bed?'

Steve stared at her for a long moment before answering. 'I don't think you have any right to accuse me of infidelity. Your track record speaks for itself. You have a lot more notches in your belt than I have, even though I'm five years older than you.'

'That's not an answer. Did you have it off with her?'

Once again, Steve hesitated. Did he have it off with Suzi? No, not in the context of a casual sexual encounter. It had been entirely different from the sexual experiences he had enjoyed with other women over the years. What he had shared with Suzi wasn't about sex, it was something deeper. Much deeper. He looked at Kirsty as she waited for his answer.

'No, I didn't,' Steve replied, guardedly. 'I didn't have it off with her or anyone else while I was away. Okay?'

As she turned away he felt a pang of guilt. He was pleased that Kirsty hadn't asked him if they had made love to each other. Technically, it was the same, but he was prepared to argue that it was different if you loved the other person. However, he felt sure that she didn't believe him.

Kirsty came home late from her reunion with Iritana and, from her condition, Steve judged she must have had a lot to drink. He helped her undress and then pushed her under the shower. 'You smell like you fell into a vat of beer,' he growled. 'And wash your hair, too, it's full of muck.'

She was still sleeping soundly when he left for work the next morning. Neither of them mentioned the episode, but the tension between them crackled like a high voltage transformer on a showery night. And Hepora wasn't due home for another couple of weeks. When she did reappear, there would be a booze-up to end all booze-ups, because the Maori girl had been her best friend for as long as he could remember.

*

He and Vince were having a coffee break that morning when the postman dropped a bundle of letters in front of them. They slit each one open and sorted them into piles. Vince sighed and slid an embossed letter across the desk to Steve.

'Pity about that,' he said.

The letter was from a company in Kuala Lumpur which had accepted a quote they had submitted some months earlier. The writer stated that due to the economic downturn they were unable to go ahead with the planned project right now, and they gave no indication as to whether they would be prepared to do business in the future.

'It could be worse,' Steve said, handing back the letter. 'At least we haven't invested too much on the project.'

'That should free you up for a week or two'

'To do what?'

'Get married.' When Steve didn't respond, Vince called his attention to another letter. 'This looks promising. The sugar mill in North Queensland that wanted some new pumping equipment is considering our tender.' He took another sip of coffee. 'If we get the contract you might have to oversee the installation.'

'How soon will you know?'

'I've no idea, but I'd imagine they'll want it before the next crushing season.'

When Steve arrived home the following Friday afternoon, Kirsty was sitting up on the bed, painting her toenails. She blew him a kiss, and asked how his day had gone. When her toenails were dry, she tossed off the bathrobe she'd been wearing and pulled on a pair of panties. Steve watched her slip into a dress, pull it off again, try another one, and then finally settle for a pair of jeans and a garish red top.

'Where are we off to, then?' he asked.

'We?'

'Well, where are *you* off to, then?' Steve said. 'It's quite obvious I'm not invited.'

'Oh, it's just a party to welcome Hepora home.' She tossed her head provocatively. 'You can come if you want, but I don't think it'd be a good idea.'

'Why?'

'I don't think there'll be many pakehas to talk to.' She laid a hand on his arm to steady herself as she slipped on a pair of gilt sandals. Then she kissed him on the cheek. 'Don't wait up for me—I'll be late.'

A few minutes later he heard her drive away from the house. As he showered, Steve wondered what she would do now that both of her girlfriends were out of jail. It wasn't a pleasant thought. He recalled Vince's account of the events that led to the young women being arrested. Kirsty thought they might implicate her, but the police had not pressed charges. Whether she had been involved was still debatable, but at least their father's connections had kept her out of trouble.

Did she intend to pick up where she left off? Steve was convinced that Hepora's influence would tip the balance one way or other. And what about Joey Ruawhane, her old boyfriend? He was still in jail, and it would only be a matter of time before he was released as well. And then what?

Chapter Seven

Suzi gave a little gasp of delight as the plane began its descent to the Cypriot airport of Paphos. It was so different from what she expected. Although she had enjoyed many a holiday abroad over the years, she felt more excited about this one than she could ever remember. Mark made a fuss about claiming their baggage and then steered her towards the taxi rank.

'Let's hope the driver knows where he's going,' he remarked tersely.

Suzi placed a hand on his arm to slow his pace. 'Calm down, Mark. We're not in a desperate hurry.'

The friendly taxi driver spoke a strange form of English, but he made himself clear enough and soon put them both at ease. Within fifteen minutes they had cleared the airport precincts and were heading towards Latchi. The man appeared to be impressed when Suzi explained that they had chosen the tiny fishing village in preference to the larger town of Polis, and he agreed that it was a much more attractive place, and only five kilometres farther away.

'All that stuff in brochure... ha, it mean no thing.' He grinned disarmingly. 'Big town spend big money, but they not better than small town.' He pulled up outside the Plaka Hotel and jerked on the handbrake. 'We are arrive,' he announced, grandly, then added, 'you enjoy.'

'It looks nice,' Suzi remarked, as they approached the reception desk.

They had chosen the hotel because the brochure stated it was set in extensive gardens and surrounded by breathtaking views of the countryside. The leaflet also assured them it was within easy walking distance of a little village called Neo Chorion, and only fifteen minutes from a picturesque fishing harbour and beach. A footnote proclaimed that it was an ideal place for nature lovers.

The receptionist confirmed their booking and handed them separate keys. Suzi had insisted on this arrangement, because she felt unable to commit herself for some reason, and saying she wanted separate rooms made it quite clear.

'Enjoy your visit,' she said, echoing the taxi driver's words, and giving them a warm smile as they signed the register.

Their rooms were on opposite sides of the hotel. Suzi's spacious apartment looked out over the bay, while Mark's faced the swimming pool and courtyard. After she had unpacked her bag, she wandered downstairs to find him waiting in the bar. They whiled away the evening in the lounge talking to a number of guests who were leaving the next day, and Mark finally escorted her upstairs. Outside her bedroom door he whispered, 'Pleasant dreams, Suzi,' lightly kissing her goodnight.

The next morning, they wandered over to the fishing village and poked around the harbour before having a meal in one of the fish taverns. The following day they strolled around the small, traditional agricultural town of Polis, and bought some souvenirs to take back to their staff. When they returned to the hotel, Suzi spent the afternoon having a sauna, massage and facial. The hotel receptionist tried hard to sell them a cruise trip on the boat Atalante, but neither felt enthusiastic about the idea so they declined.

'We could pop up to Nicosia for a couple of days, if you like,' Mark suggested. 'How do you feel about that?'

'No, I like it here. It's peaceful in these tiny villages, and it'd be a pity to break the mood and go to a bustling city even for a day.' They confined their activities to the local attractions most of the time, and Suzi was content just to laze by the pool, and enjoy the peaceful surroundings. It was all a stark contrast to the way she had spent the past eighteen months—finding and setting up the restaurant, and working virtually day and night to make it a success.

Their final evening there arrived. 'Let's dine at that little fish tavern by the harbour.'

'Yes, let's. Our first meal there was delicious.' It was a beautiful evening, and they walked hand in hand along the beach, listening to the gentle slap of the waves on the sand. It seemed idyllic. It was as they stood looking out to sea that Mark suddenly cradled her in his arms and sighed contentedly.

'I'm glad we came here,' he said, softly. 'I feel it's done us the world of good.' He brushed his lips against her hair, and gently cupped her breast. 'I think it's brought us closer together, too,' he added.

Unwilling he had become intimate, Suzi stiffened, and turned sideways to ease his hand off her breast, and then moved away in case he tried to take his fondling further.

'It's time we were getting back,' she murmured. 'I've still got to pack and I don't want to be too late going to bed.'

The next morning they caught a taxi back to Paphos for the trip back home. Their plane descended through a layer of heavy, grey clouds and taxied up to the terminal in the pouring rain. The downpour eased long enough for them to get into Mark's BMW, but then it continued until they crossed the bridge between England and Wales.

'I'll get the bags in while you brew us a nice pot of tea, Suzi.' In a short time, they were seated comfortably and enjoying the drink, both obviously trying to avoid talking about the Stow Restaurant. But it was a dismal failure. It was time to get back to work. Suzi brewed another pot of tea, while Mark phoned a few suppliers to remind them that the restaurant would re-open in two days.

*

After spending so much time in Mark's company, Suzi felt quite relieved when he finally left, leaving her free to please herself about what she did and when. She lifted the phone and rang Charlize, chatting happily for an hour before she hung up. More relaxed now, she flopped onto the squashy sofa in front of the fire and stared into the flames as if expecting to find an answer to the barrage of questions that tumbled around in her mind. What should she do about Mark? Charlize had just made it clear that she agreed with Suzi's decision not to become too involved with him, and that was a gentle reminder of her own original concerns about Mark. Caution was needed where he was concerned.

However, his unobtrusive approach had almost undermined her determination to keep him at arm's length. She had been disturbed at his attempt to caress her on the beach, but he had not taken exception to her gentle rebuff. It was then that memories of Steve flooded her mind, and how ready she was to accept his caresses. She continued to stare absentmindedly into the fire, remembering their lovemaking and the depth of feeling he had generated in her. Once again she was tempted to contact him, but common sense prevailed and she decided to leave things as they were.

Sorting through the mail, Suzi found a letter from Mr Duncan. She opened it eagerly and scanned it quickly the first time. It informed her that both she and the other claimant, a Mr Steven William Pardoe, of New Zealand, had equal rights to the Caxton Manor estate. Suzi's jaw dropped in sheer disbelief as she read the words. Steven Pardoe. Steve?

'But, he didn't say…' Her strangled words stuck in her throat. She could feel her face flush at the news. When he arrived in the country, had Steve Pardoe already been aware that she had filed a claim to Bartholomew Armitage's estate? If so, why hadn't he said something when they first met? Had he deliberately kept quiet about it?

She recalled his account of how he had noticed the wrought iron gates of the manor were ajar, and saw the securing chains lying on the ground, which made him decide to investigate. However, he had not mentioned he was there because he had a vested interest in the place.

A wave of resentment swept over her, only to be replaced by a feeling of remorse. Fully aware she had said nothing of her interest either, she realised it was tit for tat. She hadn't been frank about her visit to the old house, either. Then she recalled the solicitor's off-hand rejoinder about another claimant. Maybe he hadn't informed Steve that there was anyone else involved at that time. Even if he had, the solicitor would have kept them both ignorant of each other's identity.

'Oh, Steve,' she murmured, staring blankly at the letter on the floor. 'If I'd only known.' But 'If only' seemed out of place now as conflicting thoughts continued to run through her mind. She had to decide what to do about the situation. It would be stupid to declare her love for him, and rather silly to ask him to come back and live with her in the house. She raised her brows at the boldness of her thoughts. *What was she thinking?*

Still, even though he had made it clear he wasn't married, he had intimated he was committed to someone in New Zealand. 'He must love her, or he wouldn't have left me and gone back to her,' she murmured, tearfully. 'He must have realised he had a choice, so that's that.' Her mind flew back. At no time did he declare his love for her, and she had not used the word love either. She recalled what he really had said: 'You've touched something deep inside me, Suzi Lysle Spencer.' Those words were still ringing in her head. It had been a lovely way to express what he felt, but it was ambiguous, and that was it, beginning and end. Oddly enough, that was exactly how she felt as well.

She picked up the letter and continued to read the rest of the contents.

When you were informed that there was another claimant, you intimated that you might be prepared to buy that other person's share . Do you wish me to convey that offer to Mr Pardoe ? Should he agree to your proposal , it will be necessary to have the property evaluated to fix a price.

There was a bit about his intention to make sure it was settled amicably, and so on, but it was just so much claptrap as far as she was concerned.

'Stupid, that's what I was, to say such a thing. I don't have enough money to even buy the front door, let alone a whole half of the house. Real stupid,' she muttered as she sat down and carefully considered the situation. *Could there be a way to do it? Of course he might not want to sell. What then?* She bit her lip; she didn't want to lose the house she loved, but she couldn't see any way to afford to hang on to it either. It was an impasse.

Suddenly, Suzi jerked into life as an idea popped into her head. Maybe he would allow her to develop it into a business. Surely they could work out something between them; a lease, a share in the profits, or whatever? But even as the thought took root in her mind, she dismissed it, for that would mean taking out a bigger mortgage to pay for alterations, and she couldn't expect Steve to agree to that. After all, why should he jeopardize his share of the property?

As another tear rolled slowly down her cheek, she sat feeling forlorn and dejected. She did not want to see the lovely old house sold off to a complete stranger. Surely she could do something? She thought, racking her brains. At least, maybe she could talk to Steve about the situation. She reached for the phone and then gave a bitter little laugh as she gave herself some sound advice. 'I don't think that's a real good idea either.'

Unwilling to dwell on the upsetting letter she turned on the television and began surfing the programs. A documentary on New Zealand caught her attention and she watched the whole program. When it finished, Suzi ran a hot bath and then made her way to bed. She would phone Duncan first thing in the morning and find out what could be done about the situation.

Her dreams were full of conflicting scenes in which Steve played a pivotal role. First of all he would gather her into his arms, declare his undying love, and then carry her up the sweeping staircase of Caxton Manor to consummate their love in the antique four-poster bed. In the next dream he would stand at the front door, brandishing a gnarled walking stick and warning her never to set foot in the house again. She woke up during the night in a sweat and feeling quite exhausted.

*

When Kirsty finally returned home late Sunday afternoon, she was carrying her pretty sandals, with a heel missing on one of them. Her hair was piled up and tied with string, and her garish red blouse had been replaced by a tee shirt with a rather obscene picture on the back. On top of that, she looked as if she hadn't slept the whole weekend.

Steve was about to remonstrate with her when Norah intervened.

'I'll see to her.' She pushed him away gently. 'You take Vince down the club for a drink.' By the time they had returned, Kirsty was fast asleep in her bedroom.

'Just leave things be,' Norah counselled Steve, as they sat around after dinner. 'I'll have a talk with her tomorrow.'

'I was hoping that she wouldn't take up with that crowd again.' Vince's voice was tinged with sadness. 'She promised me faithfully, but I suppose it was only because I managed to keep her name out of things.' He sighed deeply. 'At least they didn't implicate her in the crime, otherwise she'd have been put away too.'

'Why didn't you stop her associating with them?' Steve looked directly at his father. 'Surely you must have known what she was doing.'

Vince sighed deeply again and shook his head. 'Easier said than done. Maybe if you'd been home at the time it would have been different. You might have been able to keep an eye on her… who knows?'

'We didn't take too much notice of it at first,' Norah continued, when Vince paused. 'We thought she'd get it out of her system as she grew older. The trouble is we don't understand how she thinks.' She stopped and spread her hands out wide. 'She's a Maori, and their culture is poles apart from ours.'

'But you knew that when you adopted her.'

'Yes, but we thought that if she was raised with a white family she would adapt to our lifestyle.' When Norah began to weep softly Vince took up the narrative.

'We reasoned that if she didn't associate with them she wouldn't be influenced by their way of life.' He shook his head. 'We were wrong.'

'Do you still want me to marry her?' Steve looked from one to the other, his face drawn tight. 'Is that the answer, or is it just a long shot that it might slow her down for a while?' He turned to his father. 'She knew your situation, and how her actions could have jeopardized the business, but it didn't seem to make a scrap of difference, did it?'

'No, I guess not,' Vince replied, sadly. 'It would appear that she didn't give it a second thought.' Another sigh. 'And probably still doesn't.'

'So she wouldn't feel obliged to change her ways because we were married?'

'I don't know, Steve, but she seemed to settle down after you agreed to marry her.' Vince looked at this wife. 'Norah will tell you… we think it made a world of difference.'

'Yes, but at that time all her troublesome friends were banged up in jail, weren't they?' Steve slammed his fist on the table to emphasis his words. 'She had no contact with them and so I filled the gap in her life. But now they're back, what next, eh?' He shook his head slowly. 'I'll do what I can to help, but I…'

'But what?'

'But I have no intention of cleaning her up every time she comes home from one of their booze-ups.' Steve glared at his father. 'And I don't like the idea of you having to bail her out of trouble again, because that's what's going to happen again, and again, unless this is nipped in the bud. The next time, it could be something far more serious. And what then?'

'Maybe Hepora and Iritana have learned their lesson. Kirsty was really upset when they were sent to prison.' Norah sighed. 'Apparently everyone thought they'd get a caution or some community work, or whatever.' For another hour, they continued to discuss the best way to handle the situation. Then Vince suggested that they sleep on it and talk about it again the next day but, as they stood up, Steve spoke again.

'There's another aspect to it that has to be considered. If she continues to spend time with those people, she's going to start sleeping around again. I don't care what she did in the past, but it's different now. If she picks up with one of those guys who's been messing around while he's been in the nick, then she's leaving herself wide open to all sorts of infection. To put it bluntly, I'm definitely not going to put myself at risk by sleeping with her. I'm clean, and I want to stay clean.'

Another tear slid silently down Norah's cheek. 'She fitted in so well when we brought her home,' she said, quietly. 'We thought she would turn out like you, Steve, and we've been so proud of you.'

Steve thought of her words as he climbed into bed, and spent hours staring at the ceiling as he tried to think of what to do. Finally, exhausted by his conflicting thoughts, he turned over and fell asleep.

Chapter Eight

Kirsty stared at Norah as if she was trying to understand what her foster mother was saying. She seemed unable to concentrate. It was quite obvious that her mind was still blurred with the alcohol and drugs she had consumed over the weekend. Then the haze lifted enough for her to listen to Norah's voice which now held a note of exasperation.

'You know we love you, Kirsty,' Norah said. 'We don't want to see you destroy your chance of happiness.'

'What do you mean… destroy my chance of happiness?' Kirsty peered at Norah through bloodshot, narrowed eyes. 'I'm happy with my life. I'm not destroying anything.'

Norah gazed at her in amazement. Couldn't Kirsty see how she was abusing her body? Didn't she understand that what she was doing was totally unacceptable in a normal society? How did she expect to keep out of trouble if she continued to associate with people who had no regard for the outcome of their illegal actions?

'But, Kirsty…'

'Don't "but Kirsty" me,' she said, pulling her hand free. 'You don't understand, do you? Not one of you understands me, and you never will.'

'We've done everything we could for you. We've treated you like our very own daughter, and Steve has been just as loving. You can't point an accusing finger at anyone in this house.'

Kirsty stood up and paced over to the window to look out on the broad expanse of sea visible over the rooftops of the neighbouring houses.

'You're right,' she admitted. 'You've given me the best of everything, and I know you've tried to make me feel part of your life. When I was younger I never questioned my place in the family, but all that changed as I began to discover my true identity. Now I feel trapped.'

Kirsty was well aware that, initially, she had been proud to be part of a white family, but, as she mingled with Maori children, she realised she had a preference for their friendship. Their concept of living for today appealed to her and she was happiest when she was in their company. It was as if that side of her nature was stronger than the European part.

Then she thought of Steve. She did love him, although it was a different type of love than she had for Joey Ruawhane. Steve embodied all the good aspects of her foster parents, and had provided the much needed physical love she required, but she didn't have the same depth of feeling for him as she did for her Joey. She had agreed to marry Steve because it seemed to be the only way she could have the love and support she needed, but she knew in her heart he was her second best. Joey was her first and only true love, and always would be. But she knew he would never be accepted by this family.

Norah walked up behind her and slipped an arm around her shoulder.

'What do you want to do Kirsty? What does your heart tell you to do?'

Kirsty shrugged in an effort to appear nonchalant, and then she turned to face her foster mother. She gazed into the older woman's face with its genuine expression of love in her eyes. 'I feel so totally lost and desolate, it's like a blanket of doom sweeping over me.' She buried her head on Norah's breast and began to sob.

'I don't know. I don't want to upset you and Pap, or Steve, but I feel as if I'm being torn down the middle. One half of me wants to fit into your lifestyle and the other…'

'We thought that in time you'd come to terms with that,' Norah said, stroking her hair. 'You seemed to settle down after…' She paused and then continued, 'After what happened to Iritana and Hepora. You know that if it hadn't been for Vince, you'd have probably gone to jail as well.'

Kirsty shook her head disconsolately and reached for a handkerchief to dry her tears. 'I appreciate what he did, really I do, but it doesn't change how I feel inside. It's as if the other part of me is crying out to be heard, it's like my ancestors are calling me.'

'Your ancestors?'

'Don't you understand? I'm Maori and I belong to my people,' Kirsty's voice was pitched low and she spoke in a slow, deliberate manner. 'I just got mixed up somehow. I should be part of a Maori family. That's where my heart belongs.'

Norah could think of nothing to say in answer to that, so she grasped her hand and led her into the kitchen. 'Come on, let's have something to drink.' After she had made some coffee, she added a slug of cooking brandy. 'You could probably do with a hair of the dog, and I need something to help me cope with things.'

*

When she had finished the drink, Kirsty went back to her room, and sat on the side of the bed to stare at her reflection in the dressing table mirror—deep, soulful, brown eyes looked back at her from a softly square face with a tanned complexion. Her pleasantly full lips parted to reveal large, well-formed teeth that gave depth to her naturally enchanting smile.

She pushed her fingers through a mass of dark hair with a swathe on one side dyed grey, and grimaced. It was a mess. Her eyes ranged down to her well-rounded figure, and she wondered why she couldn't accept herself as she was. Everyone agreed she was attractive, and the men were drawn to her like bees to a honeypot, but that wasn't enough; something important was missing.

Kirsty let out a deep sigh. She accepted that her foster parents had done everything possible to help her fit into their world, but it hadn't changed her, or her way of thinking. She didn't want to upset them, and she had never deliberately done things out of spite, even if they might think otherwise.

They just don't understand that I see things differently. Everyone sees things differently, she thought, twisting the dress ring on her finger. Like this ring that Steve had bought for her on a trip to Melbourne, and he'd bought an identical one for himself. She had seen it as a confirmation of their relationship, but she guessed that Steve had not attached any great significance to it.

'I wonder what he did with his?' she muttered. She felt annoyed that he had come back from Britain without it. She didn't believe he'd lost it. 'Maybe he's given it to some woman as a token.' Then she gave a short bitter laugh. 'That's stupid, you don't give a man's dress ring to a woman.' But the thought wouldn't go away.

She went out to meet Steve when he came home from work that afternoon. He hesitated when she called his name, and for a minute Kirsty looked downcast, as if she thought he would ignore her. When he accepted her kiss on the cheek, she slipped an arm around his waist.

'Did you have a good day?'

'I suppose so,' Steve nodded. 'The usual problems, but that's normal.'

'Want to tell me about it?'

Steve shrugged his shoulders.

'You know me, all techno talk. You probably wouldn't understand it anyway.' Then he caught the look of disappointment on her face. 'A picture is worth a thousand words—come on, I'll show you rather than try to explain it.'

He grasped her hand and led her into the study. After the computer brought the relevant material onto the screen, Steve described the broad outline of a pump they had designed for a particular application and then enumerated the problems they were up against.

'In other words it doesn't work?'

'Well, it would if the company had given us the right information,' Steve replied. He gave a snorting laugh. 'They want it done as cheaply as possible and so they didn't tell us all the problems that had to be overcome. However, it'll cost them more in the long run. It's what is called false economy.' He turned away from the screen and looked at her. 'Did that make any sense to you?'

'No, but thanks for explaining it.' She turned her head away knowing she was close to tears.

'That's okay.' He touched her on the shoulder and she swivelled around to look into his eyes. 'Kirsty, Kirsty,' he murmured, gathering her into his arms and rocking her like a baby. She laid her head on his chest for a minute, savouring the tenderness of the moment. Then she looked up into his eyes. 'Love me, Steve. I want you to take me to bed and love me.'

Hesitating at first, as though this was almost against his will, Steve followed her into her bedroom, more from habit than for love now. As she slipped out of her jeans the sight of her nubile, naked body stirred him yet again, as it always did. She was particularly sensitive to his mood, and they spent a long time lying quietly in each other's arms after their passion had abated. An hour later, they finally rolled off the bed and made themselves respectable to go and join the other two.

Norah got up from the table as they entered the dining room.

'We've only just started our meal,' she said. 'Yours is in the oven.'

They all made an extra effort to be jolly, but the jokes fell flat and the old anecdotes didn't seem so funny the second time around. Vince opened a second bottle of wine and then a third. By the time it had all been consumed, everyone seemed more relaxed. Kirsty coaxed Steve back to bed soon afterwards and curled up in his arms again.

'I do love you, Steve,' she murmured into his hair. 'I really appreciate what we have, it's just that sometimes…' She stopped trying to explain why she felt the way she did.

Steve twisted his head and kissed her lips. 'I know, Kirsty, really, I do know what you're trying to tell me, but forget it for now.'

Kirsty's breathing slowed as she fell asleep, and Steve wondered what Norah had said to her. Had she convinced her that this association with her Maori friends could only lead to more trouble? Or was this just Kirsty's way of trying to make amends? As he stared blankly at the ceiling, his thoughts turned to Suzi Lysle Spencer once again. He sighed softly. He had no right to judge the woman in his arms when his heart longed for another.

*

Suzi phoned Mr Duncan early the next morning. The solicitor was brusque, but not unkind, when she explained that although it would solve a problem, she found it impossible to consider buying Steve's share of the property at the moment. She asked him to put everything on hold to give her extra time to think more about the matter.

When she arrived at the restaurant, Mark was restocking the refrigerator, but he stopped to make two mugs of tea and then carried them out to the reception area. He put one down in front of her and kissed her cheek, then directed her attention to the pile of mail. 'That'll keep you busy for a while.'

Suzi had plenty of time to go through it all, for only a few people turned up for lunch. It had never been so quiet. Mark joined her at a table by the window.

'Not a brilliant start to the day, is it? Half a dozen for lunch won't pay the bills.'

Suzi forced a laugh. 'Let's hope it picks up in a day or two.'

'I've just thought of something,' Mark said, picking up a copy of the local paper from amongst the assorted pamphlets and discarded envelopes lying on the table. 'I wonder if…' He skimmed through the pages. 'Ah, yes, I thought as much—they haven't run the second advert.' He threw the paper down. 'I'll give them a blast they won't forget in a hurry.'

'Leave it to me,' Suzi urged him. 'You might wind them up too much.'

'Okay.' He was just about to climb to his feet when he stopped. 'I got a letter from Mum. She and Dad are heading down this way in a couple of weeks' time, so I'd like to organise some time off while they're here. I'll see if Gary Hyland's available. He can handle the lunchtime trade and maybe do some of the evening preparation as well.'

'Is Judith coming too?'

'I hope so. I haven't seen my kid sister for ages.'

'She might be your kid sister, but she used to be my best friend.'

'Yes, well…'

Suzi was about to say it must be nice to have a family, when she stopped, suddenly feeling very much alone. Her father had died when she was young, and she could hardly remember him. She had not enjoyed a particularly good relationship with her mother, who had been very self-centred and preferred her own company. In fact, she had welcomed Suzi's decision to move out of the family home, and her only high spot during those years had been her relationship with her great Uncle Bart. He had treated her like a daughter and she had always been welcome at Caxton Manor. It had been a sad day for her when he died, because, without him, there was no other family to turn to.

Mark's cheery goodbye cut into her thoughts, so she gave him a brief wave and opened up the book that contained the names and telephone numbers of people who had dined at the restaurant over the past year. Slowly and methodically, she worked her way backwards through the pages reminding everyone that they were back from holidays and that they had just drawn up a new menu. A half hour later she put the phone down and felt greatly relieved at having just taken twenty-three bookings for the next few days.

She let herself out of the building and slipped in behind the wheel of her brightly coloured Honda. She stared blankly through the windscreen and tried to relax, for the feeling of being neglected had returned with renewed vigour. It was as if she had just become aware of her aloneness in the world, but it wasn't as if she had no friends. She knew Charlize cared about her, and she reciprocated those feelings. She frowned as she suddenly wondered if she should marry Mark and become part of his family—after all, she had always enjoyed a good relationship with Judith. She quickly shook her head. 'Now that would be stupid—all the wrong reason for a start,' she murmured, and dismissed the idea as ridiculous.

Within a few days the restaurant was overflowing with customers and all her self-destructive thoughts dissipated like the morning dew. She and Mark resumed their former pattern of a day out together, or an evening meal in one of the many inns that abounded in the area. He seemed fairly content with himself and she wondered if he still expected to form a more intimate relationship with her, but he did not put her under any pressure, so overall, things were as well as could be expected.

The only cloud on the horizon was the dual ownership of Caxton Manor. She had no idea how was she going to resolve that.

Chapter Nine

Mark's parents stopped off at the restaurant to say hello before going on to their hotel in a nearby town. As Suzi watched them embrace him she felt more than a little twinge of envy. While Mark gave Ben and Jane Brinstead a tour of the premises, Judith plopped down on a nearby chair.

'How've you been Suzi? It seems an age since we spent any time together.'

'Busy.' She gestured at the dining area. 'It keeps us on our toes, but I'm not complaining. What about you? Mark tells me that you're engaged… is that true?'

'Yes.' Judith held out her left hand to display a diamond ring. 'Isn't it beautiful?' She spoke about how happy they were and then went on to say that her fiancé, Jonathan, hoped to join them later in the week. 'And what about you?' she asked, peering intently at Suzi. 'How are things between you and Mark? I believe it's getting a bit serious.'

Suzi was about to reply when Mark came bustling into the dining room bearing a tray laden with coffee and a large plate of sandwiches. When he sat down next to his sister, Suzi found herself comparing them again. She had almost forgotten how closely they resembled each other. In her opinion, they could easily pass for twins, even though there was a three-year age gap.

'You both seem to have done very well here in such a short time, Suzi.' Ben said, selecting another sandwich. 'Mark tells me you're hoping to move into bigger premises in the New Year.' He nodded his head and winked at the same time. 'That's the ticket, don't rest on your laurels. Get out there and make things happen.'

Suzi stole a look at Mark, but he made no sign that he had heard what his father had said. She wondered if it was just a passing remark or whether Mark had been secretly planning something without her knowledge. Ben always gave the impression that making decisions was a man's prerogative. Her thoughts were interrupted as Jane spoke again.

'What did you like most about Cyprus, Suzi? I've heard it's a romantic place.' She glanced quickly at her son. 'Mark tells me you're both out and about whenever you can make the time, so are you planning anything over Christmas?'

Before she could answer, Ben climbed laboriously to his feet and pointed at the ornate clock behind the reception desk. 'We'd better let these busy people get on with things.' He grasped his wife's arm and urged her up off the chair, and then looked meaningfully at Judith. 'It's time we were on our way.'

As they were saying goodbye, the first customers arrived for lunch, and the steady flow of people didn't stop until it was time to close for the afternoon. Mark slipped off straight after preparing the last meal and did not return until it was nearly time to open for dinner. He bustled around the kitchen hurriedly catching up on the work he had neglected that afternoon. His manner made it clear he had no time to talk, which gave Suzi no chance to query him about his mother's remarks.

It'll wait until they've gone home, I suppose, she thought, as she walked back into the dining room, hoping that Mark wouldn't think he could take control just because he was currently more personally involved with her.

*

She had barely opened the door next morning when Gary Hyland breezed in and gave her a friendly peck on the cheek before making his way into the kitchen. He had worked for Mark in the past and was quite capable of maintaining the high standard that was expected by Stow Restaurant's customers. Suzi liked his cheerful manner, but she was well aware that Gary saw all women as potential bed-mates. The young waitress would have to be on her guard while he was around, and one or two older ones as well.

She accompanied Jane and Judith on a shopping expedition the following afternoon while Mark and his father attended a local point-to-point meeting. Suzi tried to fit in as many trips with Mark's family as possible, but felt relieved that the business limited the number of activities. She had enjoyed those she had joined, and she felt very comfortable with Mark's parents; she liked Judith's fiancé as well, and seriously considered how she would feel to be related to them.

However hard she tried to convince herself, she could not see herself as part this family. Admittedly, she was very fond of Mark, but spending extra time with Mark and his relatives soon made it clear that she did not want to marry him; she simply didn't love him—that little X factor was missing.

Mark's family called into say goodbye the following day and things quickly returned to normal. Pre-Christmas parties had to be catered for, and the number of bookings seemed to increase from week to week. By now, the pace had become quite hectic.

Suzi moaned aloud when she received a letter from the solicitor again. He explained that the legalities of the inheritance had not been satisfactorily dealt with yet, and stated that although Steve had initially expressed a willingness to sell her his share, his solicitors had not yet indicated that he still wished to pursue the idea. However, Mr Duncan promised to keep her duly informed, so that was that.

Gary must have been able to see how frustrated Suzi had become, and he sidled up to her one morning.

'Don't worry,' he said, 'You can rely on me to help out over the festive season. In fact, I'll handle the restaurant trade so that Mark could be free to cope with any extra work that turns up.'

*

'It's a lot more demanding this year,' she lamented to Charlize when they met at their favourite rendezvous for a morning coffee. 'I find it hard to drag myself out of bed each day, so thank goodness Gary Hyland has agreed to help out. It would be horrendous otherwise.'

'And how are things with Mark?'

'You mean…? Oh, our social life is almost non-existent now. Mark's too busy organising things, chasing up deliveries, checking on a thousand and one things to have much time for anything else.'

'How do you feel about that?'

Suzi gave a little laugh. 'It's okay. I don't mind except when he gives me a little broadside.'

'What do you mean?' Charlize asked, an inquisitive look on her face.

'Oh, he's still on about moving into larger premises,' Suzi replied, 'and every time we have to set up in a hall somewhere, he moans about the inconvenience.'

'I suppose he would have been a lot happier if you'd inherited Caxton Manor totally?'

'No doubt, but as you know I'd be putting my head in a noose by mortgaging the place, even if it was all mine.' Suzi pulled a face. 'Mark has hinted that he might be able to raise enough money to buy Steve Pardoe's share, but I think it's all talk. He's in the same position as me—hocked to the hilt—almost.'

'Have you heard anything more from your solicitor?'

Suzi pulled another face. 'That silly old so-and-so huffs and puffs, but does nothing.'

'If you'd known about this Kiwi chap earlier you might have been able to work something out with him while he was here.'

'Amen to that. It's a pity Duncan refused to disclose his name at the time.'

'Don't worry. I expect it will work itself out okay.'

'I still don't know how I really feel about Mark,' Suzi stated abruptly. 'He can be good fun, but I can't bring myself to be intimate with him. There's that something special missing.'

'Well, that's a jolly good enough reason not to marry him,' Charlize remarked, sagely, 'and you must remember how many marriages flounder because people never get away from each other. They get sick of the sight of their partners.'

'You're right. It's a stupid idea.' Suzi glanced at her wristwatch. 'Good grief, is that the time? I must dash.' She jumped up and kissed Charlize on the cheek. 'See you later.'

As she made her way back to the Stow Restaurant, Suzi reviewed her relationship with Mark. She knew he had done everything in his power to make the business prosper, and he would probably try just as hard to make the marriage work. But, and it was a big but, was she prepared to make the same effort? Maybe I need to be a bit more loving, she mused. Maybe I should let him sleep over one night and see what happens, she mused. But, even as the thought crossed her mind, she rejected it out of hand because she just could not imagine herself in bed with him.

'Let's get Christmas out of the way,' she murmured. 'Maybe things will sort themselves out.'

Chapter Ten

Steve had not seen much of his friend Jock MacTavish since their last year at Dunedin University. The strong bond they had formed whilst attending college had strengthened over the following years, and Jock had gone into the family engineering business. He surprised Steve by phoning one evening to ask for advice.

'We had a piece of pumping equipment imported from America some years ago. It's been okay until now, but it's no longer working properly.' He sounded frustrated over the phone. 'On top of that, the company has gone into liquidation and their spare parts division no longer exists.' He paused for a few seconds. 'Any chance you can help?' The two friends had a lengthy conversation about the problem and then Jock rang off. Three days later he called again. The detailed sketches that Steve had sent to help him sort out the problem had not relieved the situation.

'Surely you can fix a pump,' Steve protested. 'You don't need me to tell you how?'

'I thought so, but maybe it's just that I can't read your handwriting.'

'Thanks a bunch.'

'Would you come down and sort it out for us? We haven't spent much time together over the past few years, so it'll be a good excuse to meet up, have a few beers and catch up on the news and all that.' There was a pause. 'We'll pay your airfare and you could make a little holiday out of it. How about it, eh?'

Steve agreed. It would be a welcome break away from the awkward situation with Kirsty; he knew he needed time to himself. And now as the plane began its descent he looked down on the small town that nestled at the bottom of South Island, and smiled. He was looking forward to the reunion with a great deal of pleasure; it would be good to see his old friend again.

Jock was waiting in the reception area.

'Well, Stevie,' he said, clasping his friend's hand tightly. 'It's so good to see you again. Come on, the car's outside. I've done my licence in by too much drink, so Jenny had to drive me here.'

'Jenny?'

'My kid sister.'

'Ah, I vaguely remember a youngster—skinny, obnoxious and under your feet all the time.' Steve laughed. 'I suppose she's changed by now?'

'You'll soon see for yourself.'

Jenny acknowledged Steve's hello and then shoved the Mitsubishi into gear and accelerated fiercely out of the airport parking lot. She glanced at him from time to time as she drove towards the MacTavish home, but made no effort to join in the conversation. When she jammed on the brake outside the house, she turned to her brother.

'Will you be monopolizing Steve the whole weekend?'

'Go away with you,' Jock growled, softly. 'Leave the man be. You've got boyfriends aplenty.'

After she got out of the car Jock handed Steve the car keys. 'You can drive us to the factory.'

Jock's father looked up as they entered the office, and seemed pleased to see Steve again.

'I wondered why my son couldn't sort out our mechanical problem himself,' he said, grumpily. 'It's a bit silly to drag you all this way.'

'Well, come on, let's have a look at that pump,' Steve said, shrugging himself into a pair of overalls. It took longer than he had anticipated to isolate the problem, and he had to fabricate a piece to replace a damaged part, which meant it was nearly five o'clock before he finished.

'That's it,' he said, wiping his hands clean on cotton waste. 'You'll just have to insert the O rings when they arrive. I'll put them in the post first thing Monday morning.'

'Thanks, Steve. I suppose I could have fixed it myself and kept the old man happy, but you've always been more of a hands-on man than myself.' Jock slapped him on the back. 'Anyway, it was a good excuse to catch up with you. Now, I don't know about you, but I could use a drink. Let's find a pub.'

*

After they had dined, the two friends retired to the study with a bottle of malt whiskey.

They were nearly halfway through the bottle when Jenny poked her head around the door after saying goodnight to her date.

'Are you going to invite me in for a drink?' she asked, tossing her head provocatively, 'or are you keeping it all to yourself?'

Steve studied her in the subdued lighting, noticing that every aspect of her face seemed a little out of proportion. Her blue eyes were too large, her freckled, upturned nose too small, and her mouth too wide. Even her limbs looked awkward, her long shapely legs ending in a tucked-up, seductive little bottom. However, as a whole, she was incredibly attractive, and quite unusual. She caught his eye and smiled.

'So, Steve, what are you going to do with yourself for the rest of weekend?' she asked, in her soft Scottish brogue. 'Are you going to stagger from pub to pub with my dear brother, reminiscing about the good old days?'

'Have you any better suggestions?'

'Aye, but you'll need to ask,' Jenny said, quietly, peering at him over the top of her glass. 'Na tim'rous beastie a gud enow, m'loon.'

Jock laughed uproariously, but refused to comment about her choice of words, except to say that he had misgivings about her morals. 'Many years ago, she decided to live up to a redhead's reputation rather than live it down,' he said, and laughed again. 'But don't get me wrong, she's a bonnie lass and I love her dearly.'

The two men spent the next morning fishing off the jetty, and then lunched at a nearby pub. Mindful of Jenny's admonition, Steve steered his friend away from the bar afterwards, and went for a drive in the country. By the time they returned to the MacTavish house, it was late afternoon, and Jenny met them at the door.

'Maureen said she'd love to meet your old flat mate,' she announced, looking meaningfully at Jock. 'And she's looking forward to having dinner with you both this evening.'

Jock took a deep breath, and then let it out slowly.

'Women! Bah, they'll take over your life given half a chance.' He turned to Steve. 'Maureen and I have an agreement of sorts.'

'Yes,' Jenny agreed, a trifle sarcastically. 'She has to chase after you. If she didn't take the initiative, she'd never get her hands on you.'

'So you decided to give her a helping hand?'

'Aye.' She grinned mischievously and then turned to Steve. 'I've lined up the most sought-after woman in Invercargill for you.'

'That's kind of you, Jenny.' Steve said, trying to keep a straight face. 'I hope you've found a date for yourself as well.'

Jenny laughed softly. 'Touché.'

They managed to get a table at one of the better restaurants in town. The food was good, but the service was better, and the wine waiter kept their glasses full. Jock and Maureen seem to complement each other perfectly, and Jenny hinted that they would probably tie the knot next year.

Like all restaurants in provincial cities, it closed the doors at ten o'clock, and as they made their way outside Jenny slipped her hand into Steve's. 'It's too early to go home. Let's go for a drink somewhere.'

He looked into her upturned face and smiled. 'Yes, the night's young.' Steve was about to say, 'Have you any ideas, Jock?' when Maureen spoke up.

'Jock's taking me home while he's still sober.' As she pulled Jock towards the car, Maureen waved them a farewell with her free hand. 'We'll catch up tomorrow.'

They watched them drive away, and Jenny gave a lilting laugh.

'Poor old Jock, he irons himself out and then he's good for nothing, so Maureen ends up even more frustrated.'

'Why does she put up with him then?'

'Why does any woman put up with any particular man? Usually

because she loves him.' She paused and then added. 'Too much.'

'And you? What about you?'

'I haven't found the man I want to spend the rest of my life with, not yet,' she replied, seriously. Then on a lighter note she added. 'Come on, we're wasting time. There's whiskey to be drunk.'

The first pub they chose was too dismal and almost deserted; the second was full of roistering drunks, and rather than risk another disappointment, Jenny suggested they should go home. As she drove back to the MacTavish house, Steve studied her profile again, and, with her vital personality, it was easy to see why she was so attractive to men. She led the way into the house and headed for the study.

'Let's hope there's some whiskey left,' she said, switching on the light. She held up the bottle. 'Aye, there's enough for one, or maybe two each.'

Steve raised his glass. 'What do the Scots say? Here's looking up your kilts?'

'Slainte mhaith.' Jenny laughed and clinked her tumbler against his. 'Slainte mhaith means good health.'

When he stood up and placed the empty glass on the table, she moved to his side. For a brief moment she looked up into his face and then wrapped both arms around his neck.

'Kiss me, Steve,' she breathed, huskily. 'Kiss me like you really mean it.' Then she drew his head down until their lips met.

Her tiny tongue sought his and the sensation sent shivers down his spine. He placed both hands on her buttocks, and pulled her closer to himself as she pressed her slender body against his. When they finally pulled apart he drew in a deep breath as the feelings generated deep within him threatened to explode. Totally surprised at her boldness, he gazed at her in silence.

'That's only for special guys, m'loon,' she said, softly. 'And you're very special.'

'But, you don't...' Steve began.

'You may not think so,' Jenny said, quietly. 'But from the moment I saw you, it was as if I were propelled towards you.'

84

As Steve tried to think of a reply, Jenny turned off the light. 'Let's call it a night.' She laughed softly. 'I'll not be responsible for what happens if you let me kiss you like that again.'

'But, I…'

'I'll not come between you and Kirsty, but that relationship is not going to last forever, is it?'

As he climbed into bed later, Steve reviewed the evening. Jenny had dominated his thoughts and desires all evening, and it was only now that she was out of his sight that he was able to think about the other woman in his life. Almost at once he recalled a similar situation with Suzi Lysle Spencer. When they had been together in Wales, all thoughts of Kirsty had disappeared from his mind. What am I trying to tell myself? How can I just push the memory of Kirsty into the background as easily as that? He wondered.

He was just dropping off to sleep when the memory of Jenny's kiss flooded back. When he finally fell asleep the night was filled with dreams of the women in his life. As he watched the scenes his mind was playing, he noted how the dark, almost sultry comeliness of Kirsty contrasted with the fresh natural beauty of auburn-haired Suzi. Both of them were a world apart from Jenny's brazen attractiveness. Steve broke out in a cold sweat when in his dream he had to choose between them, and was still agonising whom to pick when someone called his name.

A gentle tap on the door was followed by Mrs MacTavish's repeated question. 'Would you no' like a cup of tea, Steve?' When he answered, the woman said. 'I'll leave it by the door, then.'

Jock didn't return until mid-morning. He looked slightly embarrassed, and tried to make a joke of his nocturnal habits, but they fell flat. Jenny was nowhere to be seen. Steve felt both relieved and a little disappointed, and suggested that he and Jock should take a drive before Sunday lunch. When they returned for the meal an hour later, Jenny was waiting for them. 'You're just in time. Come on, it doesn't do to keep Mother waiting.'

Once lunch was over, the three of them settled in a comfortable spot in the garden, but a few minutes later Jock went inside to make coffee. Jenny took advantage of his absence and slid over to sit beside Steve, putting her face close to his. 'So when am I going to see you again?'

Steve was searching his mind for a suitable answer when Jock returned, bearing a tray of coffee. He wagged his finger at Steve. 'We'd better be going soon, so drink up, or you'll find it's a long walk to Auckland if you miss that flight.'

86

Chapter Eleven

Kirsty watched Steve drive away from the house with mixed feelings. She had done everything possible to please him and her foster parents during the past two weeks. Whenever Hepora or Iritana phoned, she had limited the conversation to a few minutes.

However, the battle within raged on. She greatly appreciated all that Vince and Norah had done for her, and in her own way she loved them both, but she was always conscious that they would never fulfil that inner need. And Steve? Well, he was a wonderful guy, and she loved him too, but not in the way she loved Joey. Steve did not understand how she felt, nor did he realise what was really important to her. It was only when she was with her Maori friends that she felt truly happy.

She had wondered if he was going on the trip to get away from everything, but he had assured her it was to help out an old friend. Norah had suggested that they visit her sister, but she didn't fancy sitting around all weekend, so she bundled some clothes into an overnight bag and left a note on the kitchen table, saying: 'I'll be back Sunday.'

Then she let herself out of the house and drove across town to the predominantly Maori area of the city where her friends lived, determined not to get drunk or take any dope. If she kept to that plan she would be all right.

Hepora greeted her with a kiss as she opened the door of the communal house. 'Well, hi, Kirsty, come on in.'

Iritana and her boyfriend turned up soon after and they all went down the pub for a drink. After they had each bought a round, Hepora's boyfriend picked up a case of beer to take back to the house, and they soon piled into it, sharing it with a few other friends who had dropped in to say hello. Kirsty had enjoyed some beer, but when marijuana was produced she pleaded a headache and went to the bedroom.

The next morning the house was quiet when she awoke, so after swallowing a quick coffee, she grabbed a plastic bag and was collecting the empties that littered the rooms, when she heard the sound of an approaching car. Through the front window she saw a battered Chrysler Valiant cruising slowly down the street. It came to a halt outside the house and as she watched, a heavily built young man climbed out. Joey. 'Joey Ruawhane,' she cried, opening the door and flinging herself into his arms. 'Oh, Joey.' All the emotions she had tried to suppress shot to the surface as the big man held her close. After a few moments, he raised Kirsty's head and looked into her tearstained face.

'I was afraid you might have forgotten me,' he said.

'Never.'

'Can we talk?'

Kirsty pulled him into the house gazing lovingly at him as he perched on a kitchen stool.

'It's so wonderful to see you again, Joey. When did you get out?'

'Yesterday. I rang your folks, and your mum just said you'd gone away for the weekend, but they didn't know where. I guessed you might be at Hepora's, so here I am.' He drew her to him and gently cupped her bottom in one large hand. 'It's been a long time, Kirsty. Too long.'

Over the next fifteen minutes Joey explained that his sentence had been reduced for good behaviour but, before she could question him further about life in prison, Joey grabbed her hand. 'Come on, let's go say hello to my folks.'

'What are you going to do now, Joey?' Kirsty ventured to ask.

Once again he turned her question back on her. 'What about you, what have you been up to?'

'It's a long story, but I'll try to keep it simple.'

When she had finished, he sighed,

'It must have been hard trying to please everyone. Like you say, it's a pity you weren't born into a full Maori family.'

'I know, but they've been so good to me and that's why I feel guilty about it all.' She grabbed his hand. 'I don't know what to do, Joey. I tried to explain to them, but they don't understand my need to be with my own people.'

'So what will you do? Is there anyone you can go to?'

Kirsty looked at him coyly then touched his cheek with the tips of her fingers.

'You. I want to be with you.'

'Do you really mean that?' Joey asked, stamping on the brakes.

The incredulous look on his face brought tears to Kirsty's eyes. Barely able to speak she merely nodded her head.

'That changes everything,' he said firmly, shoving the car into gear and letting out the clutch. 'Yes, that really does change everything.'

*

Suzi placed her coffee on the table by the window, her favourite spot, where she had a view of approaching guests, as well as allowing her to watch the changing pageant of pedestrians who thronged the crowded shopping area. It had been a particularly busy week, and she was pleased that Gary was there to help out. People were still enquiring about Christmas dinner, and it looked as if they would have to arrange two sittings.

Gary joined her after he had called his bookie again. 'Don't know why I bother with this treadmill of an existence,' he said, as he sat next to Suzi. Noticing her sudden look of concern, he laughed. 'Don't worry, I won't quit before Christmas.'

'Can you support yourself by gambling?'

'I don't call it gambling,' Gary replied, testily, 'it's a form of investment, like the stock market.'

'But surely it's more risky?'

'Only if you don't know what you're doing.'

Suzi stared at him as she thought about his words, and was about to comment when Mark bustled in. 'It's mighty cold out there,' he muttered, peeling off his coat and rubbing his hands together. He poured a coffee and pulled up a chair. 'Well, how did we do today?'

'Good,' Suzi replied. 'We had a big lunch crowd and more enquiries about Christmas dinner.'

'We've got two up so far, and both at a good price,' Gary said, grinning.

Suzi looked at him with a puzzled expression.

'What do you mean, two up so far?'

'Two winners,' Mark replied, grinning broadly.

'Oh? Don't tell me you're betting on horses, too?'

'I'm giving him a few tips.' Gary laughed again. 'There's more than one way to skin a cat.'

'But…' Suzi began, and then stopped.

'Look, if Gary can afford a Porsche and holidays on the Côte de Azure, it's gotta be worth the gamble,' Mark hastily added. 'All I want is to pay off my bank loan, and what I borrowed from my folks.'

Rather than get involved in a discussion about horse racing, Suzi turned the conversation back to the restaurant, happy that Mark assured her everything was in place for the wedding reception on the following weekend.

During a lull that afternoon Suzi phoned Charlize and voiced her concern about Mark's intention to augment his income by betting on horses.

'Don't worry. Mark'll lose interest when Gary leaves—it's a phase some men go through.'

When Suzi got home that evening she checked the answerphone and found a message from Charlize.

'Suzi,' she shrieked. 'I've won that holiday for two in Australia. Call me straight away.'

Charlize was still bubbling with excitement when she answered the phone.

'Isn't it fantastic?' she cried. 'An official letter from the distributors of Castlemaine Fourex was waiting for me when I got home.'

'You mean that slogan you scribbled on the back of the pub coaster won first prize?'

'It did, so we're both off pretty soon. I'll arrange time off, and you'll be all right, being your own boss, won't you?'

'I don't know. Two weeks away will be stretching things.'

Not to be put off, Charlize enumerated the various excursions that were part of the fully paid holiday in Australia. The prizes included a trip to the Barrier Reef, a visit to a crocodile farm, and a ride on the scenic railway through the rain forest. It sounded wonderful.

Suzi thought about arrangements once she replaced the phone; Narelle could take over as hostess and Mark could do the books and banking. She leaned back against the sofa and wondered why she felt so stressed. The business with the inheritance still rankled, but Steve Pardoe had every right to make a claim. If only he had missed the solicitor's advertisement and she had never met him, life would be much simpler right now.

'Blast you, Steve Pardoe,' she muttered. 'You should have stayed where you belong.'

Chapter Twelve

Steve spent most of his flight north to Auckland thinking about the weekend with Jock. It had been good to see Jock again, but his thoughts were centred on Jenny. She had dropped him off at the airport and kissed his cheek as Jock shook his hand. Then as he began to walk into the terminal she had slipped a note into his hand.

When the plane became airborne he pulled it from his pocket.

Dear Steve,

Words can't express how much I enjoyed your visit. I feel as if a whole new chapter of my life is about to begin. Were you the catalyst? I think so. Maybe you only see me as a precocious redhead who enjoys male attention, but I long for something more meaningful. I don't believe in love at first sight, but something has happened to make me reconsider the possibility. Do you believe in déjà vu? Please keep in touch.

He recalled their conversation of the previous night, when she spoke of starting a new job in Auckland in the New Year. If she moved to the northern capital it would complicate things, and, although the prospect of a sexual dalliance with her was exciting, it would be unwise. After all he had to consider Kirsty. He folded the note and stuffed it back into his pocket.

Life had become too complex lately. There were times when he wished Vince had never seen that advertisement in the newspaper and urged him to write to the Welsh solicitor. He had never considered he might have relatives in the UK, and knew little about his natural parents' background.

Vince and Norah were his parents—he knew no others. They had urged him to claim the inheritance, even suggesting he should present his case in person. He probably would have ignored their advice if his Dutch friend, Pieter Boersma, hadn't written again to ask when he was going to visit them in Holland; it had helped him make up his mind.

He thought about his visits to places of interest in London, and how he had become embroiled in the break-in at Caxton Manor. He wondered what would have happened if things had happened differently; if he had never gone to the manor house and encountered the burglars or Suzi Lysle Spencer.

All the if onlys and what ifs ran wild through his head. If he had not become sexually involved with Kirsty and promised to marry her, he would have been free to pursue another path. He might even have considered sharing the manor with Suzi and having the chance to make a new life for himself in Britain, but he had to consider Vince, who had come to rely on him so much lately. Besides, he loved New Zealand, and couldn't imagine living anywhere else. The cabin steward's call to fasten seat belts for landing interrupted his thoughts.

He collected his car from the car park and threw his bag onto the back seat. As he headed out of the airport complex he felt reluctant to go straight home, and found himself driving towards the local club. As he walked into the main bar, he saw Vince drinking with a couple of his friends.

'Steve,' he called, 'come and join us.'

The other men drifted away one by one until only Steve and his father remained. Now that they were alone Vince asked about Jock and his family, and then voiced his concern about Kirsty.

'Norah found her note when she came home on Friday,' he said, quietly. 'All it said was, "I'll be home Sunday".' That evening a man rang up and asked to speak to her.' Vince looked worried.

'Do you have any idea who it was?'

'No, but I wondered if it was that this Joey that Kirsty was so involved with—if he had been released from prison. Your mother and I did everything we could to dissuade her from seeing him, but you know what she's like.'

'Do you think she's with him?'

'I'm inclined to fear the worst,' Vince said as he downed the last of his beer. 'Come on, we'd better go home before I drink myself over the limit.'

*

A surge of joy swept through Kirsty as she looked into Joey's face. The words: 'I want to be with you' had completely transformed him.

'That's the best coming-out present anybody could ever want,' he said, holding her in his massive arms. Kirsty's tears slid unchecked down her cheeks as their lips met. His response to her declaration of love brought forth a tenderness that caught her by surprise. She did not know he was capable of such emotion.

When they arrived at his parents' house she was greeted like a long lost daughter.

'Kirsty, hey, where've you been?' Joey's mother, Kathy, folded the young woman into her voluminous bosom. 'You know you was always welcome here, girl. No need to stay away because our Joey was doing time.' She stepped back and smiled. 'Now you come say hello to all the folks here.'

Joey's homecoming was an excuse for a party, and as soon as the word went around that he was home, friends and relatives dropped in to say hello from all over. Someone organised a hangi. They broke it open late Saturday afternoon, and descended on it like a swarm of hungry locusts. Some time during the night, Joey pulled Kirsty away from the party and led her into the house next door where one of his relatives lived.

'It'll be quieter here. Huey won't be home until the booze runs out.'

Kirsty slipped out of her clothes and drew Joey down onto the bed. Their excitement tipped them both over the edge within minutes, and it was only as the sun peeped over the horizon that they finally drifted off to sleep, wrapped in each other's arms.

Their relationship had waxed and waned over a period of years because Kirsty's foster parents had disapproved of him and tried to keep them apart, but every now and then Kirsty rebelled, sought him out, and renewed their association. She had attended court the day he had been sentenced, and cried bitterly as he was led away.

She knew there had been times in the past when he had considered taking her away somewhere, but she also knew that the longing to be close to his own family always put an end to such plans. Joey knew where his roots lay, and the traditional link to the past was important to him, as with all Maoris. Although she did not expect to see him again, Kirsty had hoped against hope that he would come looking for her when he was released.

They spent Sunday visiting friends, and it seemed as if everyone wanted to have a drink with them. It was late afternoon before they found time to talk about what lay ahead. He watched the tears well up in Kirsty's eyes as he told her that he intended to mend his ways and make provision for the future.

'Bobby's promised me a job driving the van,' he said, clasping her hand. 'It's a start, eh?'

'That's great, Joey, really great.'

'Hey, and maybe you and I could…?' Joey fumbled for his words.

'I'd like that,' Kirsty said quietly. 'Yes, that would be really great.'

'But what about your folks, and Steve?'

Kirsty looked at the huge man by her side, and sighed softly. 'They know I'm having difficulty in accepting their lifestyle, and I know they don't understand why. Norah and Vince have been wonderful to me, but they can't give me what I need. And Steve, well, I could never be the wife he wants. He needs someone quite different from me.'

Joey listened patiently. 'Look, I know you don't want to hurt anyone, Kirsty, but…'

She looked at him imploringly. 'What am I going to do, Joey?'

'Kirsty, I'll do anything to help. Just ask, eh?' he said with sincerity.

'I'd better go home now. I'll get a cab,' she muttered. While they waited for the taxi, Joey held her tenderly in his huge arms as though she were a newborn babe. The bond between them had never been stronger. He helped her climb into the vehicle and whispered his promise again. 'Anything, Kirsty. Just ask.'

Norah opened the door as Kirsty pushed the key into the lock.

'I said I'd be home Sunday,' she said, defiantly. 'And here I am.' She glanced at the two men sitting in the lounge. 'Don't ask where I've been, because I won't tell you.'

'But Kirsty, we're only trying to…' Norah stopped as she pushed past her and headed quickly towards her bedroom.

'Something's happened to make her change her mind,' Norah said, as she returned to the sitting room. 'What are we going to do, Vince?'

Chapter Thirteen

It was mid-morning before Kirsty struggled out of bed. Her dreams had been full of Joey gently cradling her in his arms; Joey making love to her; Joey promising her anything to make her happy. And now as she padded into the bathroom, Kirsty wondered how she should break the news to Norah and Vince. And most importantly to Steve. She had to tell them that it was time for her to go, time to get on with the rest of her life, regardless of the outcome.

After a shower, Kirsty began to pack her belongings. As she sorted through the accumulation of odds and ends that she had collected over the years, her eyes filled with tears. Unable to continue, she went and made herself a drink, and while she sat there, staring into space, Steve walked into the room. He hesitated as though surprised to see her still in the house, but before he could speak she confronted him.

'Why are you here?' she demanded. 'I thought you'd be at the factory.'

'I had to pick up my laptop.'

'Do you want coffee?'

Steve looked at her in amazement, well aware now that their whole future was hanging in the balance and she had just asked him a couple of mundane questions as if everything were perfectly normal. He studied her profile. The dark rings under her eyes were probably due to alcohol and lack of sleep, but they also made her look as though she had been crying.

'Yes, please,' he said after some hesitation.

Without a word Kirsty made the coffee and pushed it across to Steve. She opened her mouth to speak, but nothing came out. Tears welled up in her eyes, and slowly rolled down her cheeks.

Steve moved quickly to her side, but she turned her head away. The tableau seemed frozen in time as they both wrestled with their own thoughts. Kirsty wept softly as she left the room, but, unwilling for her to push him out of her life without an explanation, Steve raced after her, and gently turned her around to face him as she was about to enter her bedroom. 'Talk to me, Kirsty,' he insisted. 'At least say something, even if it's just get lost.'

As she looked at him in silence, Steve sensed she was fighting a despair that seemed to overwhelm her. Silently, she reached out and touched his face with her fingertips, then nodded her head as if agreeing with herself about something. Finally, she spoke.

'Would you run me over to pick up my car?'

'Sure, we'll go now if you like.' He clasped her fingers and pressed them to his lips. While he waited for her to put on some make-up and tidy her hair, Steve went to his room and picked up a jacket soiled with coffee on the trip to Invercargill. He stopped outside the dry cleaner's, grabbed the jacket off the back seat, and slung it over his arm. As he ran to the shop, the note from Jenny MacTavish fell out of the jacket pocket and onto the ground.

Kirsty jumped out of the car and picked it up. Without thinking, she unfolded the piece of paper and read it. Within minutes, Steve was back in the vehicle, and she the thrust it at him with an angry look in her eyes.

'Who's Jenny?' she demanded. 'And what's this déjà vu business?'

*

Suzi received a phone call from the police to notify her that the four-poster stolen from Caxton Manor could now be reclaimed. When she identified the furniture, the officer told her that she would have to make her own arrangements to have it returned to the house.

'It's out of our hands now,' he said.

After she had completed the necessary forms, Suzi rang a removal firm and arranged for it to be collected. She picked up the phone to ask Mr Duncan if it was all right to enter the house, and then dropped it back on the cradle. Why should she wait for him to ponder over the legalities of her action, and then make a special trip to his chambers to pick up a key? She knew where Uncle Bart had hidden a spare in the garden, so she would have no trouble in letting herself in. And the solicitor would be none the wiser.

However, she felt strangely apprehensive about entering the building alone. The removal firm had promised to be there on the hour, but there was no sign of them yet, and it was nearly ten past. Unwilling to wait any longer, Suzi turned the key in the lock and swung open the door. An overpowering feeling of neglect impressed itself on her mind as she walked from the vestibule into the hall.

Suzi pushed open the door that led to the sitting room with a feeling of trepidation. In her mind's eye she could picture Steve Pardoe lurching towards her before he collapsed on the floor at her feet. There were no visible signs of the break-in. In fact, it looked as if the house had been undisturbed since it was closed after Uncle Bart's funeral. Her eyes pricked with tears at the memory of the eccentric old man she had loved so dearly.

The sound of a heavy vehicle backing up to the house cut into her reverie. The slightly overweight driver slid out of the cabin and then reached back in for the paperwork. However, as soon as he saw Suzi he made a conscious effort to straighten up.

'Right,' he said, in an authoritative tone. 'I'll need you to sign for this.' He peered at the delivery slip as if to check it was the right address.

Suzi quickly scribbled a signature in the space provided, then gestured at the open door. 'I'd like you to put in the second room on your right upstairs.'

After the lorry had gone, Suzi walked through the house again. Memories flooded her mind as she went from room to room, recapturing the emotions she had experienced as a young girl eagerly exploring the wonderful old manor. Uncle Bart had proudly explained everything to her in detail, pointing out the original old cottage that predated the rest of the house. The enormously thick internal buttressed walls contained just two tiny windows that opened onto the corridor leading to the breakfast room.

Then he had taken her down into the cellar. The flagstone floor had not impressed her at that age, but she had become very excited when she saw the shining fragments of crystal in the huge solid boulders that made up the wall. Her uncle had chuckled when she asked if they were diamonds. She had since learned that they were a clear indication that the foundations were bone dry and, no doubt, this had helped preserve the old house over the years. She walked over to the section of wall that seemed to have been bricked up and ran her hand over it. Knowing there was a huge mound in the garden outside that could well have been a Bronze Age burial mound, she felt convinced that this had been an entrance into a chamber inside the mound. She made up her mind to find out for sure one day.

One of the highlights of her early visits had been to race up the spiral stone steps, run across the cottage area and then clatter down the great sweeping Victorian staircase to the main hall. And now as she climbed the steps, she wondered what would become of this magnificent building. She had taken stock of the place since the funeral, mentally calculating the cost of replacing the old Victorian drapes and incorporating some form of secondary glazing. The figures had been daunting. She could never afford it under the present circumstances.

Suzi made her way to the ground floor and paused by the front door. Once again she recalled the excitement that had swept over her when she had thought about using the lovely Victorian house for receptions. That feeling had been replaced by one of frustration when she learned that she was not the only claimant to the property. If only Steve Pardoe had not contacted Duncan, the inheritance would have been all hers.

The idea of including him in some form of partnership seemed not only remote, but rather foolish. Mark would not agree to such a proposition, and certainly he would not want Steve hovering in the background. Anyway she did not really want a third party involved in the enterprise.

As she walked back to her car she glanced at the grass-covered mound that rose fifteen feet above the rest of the garden. A local historian had suggested that it could be a Bronze Age barrow, but of course the council had ridiculed that idea when they had needed to build an access road through that side of the garden. The ancient monuments department had given her a disappointing answer, but she felt quite certain she was right in her guess that there was access from the cellar to a chamber inside it. She thought about it the response the department had given her again.

'That's not important. It's just a pile of Victorian building rubble,' the clerk had stated, in a know-it-all manner. 'Instead of carting it away they merely turfed it over.' He had laughed sardonically. 'Don't expect to find any treasure or artefacts under that lot, madam. It's only rubbish.'

But Uncle Bart had thought differently. He claimed that the Victorians would never have tolerated a great pile of building rubble directly outside their beautiful dining room window, and if only to justify his views and prove him right, she would arrange an archaeological dig on it one day.

She threaded the new chain through the wrought iron gates and snapped the padlock shut. Climbing back into the Honda she drove away, deep in thought.

*

Mark looked up as she walked into the kitchen.

'Everything okay?' He glanced at the clock on the wall. 'I expected you back long ago.'

'Is there a problem?'

'No, just that there's a lot to do,' Mark replied, testily. 'We've got the Women's Institute luncheon and the party tonight and the…' He stopped as she pulled a face. 'I'd appreciate a hand, that's all.'

'Hey… have you forgotten I never agreed to work in the kitchen? It's your domain,' Suzi said, with emphasis. 'That was never part of the deal. If it's too much for you we'll cut back on bookings, but don't expect me to don an apron. Not now, not ever.' She turned on her heel and walked back to the restaurant.

She had barely reached the front desk when Mark caught up with her.

He laid a hand on her arm and sighed. 'Sorry, Suzi, I didn't mean it that way.' When she nodded, Mark kissed her cheek lightly. 'Could you find time to go to the Co-op for me?' He laid a list on the desk. 'It's urgent.'

By the time she had returned with the oddments he needed, the first few members of the local Women's Institute group had arrived. Pushing her thoughts to the back of her mind, Suzi greeted them one by one, and conducted them to the area set aside for their luncheon. The next few hours were frantic as an unexpected rush of casual diners stretched their resources to the limit. When they finally closed the door that afternoon, she heaved a big sigh of relief.

As the waitresses said their goodbyes, Suzi called to Narelle.

'I'd like you to handle the lunchtime guests for the next few days. I need to give Mark a hand setting up the village hall for the next booking, amongst other things.'

'Oh, thank you.' The woman's face lit up as she spoke. 'I've been hoping you'd give me another opportunity to prove I'm up to the job.'

'Good.' Suzi smiled warmly. 'I may need to take some time off in the New Year, so it'll be good to know I can rely on you.'

'Will you be employing another hostess when you move into bigger premises next year?' Narelle watched her closely as she waited for a reply.

'We're undecided as yet. Rest assured you'll be told if we do.'

Suzi watched the woman close the door behind her, and grimaced. Why had Narelle asked such a leading question? Had Mark been discussing his ideas with Gary, who might have passed them onto Narelle? She had specifically asked him not to divulge any details of their plans or business arrangements to any of the employees, but it seemed he had done just that.

'I'll have a word with him later,' she muttered.

Chapter Fourteen

When Suzi voiced her concern about staff gossip, Mark hinted that Gary might have passed on something to Narelle. This confirmed he must have told Gary something, but she kept her peace: they could ill afford more problems at the moment. As Christmas approached the pressure continued to mount, and their relationship gradually reverted to a purely business one again, which suited her fine.

Gary's feverish pace seemed excessive at times, but he was as good as he was fast. When he had finished for the day, he would grab a couple of beers from the bar and throw himself into a chair by the window. After he had calmed down he would methodically work his way through the racing papers, circling his selections with a red felt tip pen. Suzi saw no reason to complain, but wondered if he was still passing on tips to Mark.

By now, Narelle had slipped into her role as hostess with the minimum of fuss, and that had released Suzi to attend to other matters. She felt confident the woman would cope when she went on her trip with Charlize.

Her friend popped into the restaurant to discuss the matter one afternoon.

'I've arranged my time off in February, so I'll notify the prize draw committee and ask them to organise the tickets.'

'That should work out well for me too,' Suzi agreed. 'I'll have a couple of weeks to wind down after the Christmas and New Year rush.' She gave a little laugh. 'All I've told Mark is that I want time off in the New Year. I haven't told him where I'm going, but I'd better say something soon.'

'He won't cause any problems will he?'

'I hope not. It's just that he's come to rely on me too much lately, and gets a bit touchy if I'm not around to hold his hand.'

'And what about Caxton Manor? Have you heard from that New Zealand fellow yet?'

'Steve Pardoe? No, the solicitor hasn't received a reply to the last letter he sent. Things have gone quiet and I'm a bit concerned.'

'What happens now?'

Suzi shrugged. 'I don't know. I'll just have to wait and see, I suppose.' Then she laughed. 'If he hasn't answered by the time we go on our trip, maybe I'll might pop over to Auckland and confront him in person.'

After Charlize left Suzi sat deep in thought about Caxton Manor possibly attracting more thieves if it remained empty. The previous burglars had by-passed the alarm system to gain entry, and they might choose to pay another visit. She decided to phone Mr Duncan first thing in the morning to see if he could arrange for her to move in as a deterrent to any further break-in.

Having settled her mind on that, she went to the kitchen and found Mark preparing chickens. He straightened up and sighed.

'How's everything?'

'Fine. I think I told you about Charlize's holiday win to Australia, and that she could take someone with her.' Suzi hesitated for a moment, but Mark made no comment. 'She's given the holiday organisers a firm date in February, and I said I'd go with her. I may as well, it's a free holiday, so is that okay with you?'

He shrugged and turned back without comment to work his way steadily through the pile of chickens in front of him.

*

The job completed, he wiped his brow with the back of his free hand and hoped that Gary wouldn't be late because there was still a lot of preparation to do for the party that night. Then he thought of Suzi. They had not been out together for ages because of the pressure of business. Inasmuch as he was pleased with the success of their venture, he wanted to cement their relationship. He would have to make a point of their having a drink together at least once or twice a week when the festive season was over.

His thoughts were interrupted by Gary's cheery hello. 'Hi, Mark, how's it going?' He threw a newspaper on the stool and laughed. 'Just as well I've got something else to keep me busy. I haven't seen anything that looks like a winner all week.'

'Surely there's something worth backing?'

'I don't bet for the sake of betting,' Gary's serious tone sounded ominous. 'That's a mug's game. I don't put my money on anything that doesn't stand more than an even chance of winning.' He tapped the paper. 'I wouldn't like to have to pick a winner in any of these races.'

Mark watched him slip on an apron and begin to sharpen his knives.

'You'll have to explain it all to me again,' he said. 'I was under the impression you had at least one winner on every card.'

As they worked, Gary explained again how he worked out a horse's chances by the weights it carried in comparison to the other runners. He told Mark he kept a record of the horse's performance over a variety of distances, and a dozen other variables that affected its chances. Finally, he repeated the old adage: odds on—look on.

'I don't bet on odds-on favourites, not ever.'

Mark tried to absorb what his friend was saying, but still failed to understand all the racing terms and the jargon used by commentators and sportswriters. Within ten minutes there was no time to think about anything except getting the meals out to customers. When they finally hung up their aprons and said goodnight, horse racing was the last thing on his mind.

*

Steve looked at Kirsty for several seconds without answering her question. He had forgotten about Jenny's note, and now he wondered why he had not destroyed it straight away instead of stuffing it into his pocket. Of course it was easy to be wise after the event. As he attempted to take it from her hand, she moved away.

'Who's Jenny?' She repeated her question. 'And what's this all about?'

'She's Jock's sister,' Steve replied, squirming in the seat as he coughed self-consciously. 'She rather fancied me, that's all.'

'Ha, just rather fancies you? Oh yeah?' Kirsty's tiny laugh had a brittle edge to it. 'Sounds a bit more than that to me.'

Steve sighed again. The roles had suddenly been reversed. Whereas he had seen himself as the one who had been betrayed, now he realised that although he had done no more than kiss the girl, he was also at fault. He knew Kirsty had spent the weekend with Joey Ruawhane, but that was of no matter now, because she could accuse him of being unfaithful, too. It was an impasse.

'First of all it was this Suzi Lysle whatsername and now it's Jenny Mac whatever. Unless, of course, there's also someone else I don't know about.' Kirsty screwed up the note and threw in onto the floor of the car.

'I've got the feeling that no matter what I say you're not going to believe me. I could try to explain it, but…' Steve stopped. To him, it seemed as though a sense of freedom had suddenly swept over her—as if she had been given a heaven sent opportunity to make the break from the past that bound her to him, his family, and their way of life. He sensed she couldn't care now if he had indeed slept with the girl or not. He felt convinced that what had happened had unwittingly liberated her.

Kirsty climbed out of the car. 'Carry on. I'll catch a cab,' she said, and slammed the door shut before Steve could stop her. Then she ran lightly down the street and hailed a passing taxi.

*

'You're in a happy mood,' the driver remarked, as she slid into the front seat, smiling broadly. 'Have you won the lotto, or found a new boyfriend?'

'Better than that,' she replied, quickly. 'I'm free at last.'

The cab driver looked at her sideways, but made no comment. Twenty-five minutes later he pulled up outside Hepora's house. 'Here we are, love,' he said, and wished her well as he accepted the fare. 'You hang onto that freedom now, you hear? Don't let anyone take if off you again.'

Impulsively, Kirsty leaned over and kissed his cheek.

'You better believe it mister.' Then she bounced out of the cab and ran up the garden path to the house. Kirsty followed her friend into the kitchen and related what had happened since she woke up that morning. She spoke about her feelings as she had gone through the gifts Norah and Vince had given her, and recalled their kindness over the years. Then she spoke of the guilt that had almost overwhelmed her when she realised that her relationship with Steve had to be terminated. Finally, she ecstatically related how the note she had found gave her a way out of it all.

When she finished, Hepora laughed softly.

'Well, it certainly let you off the hook. I'd say it's all been handed to you on a plate.'

'Yeah. Looks like it was meant to happen.' It was only after she had told Hepora the whole story of the way she felt that she headed for the only home she'd known for years.

*

Steve watched her climb into the cab with mixed feelings. On one hand, he was relieved that she had found the note; it had helped her come to grips with her situation. He still cared deeply for her, but deep down in his heart he knew that this development was the best for them both. It was her choice, and he had no right to deny her that.

He stared into the middle distance for a while before starting the car and driving to the factory. Vince looked up as he walked into the office.

'Everything all right?'

'Yes, and no,' Steve replied, and then told his father what had happened.

Vince sighed deeply. 'That's it then, isn't it?' He picked up the phone. 'I'd better tell Norah.' When he had finished speaking to his wife he handed the instrument to Steve. 'She wants to talk to you.'

Steve listened in silence, answering her questions as best he could, and then said goodbye. The two men looked at each other as if unwilling to allow their emotions to show, until Vince sniffed noisily.

'I'd sooner see her dead than take up with that man,' he said, in a strangled voice. 'She's throwing her life away.'

'But it's her life, Vince. You can't live it for her.'

Kirsty was busy heaping her belongings into the back of her car when Steve pulled up behind Norah's Mitsubishi. He hesitated before climbing out of his vehicle and walked towards her. She paused for a moment as he reached her side, but continued to shove things into the trunk while he waited patiently for her to acknowledge him. When he finally called her name, she turned to face him.

'I'm not saying anything until Vince comes home.' Her voice was strained and hard. 'I don't want to repeat myself. It'll keep.' With that, she marched purposefully into the house.

When Vince finally arrived, Norah met him at the door, and placed a finger to her lips to indicate he should say nothing before going into the lounge. Steve joined them moments later. Kirsty was standing by the window, her arms folded across her chest in a defiant manner.

'What's going on Kirsty…?' Vince began, and then stopped as Norah grabbed his arm.

'No, Vince, I promised we would listen to what she has to say first, and without interruption. Now let her be.' She pushed him down onto the sofa and nodded to the young woman. 'Okay Kirsty, we're prepared to hear what you have to say, but I hope you're mindful of the effect your actions will have on us all.' Then she lifted a hand as if to ward off any objection. 'This is not the time to air your grievances, real or imagined. Okay?'

Kirsty hesitated and appeared to deflate. It was as if her foster mother had stripped away the barrier she had managed to erect around herself. She had nothing to hide behind now. When she finally spoke, her voice was pitched so low everyone had to strain to hear what she was saying.

'I appreciate everything you've done for me over the years, and I won't ever forget it. Not ever.' She looked at each of them in turn. 'My pain is as deep as yours, believe it or not, but it is.'

'You can't…' Vince began only to be stopped by Norah once again.

'No, I can't feel your pain, Vince. Or Steve's or Norah's—it's personal to each one of you, and so is mine, to me.' She took a deep breath and began to explain why she had arrived at her decision. In short, stilted sentences, she spoke of her frustrations, of her longings, and of her desire to live with her people—the people she identified with. She acknowledged her debt to the family, yet again, and thanked them for being mindful of her welfare. 'I don't want to cause any of you more pain,' she concluded.

Her voice broke again as she turned to Steve, and she took another deep breath to calm herself. 'Now that I have taken this step I can see it would not have been right to marry you. I always felt like your kid sister, and I think you saw me that way too. I don't care whether you screwed this Jenny woman or not. It doesn't matter one way or the other, although I'd believe you if you say you hadn't.'

'Then what…?'

'It just made up my mind for me. Don't ask me why or how… I don't know, but it did. If I could go the whole weekend without giving you a single thought, then there has to be something missing in our relationship.' She paused as Steve nodded his head, evidently knowing what she meant. 'Sooner or later we would have realised we were wrong for each other and it would have been worse for us both if we were married.'

'Yes.' Steve's reply was just loud enough for everyone to hear.

'I don't want to go from here feeling bad about you.' She tried to laugh, but the sound was brittle and cracked. 'I know I had no right to accuse you of being unfaithful, because I am too. I just hope you find what you want. Maybe you should hightail it back to Britain and hook up with that Suzi whatshername.'

The ticking grandfather clock in the corner seemed excessively loud as her voice trailed off. Norah sat staring at her folded hands until Kirsty walked over to her, then she climbed slowly to her feet. The two women embraced each other for a long time. Vince choked back a sob as she turned her tearstained face in his direction, and then he placed an arm around her shoulder. She broke away from them and grabbed Steve's hands.

'I think you're a great guy, Steve, I really do. It's a pity you were born a pakeha.'

Without another word, she walked from the room. Moments later they heard the car start up and drive away from the house. It was a long time before anyone spoke, but finally Norah broke the silence.

'I need a drink. A stiff one.'

Chapter Fifteen

The next few weeks seemed excessively long. Every time the family sat down for a meal, their eyes would automatically turn to the empty place opposite Steve. Norah was more philosophical than the two men, reasoning that Kirsty would have left sooner or later, anyway.

'As long as she's happy, that's all that really matters.'

'I don't know how you can be so… so blasé about it,' Vince declared sharply. 'We've lost her, don't you realise that? We may never see her again.'

'Why don't you think about all the years that we had with her? You could try thinking about the happy times we had together and how much pleasure she gave us.'

In an effort to put an end to the conversation, Steve asked his father whether he intended to go ahead with the idea of closing the factory over the Christmas to New Year period. In the past they had made sure someone was there to handle emergency calls while the rest of the staff took their annual holidays, but it had not really warranted the expense. Once again, Norah was instrumental in the final decision.

'Let's go away this year,' she suggested. 'Book into a hotel somewhere and do something different. We've done the same thing for the past twenty odd years, and it's high time we changed our habits.'

'That's a good idea,' Steve agreed. He had not been looking forward to celebrating Christmas in the normal manner. It wouldn't be the same without Kirsty. Vince readily agreed and began to check out various sites on the Internet. There was very little available, but a late cancellation at a top hotel in the Bay of Plenty solved their problem. Vince dug out all his old fishing gear, Norah bought herself some exotic beachwear, and Steve invested in some new scuba diving equipment.

*

Kirsty only stayed with Hepora long enough for Joey to find them a place of their own. Friends and relatives provided just about everything they needed to set up home, and within a couple of weeks she felt as if they had been together for years. Joey found work on a building site while he waited for the promised driver's job, so there was no shortage of money. She had not gone back to her old job for obvious reasons and had not made much effort to find another.

'It was all meant to be,' she said softly, as they lay cocooned in each other's arms one night. 'Everything has fallen into our laps; the flat, the job, the lot. Like I said to Hepora, it's all meant to be. We're fulfilling our destiny.'

'Yeah?' Joey sounded a little unsure, but he did not argue with her and changed the subject. 'Bobby says the van will be ready next week,' he said, planting a kiss on her forehead, 'but having you is the greatest thing that's ever happened to me, and I'll make sure you'll never regret giving up everything just to be with me.'

'I didn't give anything up, Joey. I just walked away from a life that wasn't mine.' Although she would never admit to it, she still felt guilty about leaving so abruptly, and felt tempted to ring and say hello, just to tell them she was okay. But she kept putting it off, deciding instead to write a note and pop it in a Christmas card to let them know she was okay.

*

Suzi set the alarm and switched off the lights of the Stow Restaurant with a sigh of relief; it had been a hectic day. She glanced at the time: five o'clock—plenty of time for a long soak in the bath before getting dressed to go to Charlize's New Year's Eve party. As she drove home she thought about Mark's determination to keep the Stow open; he had argued that their customers expected it, but Charlize had finally rounded on him and told him in no uncertain terms that Suzi needed a break. Then, to his surprise, she invited him to her party.

When Suzi arrived at Charlize's flat, Mark was already there. He made an effort to mingle with the other guests, but it was quite obvious he felt out of place because they were all friends of Charlize. However he loosened up after a few drinks and even began to mix more freely.

At midnight they all linked hands, sang Auld Lang Syne, and kissed each other with seasonal enthusiasm, but it was just then that Suzi had the distinct impression that Mark would have preferred to be alone with her instead of standing in a stranger's house surrounded by people he barely knew. As she returned his kiss she noticed how misty eyed he looked, and wondered why; was it seasonal emotions affecting his feelings, or something deeper?

They both left fairly early and said goodbye as they stood beside their respective cars. Mark had wanted to pick her up, but Suzi had refused his offer because she wanted to be in control of things. If he had driven her home he would have expected her to invite him in for a nightcap or coffee, and maybe he'd have tried to push his luck. She had already decided that if they ever went to bed together, it would be only if she wanted to, at a time she chose, and certainly not when he was feeling horny because of booze.

They opened as usual on New Year's Day, but the number of diners was below expectations so they closed reasonably early. Gary came by to wish them well for the coming year, and, as Suzi shook his hand, she thanked him profusely. 'Thanks, Gary for all your help. And remember, there's always a welcome here for you. Drop in at any time you please.'

He gave Mark a folder containing papers covered in names and figures.

'Okay, you're on your own now,' he said, grinning broadly. 'I'm off to New York the day after tomorrow for a well-earned holiday.' He patted his hip pocket. 'The bookies are paying all my expenses.'

Suzi waited until the following Monday before she phoned Mr Duncan, who was polite, but of little assistance. He had not received any further correspondence from Steve Pardoe's solicitors in Auckland, so there was little he could do to help. As she put down the phone, she decided to write to Steve herself. She spent hours drafting and redrafting the letter, and then sighed deeply as she realised it contained too much of her feelings about him, and very little about the house.

This is ridiculous, she thought; *why should I still be so affected by a brief encounter?* We were two strangers passing in the night; we met, we touched, we separated again, and nothing more. And yet in the depths of her heart she knew differently. Without thinking, she dug out the ring he had pressed into her hand the morning after their night of love, and watched as it glinted in the wintry morning sunlight. 'I must put him out of my mind,' she muttered, placing it back in the drawer. 'He's got someone else to think about, and I've got Mark.'

Even as she thought about her business partner, Suzi knew she could never love him in the same way. Their relationship had not deepened over the past few months; she found it hard to return his passionate kisses, and had avoided any further intimacy. It had crossed her mind that their close association made it impossible to engender the strong feelings of love she wanted to share with a man, but then she reminded herself that other people loved each other in similar situations.

She and Mark worked well together and complemented each other's skills, and the Stow Restaurant was proof of their success. But there were times when she regretted the involvement, the long hours, the constant pressure of dealing with the public and the ceaseless worry of attracting and holding good staff. When those thoughts filled her mind, she had to remind herself that very few people had the opportunity to realise their dreams.

In an effort to lighten her mood, Suzi went shopping, but it didn't have the desired effect. On the way home she turned off the main road and headed towards Caxton Manor. The grey winter's day seemed to cast a shadow over the old building, making it appear dark and unfriendly. The neglected garden reflected her feelings—everything was overgrown and choked with weeds. A few snowdrops were the only things to brighten an otherwise dismal scene. 'I'll take one with me,' she murmured, and then changed her mind before snapping it off. 'No, that will only make me feel worse.'

Unwilling to face the coldness of the unheated house, Suzi resisted the desire to go inside, so she walked around the outside of the building just to satisfy herself that everything was all right. She peered into the large glass conservatory, and in her mind's eyes saw herself serving morning and afternoon teas, or holding wine tasting parties. A sudden gust of wind tugged at her coat and made her draw it tightly around her throat. She gave an involuntary shudder and made her way back to the car.

'I'm really going to appreciate that sunny Queensland weather,' she murmured, turning up the car heater another notch.

Mark was busy chopping up vegetables when she walked into the kitchen half an hour later. He put down the knife and turned to face her.

'What have you been up to? Your cheeks are rosy red.'

'I stopped off at Caxton Manor and walked around the place, just checking to see that everything's all right.'

'Pity we don't have enough money to buy that New Zealand fellow's share.' Mark picked up the knife again and tested the blade. 'Maybe you could see if he would let you take out a mortgage...' He stopped as Suzi shook her head.

'No way would that be possible. Forget it. Our only hope is to win the Lottery, I'm afraid.'

'Or back a few winners.' Mark was about to continue when the phone rang. He reached over and plucked it off the wall. When he recognised Charlize's voice he handed it to Suzi. 'It's for you.'

Charlize's excited words seem to leap out of earpiece. 'I've received a letter from the organisers of the trip. Everything's been approved... airline reservations, hotel bookings, excursion passes, the lot. All we have to do is get on the plane and go. Let's get together soon and work out the finer details, okay?'

'Okay.' Suzi hung up and turned to Mark. 'Well that's it. All systems go, or whatever it is they say.'

He muttered something unintelligible and resumed his task of cutting up vegetables. She was about to remind him, yet again, that Narelle was quite capable of handling things for a couple of weeks, but then she stopped. She knew he was aware she would be away at the quietest time of the year, that there were no big parties to cater for and only one luncheon party to organise. There was no reason for him to expect her to give up the holiday, none at all.

*

After the last guest had gone, Mark spread the contents of the folder Gary had given him out on a table. His amiable friend had made it sound so easy. He tried to remember all the various factors that pinpointed a winner, but it was more complicated than he could have imagined. Besides, he had never been very good at mathematics.

'I'll go over the figures,' he murmured. If he could make them tally up with the strong possibilities that Gary had tipped, then he was on the right track. All he had to do was apply the principle that he had been shown. He wiped a hand across his brow. Fortunately, he had more time to spare now that things were quieter. 'I'll get the hang of it before long,' he muttered, as he straightened up and stretched.

Then he thought about how Suzi continued to rebuff his advances, even though she had made it clear she was willing to consider a more intimate relationship. However, there were times when his physical longing for her was more than he was willing to admit. Sometimes he wondered whether she was naturally cold or whether her excuses were a means of discouraging him. Maybe she'd had a bad experience and was frightened of getting sexually involved with anyone.

Like so many men, Mark had accepted the idea that all attractive women were sexually inclined; that if a woman was beautiful she would be even more sexually motivated. And, although Suzi was beautiful, she did not seem to fit that pattern. Maybe it's me, he thought, and then dismissed the idea because he had bedded plenty of women in the past.

'If I could raise the money to buy out that fellow's share in Caxton Manor, things might be different,' he said, half aloud. He looked at the figures again. They were his key to success; all he had to do was emulate Gary's track record at picking winners and all his problems could be solved.

Chapter Sixteen

Once Steve had pulled his luggage out of the boot of Vince's car he clasped the older man's hand. 'I'll give you a ring,' he said, 'if not tonight, then first thing in the morning.'

Vince patted his son on the shoulder.

'Now don't overdo it—take some time off. You might never get the chance to see that part of the world again, so make the most of it.'

'Okay, I hear you.' Steve said, and walked into the Auckland airport terminal. He was dealt with quickly, then the man wished him a pleasant journey and handed him a boarding pass.

As he settled back into the seat, he thought about their recent holiday in the Bay of Plenty. They had all enjoyed the break, but he knew it had not stopped any of them thinking about Kirsty. On more than one occasion he had found Norah weeping softly, and Vince would often start to say something and then hesitate. He wondered what would have happened if she came back home and wanted to resume their relationship, but it was out of the question now; she was where she wanted to be, and that had to be a good thing—for her, if not for the rest of them. And for that he was thankful.

Steve's thoughts turned to Jenny MacTavish. She had enclosed a long letter with her Christmas card, and reaffirmed her desire to see him when she moved to Auckland in the New Year. I could do a lot worse, Steve thought, as he recalled the fiery redhead's effect on him, but a lasting relationship with her was the last thing he wanted. In fact he wondered if he really wanted to see her again.

And of course the memory of Suzi Lysle Spencer was never far away; she popped back into his mind often, and at the oddest of times. As he thought about the time they had spent together, he wondered again if it was feasible to think of sharing Caxton Manor. But the thought of living in that old house was unacceptable. Even though Wales was the land of his fathers, he had no desire to live there. As far as he was concerned, New Zealand was home, and the only place he wanted to live.

His solicitor had advised him to reject Suzi's suggestion to share the property and allow her to operate the place as a restaurant and venue for receptions. The man argued against any involvement with a third party, and suggested the manor should be sold, and the money divided between them. But Steve continued to procrastinate, so a great deal of time was wasted without anything being settled.

I'll have to give them an answer one way or the other; it's not fair to leave everything up in the air. I'll do it as soon as I return from Queensland, he promised himself.

The announcement to fasten seat belts cut into his thoughts as the plane began its descent to Brisbane airport. Steve glanced at his watch and calculated how long he had before catching the connecting flight to Townsville. There was plenty of time.

Chapter Seventeen

Vince snapped on the radio as he drove away from the airport. The newsreader was just about to launch into the sports results when he paused to announce a news flash.

'A vehicle being pursued by police has been involved in a fatal accident. Both occupants were killed when the car crashed into a shaft on a building site. Police have not released the names of the occupants, but they are believed to be either Maoris or Cook Islanders. We'll give you more details as they come to hand.'

The newsreader's words went around and around in Vince's mind as he drove home. Police pursuit, a crashed car, both Maori, both dead. He tried to shrug it off, but something deep inside made him cringe.

Norah looked up as he walked in the door and gasped when she saw the expression on his face. 'Oh my God, you look awful. What's happened?'

'I don't know... it's just that I have this terrible feeling that something's happened to Kirsty.' Vince's voice was tinged with emotion. 'I hope I'm wrong, but it feels like some sort of intuition.' At Norah's insistence he repeated the newscaster's words and shook his head sadly. 'I'm afraid...' He stopped as Norah reached his side and grasped his hand. 'We'll know soon enough, I suppose.'

It was two hours before a police inspector knocked on the front door. He introduced himself and the young policewoman who accompanied him, and asked if they could come inside. He had some difficulty making eye contact, and his colleague seemed equally distressed.

Norah clung to Vince as the policeman spoke of the accident that had killed their foster daughter. When he finished speaking, she began to weep softly. Vince continued to stare stony-faced at the officer as he tried to come to grips with the hurt that tore at his insides. He would have given anything to blot out the words the man had spoken.

After he had agreed to identify the body, Vince saw the two officers to the door, and walked slowly back into the lounge. He found Norah huddled in the corner of the room, weeping silently to herself. Vince sat down beside her, placed an arm around her and drew her close. There was nothing to say, and even if there were, it was better left unsaid at this time. He bit back his desire to blame Joey, but it was a natural reaction to blame someone, anyone, whether it was warranted or not. However, he knew the man was at fault.

It was a long time before he could calm the anger he felt. He continued to sit with an arm around his wife until his eyes slowly filled with tears. He had just reached for a handkerchief when the phone rang.

'Leave it,' he said in a choked voice as Norah moved to pick it up. Then he remembered Steve had promised to ring. 'It's all right, I'll get it.'

*

Steve hung up the phone and shook his head in disbelief. Kirsty dead? He had difficulty believing it. His father had repeated the police officer's horrific description of the circumstances surrounding her death, and that seemed to make it worse. When Vince's words had finally sunk in, he made his way to the bar and ordered a drink. He sat there staring into the glass as he tried to make sense of it all.

He was deep in thought when a person sitting next to him nudged his elbow and called his attention to the tannoy. It was making a last call to board the flight to Townsville. Steve placed his glass back on the bar and headed for the boarding gate. As he made his way onto the plane, he wondered how his parents were coping with the tragedy. When he had suggested returning to Auckland, Vince had been adamant that he should continue on his journey.

'We'll be okay,' he had said. 'There's nothing you can do. I'll look after things this end.'

And now, as the plane prepared to land at the northern capital he

121

wondered what preparations were being made for the funeral. The police officer had told Vince that they would probably carry out an autopsy on the bodies. So it was no good going back until that was settled. Maybe it would be better for him to remain out of the way in case his presence added to everyone's grief.

The hire car company had reserved a Toyota for him. When he explained he wanted to visit some of the resort areas before he returned to New Zealand they agreed to his request to return the vehicle to Brisbane airport. It was a relatively short drive to the hotel, and the receptionist gave him a quizzical look when he complained about the heat. Then she reminded him that he was in North Queensland, that it was summer, and Townsville was always a hot place.

'Your room is air-conditioned,' she said, handing him the key, 'if that's any consolation.'

After he had finished breakfast the next morning, Steve rang the sugar mill to check with the second engineer. The man assured him that the pumping equipment had arrived safely and that he would be available for the rest of the day.

Kirsty's death hung over him like a cloud as he drove north out of the city. He recalled their life together over the years and in particular their recent visit to Rotorua. They had shared some good times together, and until recently they had both expected those good times to continue. Despite her battle to come to terms with herself, Kirsty had maintained an excellent relationship with them all. Her enthusiasm for life had always seemed to sustain her, even as she began to question her origins and her role in the European culture of her foster parents.

It was only when she had become more involved with her Maori friends that things had changed. But she was still acutely aware of her role in the family, and Steve believed that even though she rebelled against her lifestyle, she still loved them all dearly. And now she was gone forever. He choked back a sob as a vision of her pretty face came to mind. It was such a tragedy.

Steve pushed the thoughts to the back of his mind as he drove into the sugar mill and parked outside the engineer's office. Tony Randall was a typical northerner, and bore the marks of his years in the Queensland sun without adequate skin protection.

'G'day, mate,' he said, stretching out his hand. 'Did ya have a good trip? Where ya staying?' When Steve replied that he had booked into a hotel in town, Tony suggested he book out again. 'Come and stay with me and the missus,' he said. 'There's plenty of room.'

'That's a kind gesture, Tony, but I've already been billed for today so I'll leave it until tomorrow. It won't cause your wife any inconvenience will it?'

'Nah, it'll do her good to have someone to look after,' he joked. 'Smarten her up a bit.' Then he became more serious. 'So you reckon this pump of yours will do the trick, eh?' Without waiting for a reply, he continued. 'Is this your first visit to a sugar mill?' When Steven nodded, Tony jammed a hat on his head. 'Come on, I'll take you on a guided tour of the place.'

The engineer pointed out the rows of cane trucks lined up on the narrow gauge railway line, and explained that they were being checked over and repaired in readiness for the crushing season. Then he led the way to the locomotive shed to show him the small trams that provided the power to pull the long line of wagons bearing the harvested cane from the farms to the mill.

'Do those trams collect all the sugar cane?' Steve asked.

'No. The tramline only services the older farms. Those on the outskirts have to bring the cane in by road.' He led the way to a machine that emptied the cane trucks. 'This where it all starts. The cane drops onto a conveyer belt that carries it up to a staging station, where it's directed towards two banks of crushers.' He pointed out the huge rollers that pulverised the cane. 'Okay, that's where things get serious,' he said. 'It goes through four of those, so by the time it's finished there's absolutely no sugar left in the cane.'

'What happens to the residue?'

'The bagasse? It's conveyed up to that tall building. It's dried there

123

and then fed back down to fire the boilers.' He gave a short laugh. 'Nothing's wasted.' Then they followed the pipes that led to the centrifugal pumps that separated the remaining fluid to produce a dark brown, viscous, malt like substance. Tony pointed to some storage tanks. 'From there it's taken to the refinery, but I'll show you that another time.' Then he looked at his watch. 'Come on, it's time for lunch.'

Steve followed the man to a modest three-bedroom cottage on the far side of the property.

'This Stella, my wife,' Tony said, proudly.

Stella was as small and lean as Tony was large and stocky. Her wispy brown hair had been pulled back into a chignon that highlighted the pair of large colourful earrings that seemed to sprout from the bottom of her earlobes. They seemed to make her pinched face seem even smaller. Tony gave her a playful pat on the backside as she was about to sit down.

'Now just you behave yourself,' she said, brushing his hand away, 'or you'll give our guest the wrong impression.'

Steve could see that she was secretly pleased with the attention, and their bantering talk throughout the meal added to his feeling that they were well matched and enjoyed each other's company.

'How long will the job take, Steve?' Stella asked.

'It depends,' he replied. 'If there are no problems it should be only a few days, a week at the most.'

'We'll get onto it first thing in the morning,' Tony said, as they stood up. 'Nick should have been here today, but he didn't show.' He gave a hearty laugh. 'His daughter rang up to say he'd eaten something that hadn't agreed with him, but truth be known he's been on the piss all weekend and can't keep his head up.'

Steve made an appropriate noise as he recalled his own lost weekends.

'He's a Kiwi, too.' The man laughed again. 'Your mob might be able to beat us at rugby, but you don't know how to drink.'

They spent the early part of the afternoon checking the equipment, and then Steve insisted that they drive into the nearby town to have a couple of beers. After dinner that evening, Tony took him for a run into the countryside to a place where they hunted wild pigs. They both carried rifles, just in case, but there were no animals to be seen. He left the engineer just after nine o'clock and drove back to town. He had just enough time for one beer in the garden lounge before the barman called time.

When he turned up at the sugar mill the next morning, Steve was surprised to learn that the man who was to install the pumping equipment had worked for his father. Nick Bolte had moved to Australia to be near his only daughter when his wife died unexpectedly, and it was like greeting an old friend.

'Hello, Nick,' Steve said, shaking the man's hand vigorously. 'If I'd known you were to oversee the installation I could have saved myself the trip.' He turned to the second engineer. 'Nick is the best man you could have picked for the job—he can probably still teach me a few tricks.'

By the middle of the afternoon, Steve realised that there was no reason for him to stay any longer. He briefed Nick on some of the finer points of the new design and then let him get on with the job. That evening he rang Vince and gave him the news. 'There's not much use my hanging around here so I'll pack it in and come home.'

'You don't have to rush back unless you want to,' Vince said, a trifle quickly. 'Stay there for a while and take a look around the place. If you come home now it'll only upset Norah again. There's enough tears around this place as it is, she'll start crying all over if you turn up on the doorstep unexpectedly.'

Steve drove out to the mill first thing after breakfast next day just to assure himself that everything was all right. When he said goodbye to Tony and his wife, they seemed genuinely disappointed that he was going.

'Now don't leave the area until you've seen Cairns—it's the new gateway to Australia,' he boasted. 'And take a trip in the hinterland while you're there. The rain forest is unbelievable.'

Stella brought out some photos they had taken on their recent holiday to the area. She enthused about its natural beauty, and enthused about the little train that carried sightseers up the mountain range. When she drew breath, Tony said he should warn Steve about the snakes.

'It's a bad time for snakes, I'm afraid,' he said, in a serious tone. 'There are thousands out there in the undergrowth. You'll have to watch yourself every time you step out of the car.' He tried hard to suppress a grin. 'Some of them are lightning quick and for some reason or other they'll give the locals a miss and sink their fangs into a passing Kiwi. Must taste better, or something.'

'Stop teasing the man,' Stella said, thumping her husband on the back. 'Tony yells snake at every New Zealander he meets just to see them jump.' She thumped him again. 'Silly old thing, always trying to take the mickey.'

Steve was still chuckling when he turned out of the sugar mill and headed north towards Cairns. By the time he was half way to Mackay he began to wonder if he was doing the right thing, or whether he should go home.

He had the distinct feeling that he should have been heading in the other direction, but he had no idea why he felt this way. He was tempted to turn around, but then he shrugged off the idea.

'It's silly not to see a bit of the country while I'm here,' he murmured. Like Vince had said—there might no other chance.

Chapter Eighteen

Mark took Suzi out to dinner the evening before she and Charlize were due to fly out to Australia, but it did not turn out the way he had planned. The candlelit interior looked inviting and the soft lilting melodies issuing from the baby grand piano seemed to add a romantic touch to the atmosphere. He looked apologetically at Suzi.

'I'm sorry the service here is so slow.' He glanced at the other diners' tables. 'And this food is no way as good as the Stow Restaurant's. Chose the wrong place, didn't I? Or maybe the chef is new.'

Suzi picked disconsolately at her Dover sole, but rather than spoil the evening by adding to Mark's complaints, she just agreed it could have been better. Mark looked even further irritated when he had to send the wine back because the waiter had brought the wrong bottle and, to cap it all, by the end of the meal they had become completely disenchanted with the pianist. The silver-haired man tonked out ancient melodies, and finished every piece with a trilling crescendo, which was not only irritating, but impossible to ignore.

She had not intended to ask Mark in for coffee when they returned to her house, but he looked so miserable that she relented at the last moment. They tried not to talk about the disappointing evening, but when she produced a freshly brewed pot of Moroccan coffee, Mark made another snide remark about the restaurant they had just left. A coffee laced with a shot of brandy liqueur had the desired effect of putting him in a more mellow frame of mind, and he was soon his usual self. When he hinted that it was a pity to break the mood and go home, Suzi pulled a little face.

'It's not a good time, Mark,' she said, softly, 'if you know what I mean. Besides, I have to be up early in the morning, don't forget.' When she saw the look of disappointment on his face, Suzi kissed his cheek.

'There'll be plenty of opportunities when I get back.'

'So you're not saying there's no hope for me?'

'I don't really know what you mean.'

'I was hoping that we might think about becoming engaged soon.' Mark grasped her hand and gazed earnestly into her eyes. 'You know I love you Suzi, and I really believe you could love me the same way… in time. I think we could make just as much a success of our marriage as we have of our business partnership. We could be good for each other.'

Suzi hesitated for a minute.

'We'll talk about it when I come back, okay?' Then she stood up, and yawned, looking pointedly at the clock. 'You don't want another cup of coffee before you go, do you?'

'No, I'll pass on the coffee.' He drew her to him and kissed her gently. 'Have a good night's sleep, and have a wonderful time down under.' Then he sighed. 'I'll miss you.'

As he drove away, Suzi wondered why she had allowed him to get under her guard. She had unwittingly responded to his gentle caress, and he evidently assumed that she was ready to be more intimate. Fortunately, her excuse was genuine, but he seemed convinced that things would be different when she returned. She could see that she should nip that notion in the bud straight away otherwise things might become rather awkward.

She stretched again, but didn't feel tired enough for sleep yet. I'm probably too excited, she thought. Charlize would be picking her up at about eight o'clock, and that would allow plenty of time to get to Heathrow Airport, barring any hold-ups on the motorway. After she had cleared away the coffee cups she tidied up the room, and then made her way to bed. Within minutes of putting her head on the pillow, she was fast asleep.

*

Mark had not really believed that Suzi would accompany her friend to Australia, and it came as a bit of a shock when he realised that she was determined to go. He reasoned that she would not want to leave the day to day running of the restaurant in someone else's hands, even though it was the quietest time of the year. Narelle seemed competent enough, but Suzi *was* the Stow Restaurant and people identified the establishment with her.

However, he could not deny her the opportunity to visit the antipodes on an all-expenses paid holiday. Charlize had called into the restaurant the previous afternoon to see Suzi, and it amused him to watch as they giggled and teased each other like a pair of schoolgirls.

And now, as he prepared for the lunchtime trade, he found himself continually glancing at the clock, and mentally counting off the hours until their plane departed from Heathrow. He had to admit that he was already feeling rather sorry for himself.

'Morning, Mark.' Narelle's cheery greeting cut into his thoughts as she walked into the kitchen. She glanced at the wall clock. 'They'll be taking off in an hour. Lucky things.'

Lunchtime trade was brisk, but not over-busy, and Narelle handled everything competently, much to Mark's surprise and delight. As soon as the last guest had departed, he took a coffee to the table by the window and looked at his notes. There seemed to be a strong chance that Silver Chalice could win the second last race of the day. Mark had studied Gary's notes again and again, until he was sure he had mastered the complex balance of weights, times, and distances that affected the right choice, and now he was confident that he could make it work.

The only major setback had been with the betting shop. When he had rung up to place a bet, he had been asked for an account number. He explained that Gary Hyland had placed bets on his behalf and they had been honoured, to which the man had replied, 'Ah, yes. We know Mr Hyland, but we don't know you.'

When he called into the premises two days later and asked about establishing an account, he was given a form to fill out. Mark was halfway through the questionnaire when he began to wonder if it was a good idea to have everything monitored. He did not want the bank to know anything about his activities.

'I'll stick to betting in cash,' he murmured, screwing up the form. 'It'll be less convenient, but safer in the long run.'

The first horse he picked without Gary's assistance won. It was a case of touch and go, but nevertheless it scrambled home by a short half head. He was overjoyed with the result, and when he pocketed the money he thought about Gary's remark—that it was easier than working for a living. However, he was also conscious of the man's advice not to be greedy, but to wait until the right time to back a particular horse.

As he reviewed his figures, Mark was convinced he had picked another winner. He calculated what he could expect to win if he obtained the odds quoted by the morning paper, and decided that it was a substantial amount. If he reinvested all that he had won on the last horse, he would stand to win more than a thousand pounds.

'Go for it,' he muttered, putting all his papers back into a folder. He set the alarm, locked up the premises, and drove to the betting shop. Ten minutes later walked into the nearest pub to watch the race on television.

Once again, his horse managed to hold off the opposition and win by a narrow margin. With a sigh of relief, Mark waited until it was officially declared winner, and then returned to the betting shop. When he presented the winning ticket the clerk reached for a blank cheque and asked for his name.

'I've just bet in cash,' Mark said, with a touch of aggression in his voice. 'And I want to be paid in cash.'

The clerk protested that it was company policy to pay by cheque if the amount exceeded a thousand pounds, and when Mark pointed out that it was barely over the limit, the man stated that rules were rules. After a few minutes of heated discussion, Mark asked to see the manager.

'I don't want a cheque,' he stated, emphatically. He gestured to the signs on the walls. 'There's nothing about that rule on any of these notices.'

Reluctantly, the manager okayed the payment by cash, but then he intimated that Mark should take his custom elsewhere. 'We run a law-abiding shop,' he said, sarcastically. 'We don't need people who cause trouble.' When Mark asked him to clarify his statement, the manager turned his back and walked away.

He stuffed the money into his pocket and walked out of the building, vowing never to return. The man's remarks niggled away at him all afternoon, and overshadowed the excitement of his first major win. However, by the time he closed the restaurant that evening, he had been able to push the incident from his mind, and by now he felt quite pleased with the result of his venture.

In his excitement to repeat the success, Mark eagerly applied his technique to the next meeting, but this time the system didn't show up a winner. He threw the pen down with a snort of disgust and then reminded himself that Gary often went a whole week before finding something worthy of a bet. Determined to build on his capital, Mark pored over his figures again and again, trying to convince himself that he had not made a mistake. Then three days later, he found another possibility, and he placed his bet in a different establishment.

'You beauty,' he cried, excitedly, as the horse careered away from the rest of the field and won, easing down at the post. He nudged the man next to him in the betting shop as he waited for the numbers to come up.

'How about that, eh? I just wish I'd put a bit more on it.'

A postcard from Suzi, which extolled the virtues of the Sunshine State, arrived the next morning. The semi-tropical scene depicted a smiling man sitting under a large, colourful umbrella with a fishing rod in one hand, and a beer in the other. It bore the legend:

'*Ah Queensland, beautiful one day, perfect the next.*' He turned it over and read what was on the reverse side.

Dear Mark,

Well we're here. The trip was long and tiring, but uneventful. We're both suffering from jet lag, but that'll soon wear off. We're off to the Gold Coast tomorrow to do some sightseeing. Hope you are coping all right. Say hello to everyone there. I'll write again soon.

Love Suzi

He laid the card aside and thought about their relationship. As business partners he could not wish for more. Suzi was very efficient and knew instinctively how to handle the customers. The riotous ones were firmly reminded that their behaviour was unacceptable, the complainers were placated, and the disappointed diners were promised the table of their choice next time they rang for a booking. And of course, the old dears thought she was a darling.

When she had told him that she might inherit Caxton Manor he did not really appreciate what it meant to her. After he had taken a look at the place he began to understand why she was so keen to turn it into a venue for receptions. Her original idea had been to retain the Stow Restaurant as a diner and use the old house for parties and conventions, but he soon convinced her that it would not be too difficult to utilize and expand the existing kitchen.

By the time they had begun to discuss the matter seriously, Steve Pardoe had arrived on the scene to claim half of the property. Mark had even wondered if he should write to the man himself, and offer to buy his share. But of course he had the same problem as Suzi—not enough money. And he had no collateral to borrow on.

That evening he had a long talk with his father about the situation. Ben was sympathetic, but reminded Mark that the manor had been valued at a high figure, excluding the contents. He said that even if he took out a mortgage on his modest house, it would only be about half of the sum required.

'Really, the only way is to get this New Zealand fellow to agree to part payment and the balance over a period of time,' Ben said. 'But be mindful of the high cost to make the necessary alterations to satisfy the health regulations. They're tough.'

'Yes, I know that, but the restaurant is generating a good income now, so we...'

He didn't have time to finish, before his father interrupted him.

'You've got to service your existing loan first and foremost. It's no good borrowing from Peter to pay Paul. If you're not careful you'll lose everything.' He paused to emphasis his words. 'And Suzi will, too.'

His father's admonition rang in his ears for the remainder of the night. The more he thought about the situation, the more concerned he became, because he needed to succeed, and he wanted Suzi to be a part of that success. Although she had argued against rushing into things, Mark knew she had set her heart on living in that lovely old house and turning it into a show place where she could cater for the up-market clientele who were looking for something special. If he could help turn her dream into a reality, he reasoned that then she would be a lot more amenable to marriage.

'If only I could emulate Gary's success,' Mark murmured. His old workmate lived very comfortably, staying at top hotels, flying first class and driving a late model Porsche. He groaned aloud as he reminded himself that Gary had nothing to lose if his system failed. The man was a first class chef and he could probably choose a job anywhere in the world. He drummed his fingers on the table. 'But his system hasn't failed, so it has to be good.'

He pulled a large envelope full of banknotes out of his wardrobe and counted them out onto the bed. One thousand, seven hundred and fifty-three pounds, and nearly two thirds of that had come from just one bet. If I could up the ante, he mused, start betting in hundreds or even thousands instead of fifties, I could accumulate the money a lot quicker.

His friend's words came back to taunt him again. 'Don't be greedy.' That was all right for Gary, because he was living a footloose life and had no particular goal, whereas Mark wanted to make something of his life. It was not greed; it was necessity. Even as he begrudgingly admitted it was risky, he was determined to push his luck to the limit to raise the money he needed. He replaced the box in the wardrobe and went to bed.

He lay staring at the ceiling for a long time before he went to sleep.

His night was filled with conflicting dreams. In one situation he would be see himself carrying Suzi across the threshold of Caxton Manor and up the long flight of stairs leading to a to beautifully decorated bedroom. In another scene he saw her watch him dispassionately as he wagered his last pound on an outsider in a desperate attempt to claw back some of the money he had lost.

The grey light of a new day was a welcome relief from the troubled sleep. He stamped across the frosty parking area, rubbing his hands together against the bitterly cold wind that tore at his jacket. The car was blanketed in a thick coating of frost and there were miniature icicles hanging off the rear-view mirrors. After scraping the windows clear he started the vehicle and eased it out onto the road. As he drove to the Stow Restaurant, he thought about Suzi and her friend in sunny Queensland—they had picked a good time to be out of Britain.

Yes, he mused, but I bet she'll get tired of it in a few weeks. He was sure that by the end of the holiday she would be more than keen to get back to the restaurant.

'I'll even bet on it,' he murmured, and then laughed.

Chapter Nineteen

Three days later Mark received an airmail letter from Suzi. She wrote to say they were having a wonderful time, that everyone was friendly, the food was fabulous, and it was all very exciting. They found the heat a bit unbearable at times, and she had to be extra careful about protecting her fair skin, but that seemed to be the only complaint. The rest of the letter was taken up with a short description of some of the places they had visited.

She closed with the words:

Sometimes I wish you were here to share in this marvellous experience. Maybe we can visit it together at some future date when we've made lots of money from the restaurant.

With love,

Suzi

He dropped the letter back onto the table and looked at the calendar.

'She'll be home in three days,' he mused. Narelle would probably be happy to see her back, too, because he had noticed that the novelty of being a full time hostess seemed to have worn a bit thin now.

As soon as the last customer left that afternoon, Mark began to work on the racing formula. It had been nearly a week since he had placed a winning bet, and he was eager to recuperate the money he had lost on the last wager. The horse had run well, but faded in the closing stages and was forced back to third place. It had been a bitter disappointment, because he had been absolutely sure it would last the distance, and he had bet accordingly.

However, he knew that his hope of handing Suzi a bag full of money when she came home was just a dream now. Even if he could back a winner each week, it would take quite a few months to accumulate enough to satisfy his needs. Unless of course he could find a horse

135

that he considered unbeatable, and a bookie willing to accept a bet of a thousand pounds or more.

*

Suzi and Charlize had spent the last part of the flight discussing the various excursions that were included in the prize. They leafed through pamphlets depicting some of the attractions to be seen in the various resort areas around Brisbane.

'The Gold Coast sounds like a great place to start,' Suzi said. 'It says here that although it was initially a haven for fishermen and surfers, it's now considered Australia's top playground.'

'So we go there to play?'

'Whatever,' Suzi laughed.

Charlize turned over another brochure.

'Now… we've got the choice between Hervey Bay and Fraser Island.' She read aloud the description of the world's largest sand island that boasts a fresh water lake and wild horses. 'That sounds better than leaning over the side of a boat trying to catch sight of a whale.'

'It all sounds great,' Suzi enthused, as she grabbed one of the other folders that extolled the virtues of the Whitsunday Passage. 'We're going Airlie Beach, aren't we?' She sighed. 'It's a bit hard to take it all in at once.'

Part of the package holiday included a stopover in Townsville and Cairns. From the northernmost city they would take a ride on the famous narrow track railway that had serviced the early settlers on the Atherton Tablelands. The opportunity to trek through the rainforest at Kuranda did not appeal to either of them so they crossed that one off the list.

'And there's an optional visit to museum at Longreach.' Suzi turned the brochure so that Charlize could see the picture of a huge corrugated iron building standing on the flat plain. 'I think it's a tribute to all the cowpokes who went out west.'

Charlize looked at her and then laughed uproariously.

'Good heavens, get your facts right. They don't call them cowpokes in

Australia.'

'Never mind, it still doesn't sound like a very nice place to visit.' Suzi looked at the brochure again.

They spent the first night in the heart of Brisbane and took the bus to the Surfers Paradise the next morning. After having lunch at SeaWorld, they caught another bus to the bird sanctuary at Currumbin, where flocks of lorikeets flew in to feed on the bread and honey mixture prepared by the proprietors.

The myriad beautifully coloured birds perched on anything available—usually the nearest shoulder or an outstretched arm. They watched as one even settled on the top of a man's crutches.

On the way back to Brisbane they stopped off at Bundaberg where Australia's favourite rum was produced, but neither of them could bring themselves to drink the samples on offer.

'Much too strong,' Charlize complained, putting her glass down after a tiny sip.

Wherever they went, the two women found themselves the centre of attraction. It seemed as if everyone wanted to invite them to a barbecue, or take them to dinner, or buy them a drink. They soon learned to say no, but were highly amused at the outrageous comments made by the local inhabitants.

They were sitting on the veranda of a country hotel one afternoon when a couple of workmen sat down at a nearby table.

'Hey, there's a pair of good-looking Sheilas, Trev,' one of them said, in a voice loud enough for them to hear. 'Which one do you fancy? I like the dark haired one, myself.'

'Please yourself, mate,' Trevor replied, with a laugh. 'Which ever one you choose, I'll fancy the other one.' He took a swig of beer. 'Why don't you chat 'em up, Chicka?'

The man called Chicka eased himself off the chair and nonchalantly wandered over to where Suzi and Charlize sat. He looked from one to the other and smiled.

'G'day. How's it going, girls, pretty good, eh?' But before they could respond he continued with an answer. 'Not too bad, that's good. Can I buy you a drink?'

'No, thanks,' Charlize replied, sweetly. 'But thanks for the offer.'

He turned to Suzi. 'How about you, love?'

Suzi managed to stop herself from laughing and shook her head vigorously. 'I'm fine, thank you.'

'You want keep your eye on that bloke, girls,' Trevor called out. 'He's a bit of a lady's man. Really knows his way about, he does.' He laughed good-naturedly.

'Come on, Chicka,' Trevor said, climbing to his feet, 'they're awake to you. You're not going to do any good there, so you might as well have another beer.'

As made their way to the bar, Chicka took one last look at them.

'You're right, Trev, it's a waste of time laying on the charm with those pommie Sheilas.'

'Yeah, like I said they just don't appreciate when they're on to a good thing.'

Charlize nudged Suzi again.

'Well, that's the end of a beautiful friendship, thank goodness.' She looked at her empty glass. 'I think it's your shout.'

The next day they headed north to Cairns. The hot and steamy town was full of tourists and backpackers even though it was officially off-season. Once again the two women were pleased to find that their hotel was air-conditioned. Charlize found the heat particularly hard to bear, and was almost on the point of suggesting that they should go back to Brisbane when something made her change her mind.

They were making their way towards the dining room that evening, when a man bumped into Charlize, nearly knocking her off her feet. He apologised profusely, and then offered to buy them a drink in the bar. Suzi had visions of the episode with Trevor and Chicka and tried to hurry her friend away, but then she saw a smile light up Charlize's face. The man introduced himself as Lloyd Bridgestone, from New Zealand.

After he had ordered the drinks, he looked directly at Charlize. 'So you're on holidays.' It was neither a question nor a statement, then without waiting for a reply he continued. 'It's a bad time of year to visit North Queensland. The heat is always unbearable and the insects are... well, ferocious to say the least.'

'Then why are you here?'

'No option, I'm afraid. I'm a property developer. My company is looking at this area with a view to expanding our interests.' Then he took a sip from his glass. 'But I haven't seen anything that interests me, to be frank, so I'll be more than pleased to go back home where the weather's more temperate.'

'We've just reached the same conclusion,' Suzi said. 'I don't know how people put up with this humidity.'

'I can understand your point of view.' Lloyd nodded. Then he gave them a quizzical look. 'I'm trying to place your accents. What part of England are you from?' When neither of them answered immediately, he gave a nervous laugh. 'Oops, should I have said Britain? I know the people from Wales and Scotland don't like to be called English.'

Charlize gave a small laugh.

'How right you are, but it's just a bit of national pride. We Welsh like to think we're different.'

'No, special,' Suzi interjected. 'We are special. Some of us like to think that maybe some truly ancient blood runs in our veins, the blood of the earliest pre-Celt Britons.'

Lloyd inclined his head.

'Very interesting,' he said. 'So tell me, how does it go?' He tapped his forehead with his finger. 'Croeso, er... Croeso y? Ah, yes, I think I've got it now. Croeso y Cymru.' He gave a small laugh. 'That's it isn't it? It means welcome to Wales.'

'Well done.' Charlize clapped her hands. 'You've even pronounced it correctly... someone must have taught you that.'

When he offered to escort them into the dining room she readily agreed. He seemed very knowledgeable about the restaurant industry and asked Suzi a couple of leading questions. But it was Charlize who had most of his attention. He wanted to know all about her family and her job as a PR consultant. After dinner they all moved into the lounge bar for coffee and liqueurs.

By the time they said goodnight, he and Charlize had eyes only for each other. Although Suzi was feeling a little neglected she wanted to hide it, so as they climbed the stairs to their room, she tried to sound casual.

'He seems rather nice.'

'Yes. And attractive. And intelligent,' Charlize said, dropping her bag onto the dressing table. 'And quite rich, apparently.' She sank down on the side of the bed and grinned. 'He's asked me to have breakfast with him.'

'Where? In the dining room, or in his bedroom?'

Charlize spent more time with Lloyd over breakfast than she had intended, and had barely enough time to change into something more suitable to for the day trip to Kuranda. She ran out into the parking lot to find Suzi waiting impatiently. They scrambled onto the bus just before the driver closed the doors, and had to sit on opposite sides of the vehicle. Suzi was somewhat piqued at first, but then she saw the funny side of it.

I think she would have preferred to miss the bus altogether, she mused, as she noted the faraway look in her friend's eyes. She seemed to have been very taken with Lloyd, and Suzi knew it was unusual for Charlize to become this attracted to a man so quickly. They usually had to stand in line and wait to be noticed.

They were both enthralled by the primitive beauty of the rain forest, and agreed that they would like to spend more time absorbing the tranquil setting. The train trip was entirely different but equally enjoyable and, by the time they climbed back on the bus, the ordeal had exhausted them. It had been a very long and tiring day, and the air-conditioned hotel room was a welcome relief from the heat and the humidity.

Charlize threw her bag on the bed, and looked anxiously at her watch.

'Will it be all right if I use the bathroom first? I promised Lloyd I'd have a drink with him before dinner. You don't mind, do you? It's just that…' She stopped and gave a little laugh. 'You can meet us after you've showered if you want to.'

'I don't mind if you go first,' Suzi said, joining in her friend's laughter. 'I won't spoil the party, so just you go ahead and make the most of it while you can.'

While Charlize swept around the room like a whirlwind, scattering clothes as she tried first one dress and then another in an attempt to choose the right one, Suzi brought her diary up to date. Then she took a shower and eventually made her way downstairs. Lloyd and Charlize were deep in conversation at the far end of the bar, so she found a table by the window. As she sat down they crossed the room and asked to join her.

Suzi was amazed at Charlize's reaction to the tall, blond New Zealander. He had evidently triggered something in her that no other man had done before, and he was obviously equally as enchanted with her. She felt slightly embarrassed by their open intimacy and nearly suggested that they have dinner by themselves, but Lloyd must have read her mind. He looked directly at her.

'I feel a bit of an interloper,' he said, quietly. 'I've come between you both. That wasn't my intention, I can assure you, but…' He paused and looked at Charlize for help. 'I, er… we seem to have found each other mutually attractive, and er… you know how it is.' He stopped again, and smiled engagingly.

'Yes, I do know, and I can identify with that,' Suzi said, as she recalled her own situation with Steve Pardoe. She patted her friend's hand. 'Just remember we have to be at the airport in time to catch a plane in the morning… that's all.'

As they moved away for dinner, Suzi wondered whether Steve ever thought of her. She had a feeling deep down that he had not married the woman waiting for him in New Zealand, although there seemed to be no reason for her to think that way, but she hoped she was right. It's just female intuition, she had told herself, more than once.

She could see that Charlize's situation was not dissimilar to her own; both of them had been drawn to someone almost instinctively. *I wonder what it is about these New Zealand men?* she mused. *They seem able to sweep into someone's life and turn it completely upside down.*

When Suzi finally went in to dinner, Charlize and Lloyd were nowhere to be seen. She joined an elderly couple and enjoyed a comfortable evening listening to their stories of life on a sheep farm. It was only when she returned to her room that she realised that the old man was also a New Zealander. Maybe it was coincidence, but Suzi felt it was significant.

Charlize burst into the bedroom the following morning and began throwing clothes into a suitcase. As she rushed about, she apologised for excluding Suzi the previous evening.

'I can't help it, Suzi, but I feel the need to be alone with Lloyd. I never thought I'd let a man get under my skin so completely as this,' she said, deftly applying her make-up. 'He seems to have reached the core of my being.'

'So where do you go from here?'

'Figuratively or physically?' Charlize twisted the lipstick closed and tossed it back in the bag.

'I mean right now… today.'

'You'll never guess. He's going to meet me in Airlie Beach.'

'The resort area on the Whitsunday Coast?'

'Yes, when I told him that we only had two days left of our holiday, he asked if he could spend them with me.' She grabbed her suitcase. 'Come on, he's waiting to drive us to the airport.' Then she stopped. 'You don't mind, do you?'

Suzi shook her head.

'Don't be silly. It's great to see you so excited about a man… at last.' She chuckled. Who knows, she thought, maybe at Airlie Beach I'll find a handsome Kiwi who can sweep me off my feet in the same way. Then again, maybe one has already done that.

Chapter Twenty

Suzi smiled as she watched her friend clinging to Lloyd's hand as they walked into the terminal at Cairns airport. Charlize was certainly enamoured with the tall New Zealander, and by now he appeared to be completely smitten with her. It really did look like love at first sight for them both. After he waved goodbye they watched him hurry away to his hired car for the long drive ahead of him.

It was late morning before the two women settled into their hotel at Airlie Beach and walked out onto the esplanade to enjoy the view. Charlize had booked a room in the same complex for Lloyd and told the receptionist he should arrive in time for dinner.

He wheeled into the car park just before seven, in almost record time. Fifteen minutes after he parked the car he joined the two women in the beer garden. He bought a couple of beers from the bar and drained the first without taking a breath, then carried the other one back to the table.

'Oh boy, I needed that. I'm as dry as a wooden chip.' He grinned at Charlize. 'Well, I'm here, but the whole trip was a nightmare. Mile after mile of potholes, dawdling cars, and road repairs everywhere.' He chuckled. 'But I didn't see one cop, not one, and just as well, at the speed I was driving.'

'Well you're here now.' Charlize echoed his words and laid her hand on his. 'So we can all relax.'

'What are you going to do tomorrow?' Suzi asked looking from one to the other.

'We'll fit in with you,' Lloyd replied quickly and Charlize nodded agreement.

'Well, I've never been on a sailing boat before and it sounds more exciting than a launch trip to Hook Island.'

'Oh, I thought you'd like to see the observatory.' Charlize sounded a little piqued. 'But if you'd rather go sailing that's okay with us.'

As she spoke the barman came to collect the empty glasses. While he cleaned the table, he said something about the 'Dolphin' being good value for money, and then added, 'You'll be dead lucky if you can get on though—they're fully booked most of the time.'

'Let me check it out,' Lloyd said, climbing to his feet. He returned five minutes later and handed a ticket to Suzi. 'There you are, the very last one. The young lady at the desk said they were sold out, but I persuaded her to see what she could do and she came up trumps.' He placed two more vouchers on the table. 'There was no trouble getting tickets for the Hook Island observatory.'

Charlize looked at Suzi. 'Is that all right with you? You don't mind going on your own?'

'Of course not, and for heaven's sake stop asking me if it's all right.' Then she clasped her friend's hand. 'I'm happy for you. Enjoy what time you have together.'

They drove down to Shute Harbour the next morning and left the car in a parking space overlooking the wharf complex. Charlize waved as she and Lloyd boarded the motor launch.

'See you back at the hotel for dinner,' she called.

*

Steve had only driven about twenty kilometres up the highway before he stopped in a parking bay and pulled out the roadmap to recalculate how far it was to Kuranda.

'I don't know that I want to go that far,' he muttered. The shimmering heat haze was becoming stronger by the minute and his eyes were already straining against the harsh northern sun. Maybe he needed stronger sunglasses. Maybe it was not such a good idea after all to listen to Tony Randall. He sighed noisily. Maybe he just needed to head south again and hope the weather was kinder below the Tropic of Capricorn.

Without making a conscious decision, he put the car into gear, did a U-turn and headed back the way he had come. A short while later he saw a man leaning against a road marker, with his thumb extended, hoping for a lift. Steve slowed down to have a look at him, decided the guy seemed fairly presentable, and pulled in to the side of the road. The stocky man thanked him profusely, threw his pack into the back of the car, and slid into the passenger seat.

'Thanks mate,' he said, wiping a film of sweat off his brow. 'How far yer going?'

'I'm not sure, yet,' Steve replied. 'I might go straight through to Brisbane, or I might stop off somewhere on the way. What about you?'

'Anywhere away from this heat,' the man, who introduced himself as Matt, said. 'I don't know how people put up with it. It gets hot back home, but nothing like this.'

Steve laughed at the man's expression. 'So you're a backhomer too? Where are you from?'

'Timaru.'

'Ah, a mainlander.'

The man laughed good-naturedly. 'Well, it's got more going for it than the North Island so we're entitled to call it the mainland. Besides there are more real New Zealanders down south than up north.'

The two men soon began reminiscing about their homeland. They both agreed that it was the best country by far, and they wouldn't want to live anywhere else in the world. The miles soon dropped behind them as they talked. An hour later Steve pulled into a garage to fill up with petrol, and as he climbed out of the car, Matt asked if he wanted anything from the shop.

'No, I'm fine thanks,' Steve replied, sticking the nozzle into the tank. When he returned to the car after paying the bill, Matt was licking an ice cream. 'It's a pity you bought that,' he said, pointing to a hotel across the road, 'I was going to suggest we have a beer over there.'

Matt glanced at the pub, opened the car door and, without a word, he dropped the cone into the gutter. Steve laughed aloud.

'Ice cream and beer don't really mix do they?'

It was mid-afternoon when they approached the small sugar mill town of Prosperine. As they waited for an empty cane tram to cross the road, Matt directed Steve's attention to a billboard extolling the attractions of the area. The legend read: 'Airlie Beach gateway to the Whitsunday Passage'. Underneath the message was a list of the major attractions in the area, and the tours that were available.

'I might have a look at that place,' Matt said. 'Would you drop me at the turn off, please?'

Steve glanced sideways at his companion. Although he had originally intended to visit some of the resorts on his way south, he had lost the urge to go sightseeing now. Maybe it was the oppressive heat, maybe it was because he could not rid his mind of Kirsty's tragic death—or maybe he felt that everything was wearing him down. He really needed to be alone, to purge the remaining grief that still tugged at his heart—not to be caught up in a busy tourist scene. But something was pulling him towards the fork in the road.

'Well, thanks again,' Matt said, as Steve eased the car over to the side of the road. But, as Matt went to open the door, Steve spoke.

'No, don't get out just yet. I might as well take a look at the place while I'm in the area. Who knows… I might find something interesting to do.' A little later, he dropped the fellow New Zealander off outside the camping ground at Cannonvale, and continued on to Airlie Beach where he booked into a motel. He sauntered down to the waterfront and walked along the sandy beach towards the marina. The sight of so many boats reminded him of Auckland, the city of sails, and suddenly he felt homesick.

He was about to return to his motel when he saw a man tying up a powerboat. They passed the time of day and Steve mentioned that he had originally intended to go scuba diving on the Great Barrier Reef.

'There's some good coral reefs near here,' the man said. 'I can take you out if you're interested.' He quoted Steve a price for the hire of the boat. 'You make a choice, morning or afternoon, whatever you want.'

'I'll think about it, okay?'

Steve walked to the far end of the small village and then headed back to the motel. By the time he had listened to a throng of tourists arguing with their bus driver, and watched some drunken kids hurling empty beer cans into the creek, he wondered why on earth he had bothered to come to the place. He looked into the pub and decided it was too noisy, so he bought a couple of cans of beer to take back to his motel.

The manager arranged to send a meal to his room so that he could have it on the balcony overlooking the bay. The motel was far enough away from the hustle and bustle of the main part of town to allow Steve the peace and quiet he needed. He had just finished a can of beer, when a knock on the door announced his meal had arrived.

'Put it on the table, please,' he said, as the waitress entered the room. When he had finished, Steve pushed the plate away with a sense of satisfaction. The fresh barramundi fish had been cooked to perfection, the vegetables had been beautifully prepared, and the side salad crispy fresh. His only regret was that he had no one to share it with. And even as that thought crossed his mind he realised that there was no one special in his life now. Kirsty was dead, Suzi Lysle Spencer was half a world away, and Jenny was only a vague possibility, and one he did not particularly wish to encourage.

The connection between his thoughts and the physical world around him seemed to be highlighted by the changing scene below him. A feeling of sadness swept over him as the setting sun dropped below the mountain range behind the resort area and cast long shadows across the landscape. The scene remained unchanged for about ten to fifteen minutes, and then suddenly it went dark.

Shortly afterwards the first glimmer of moonlight touched the water. As the moon continued to ascend, its silvery beam formed a new vista, one that depicted the opposite aspects of setting before him. It was as if he were being given the opportunity to compare both the reverse and obverse side of things, and that he should not judge according to the light that shone, but rather on the substance that was being illuminated.

'What am I trying to tell myself?' Steve muttered, as another wave of melancholy engulfed him.

It was unusual for him to feel so despondent. Until recently his life had been fairly predictable, and rewarding, and he had looked forward to a prosperous future. Deep in his heart he knew that marriage to Kirsty was never really an option. She probably loved him, but not enough to deny her roots, and in one respect that saddened him, but on the other hand he was relieved. He had been prepared to accept the responsibility, but he was aware that it was a responsibility forged by sibling protectiveness rather than anything else. He knew deep down that it would never have worked.

He let his mind wander. Things might have turned out differently with Suzi, if he hadn't been committed to Kirsty at the time. There was no denying the effect the pretty Welsh girl had on him. As he thought about her and relived their last night together, he was amazed at the depth of feeling it still produced in him. Her lovely face seemed to be reflected in the moonlit waves breaking gently on the sandy seashore.

Unwilling to be swamped by feelings of self-pity, Steve went indoors and snapped on the television. By the time he had watched a nature programme, the news, and a comedy, his sense of purpose had returned and he went to bed in a happier mood. He was soon asleep, and woke up feeling refreshed and ready to enjoy the next day.

'I'll stay another night,' he told the receptionist, when he came down for breakfast. 'I'm going to do some scuba diving.' The man Steve had been talking to the previous day could not take him out until the afternoon because of another booking. Rather than hang around the resort area he drove into Proserpine and introduced himself to the engineer at the sugar mill. He explained that his company, Vaxline, had currently installed some pumping equipment in another mill in the Townsville area, and outlined the advantages of their product over the existing plant.

'We have a resident fitter in North Queensland,' he said, when the engineer asked how they would address any related problems. 'He's worked for our company for about ten or twelve years. We would arrange for him to oversee the installation and check it over regularly.'

The man listened attentively and agreed to discuss it with the mill manager when he returned from a visit to Brisbane. Steve whistled a catchy tune as he left the premises. Vince would be happy to put Nick Bolte on a retainer, pay him to install the equipment, and to do any maintenance work. It would obviate sending someone over from New Zealand every time something went wrong. Steve knew that Nick would be the best man available to look after their interests and he would ensure that the work was done to their satisfaction. More importantly, it might provide the opportunity to open up new markets reasonably close to home, rather than look farther afield in the Asian countries.

Greg Chaplin, the boat owner, was waiting for him when he drove down to the marina after lunch. He led the way to a motorboat with two powerful Yamaha outboard motors on the back. When he saw Steve's appraising look, he smiled.

'We get out there quick and we come back quick,' he said, clambering into the cockpit. 'A sailing boat might appeal to your average tourist, but this baby will give you more time in the water.'

Steve slung his gear into the back and settled down beside Greg as he hit the starter button. The two engines roared into life. When they cleared the end of the marina, Greg pulled the throttles back and gave a thumbs-up sign as the boat surged forward. Within seconds they were skipping across the tops of the waves as the craft responded to the thrust of the propellers. When they cleared the nearest headland he pointed the boat towards a distant island. Forty-five minutes later they had reached the place where a natural reef ran out from the point of a nearby island.

As Steve slipped on the scuba gear, Greg cautioned him.

'Normally, I wouldn't let you dive by yourself,' he said, in a serious tone of voice, 'but you seem a pretty level-headed sort of guy. All the same, I want you to pop up from time to time just to let me know you're okay. I don't want to be fishing your body out of the sea.'

The reef was quite spectacular and far better than he had expected. Time slipped by quickly as he worked his way along the length of it, but he still remembered to surface at regular intervals to assure Greg that he was all right. When he finally thought to glance at his underwater watch he realised that there was only another twenty minutes of air supply left in the bottle. He struck for the surface and reached out for the side of the boat. Just as he clambered aboard, a sailing boat carrying a load of tourists rounded the point and prepared to go about.

As the boom swung across the sailing vessel, a crew member on board shouted, 'Keep your heads down, we're going to go about.'

However, they were unprepared for what happened next. The flapping sail knocked off a woman's big floppy hat and as she instinctively grabbed for it, the vessel shifted beneath her. She lurched towards the side of the boat and, unable to keep her balance, she slowly toppled overboard into the sea.

By the time she had surfaced, the sailing boat was a hundred metres away.

Chapter Twenty-One

Suzi was gazing absentmindedly at the small boat anchored nearby when a crewmember called out: 'Keep your heads down.' The words had been repeated numerous times during the day, but she knew that if she remained seated everything would be all right.

Directly in front of where she sat was a gap in the railing that allowed passengers easy access to the vessel. Normally it was closed off, but someone had failed to secure the chain properly, and as boat heeled over it came loose.

At the precise moment it dropped off the hook, Suzi stood up. The man shouted, 'Keep your heads down, we're going to go about,' as the boat turned into the opposite tack, but it was too late. The trailing edge of the sail caught the top of her broad brimmed hat and knocked it off her head. She tried to grab it, but the deck level shifted and she lost her balance. Almost imperceptibly she began to topple overboard—like a slow-motion movie, and there was nothing she could do about it.

Suzi's scream was cut short as she hit the water and sank beneath the waves. She had never been taught to swim properly and had always harboured a fear of drowning. Now her fears were reality. Even as she managed to kick her way to the surface and take a breath, another wave slapped against her face and forced more water into her mouth. Panic stricken, she lashed out with her arms and legs, but the waves continued to batter her face.

She had always scorned the idea that a person's life would flash before their eyes as they were about to drown, but now, as she sank into the depths, it seemed very real. Suzi had visions of her mother's funeral, and of Uncle Bart's body lying cold and stiff in a coffin in the front room of Caxton Manor. A wispy figure seemed to hover over the casket beckoning to her with a spectral hand. She had heard stories about a ghost that haunted the old house. Was this spectre drawing her into the next life?

The dim outline of the ghost faded as her vision was filled with light, a green translucent light that seemed to be speckled with bright flashes of sunshine. It was blotted out for a moment by some large object that made a fearsome noise and produced a stream of churning bubbles. Then it seemed to disappear. A moment later a face swam into view, a familiar face, the face of someone she loved. It looked strained and unearthly in the opaque light. It's Steve, it's Steve Pardoe... he's going to save me. The words formed in her mind and repeated themselves over and over again even though she knew this was an impossibility.

The person's face receded and there was nothing she could do about it. She tried to reach out to whoever it was, but her limbs seemed paralysed and everything looked blurred and tinted green. Then her eyes glazed over and she lost consciousness.

*

Greg Chaplin had not hesitated when he saw the woman fall overboard. He dragged Steve down into the cockpit of the powerboat, hit the starter button and raced towards the spot where she had fallen into the water. As he closed the throttles a woman's head bobbed above the waves.

'I'll get her,' Steve yelled, slipping off his scuba tank. But even as he jumped into the water the woman sank from sight again. He followed her into the depths, grasped under her arms, and kicked his way furiously to the surface. When his head broke water, Greg reached out a helping hand.

'Get her into the boat,' he cried.

At that moment a dinghy from the sailing boat came alongside. One of the occupants dropped into the water and helped Steve push the unconscious woman into the powerboat. As they manhandled her aboard the other person in the dinghy called to Greg.

'I'm an ambulance officer. Let's see if I can help her.'

Steve pulled himself into the dinghy as the ambulance officer took his place in Greg's powerboat and began to work on the woman. It was only as the man straightened her head that Steve thought that the woman reminded him of Suzi Lysle Spencer, only this white-faced, half-dead woman was hardly her—she was thousands of miles away.

'I'm taking her back to Airlie,' Greg shouted, and then thumbed the ignition switch. 'I'll radio for an ambulance on the way.' Then without another word, he pulled back on the throttles and swung the wheel hard over to the right. Within minutes the powerboat was just a speck on the horizon.

Meanwhile the sailing boat had come about and had motored to where the dinghy bobbed gently in the sea. Numerous hands reached out to pull Steve aboard and a couple of people clapped him on the back and said well done. The skipper, who introduced himself as Kerry, thanked him profusely for saving the woman. Someone produced a towel, and another person offered to lend him a tee shirt, while a female crewmember made him a cup of hot, sweet tea.

As he sipped the liquid, Steve spoke to the skipper again. He could tell the man was worried because he had been negligent in providing for the passengers' safety. He eyed Steve cautiously, but he could hardly refuse to answer his questions.

'Do you know the name of the woman who fell overboard?

'No I don't, but Naomi might be able to help. She usually gets to know people,' Kerry replied. He gestured at the crowded boat. 'There are twenty-three people on board today, and I barely have time to talk to half of them let alone find out their names.' He called to the young woman who had made the tea.

'I'm not sure who she is, sorry,' Naomi apologised. 'We barely passed the time of day, so I don't know anything about her, I'm afraid,' she said, using the same excuse as the skipper—that it was hard to keep track of all who came aboard.

'Did she have a bag, or anything that could identify her?'

Kerry shrugged his shoulders.

'We won't know that until we get back to Shute Harbour. If there's anything left when everyone's gone, it'll be hers.' He cast another worried look around the boat as he steered it towards the last point leading into the harbour. 'I'm in big trouble if she doesn't recover.'

When the man turned his attention back to the helm, Steve walked over to the nearest hatch and sat down. He closed his eyes for a second and when he opened them again he saw a middle-aged woman peering intently at him.

'You're the young man who made the rescue. You were very brave.' When he nodded, she continued. 'I heard you asking the captain who she was. I might be able to give you a clue.'

'Oh?'

'Yes, we had a lovely long talk just before lunch. She and her friend were on a holiday together as the result of a competition they won.' She made a funny little sound that came out like a chuckle. 'And now, it seems her friend has fallen in love with some fellow they met in Cairns. It all sounded very romantic.'

'Did she tell you her name?'

'Yes, but I'm so sorry, I've forgotten it. I always forget names. I remember she said she's from Wales, though… a part of Britain,' she explained. When Steve thanked her, the woman smiled. 'She's such a lovely girl and a very pretty one, too. I do hope she'll be all right.'

Steve's heart was thumping fast; was there a chance that the person he had just saved could well be the woman dearest to his heart? He wanted to see her, to touch her, to tell her everything was going to be all right. Yet, he could not equate with Suzi being in this part of the world, and strong doubts began to creep into his mind. There were others here from Wales—surely; this was wishful thinking.

When the last passenger departed, Kerry and his crew searched the boat, but were unable to find anything that didn't belong there. When they came back up on deck, Naomi was the first to speak.

'I think she might have had a clutch bag,' she said. 'If that's the case, maybe she dropped it and it's been picked up…' She left the sentence unfinished and looked anxiously at the skipper.

'That's what happened... somebody's stolen it,' he said, looking more worried by the minute. 'It happens, you know.' His voice had taken on a distinct whine. 'We can't be expected to watch everyone's personal luggage.'

The deck hand broke the uneasy silence.

'She might have had it in her hand when she fell overboard,' he said. 'That's more likely what happened, if you ask me.'

Kerry seized on the explanation with a sigh of relief.

'Yeah, you're right. It's probably lying on the seafloor amongst the rocks or whatever.'

Naomi had very little so say as they drove back to Airlie Beach. She dropped Steve outside his motel and mumbled a goodbye as he climbed out of the vehicle. Greg Chaplin's van was parked nearby.

'Oh, there you are.' The man emerging from the building greeted Steve heartily. 'I've just dropped your gear off.' He gave a little laugh. 'The manager might give you an earful—he wasn't too impressed to have a load of wet scuba gear dumped in front of his desk.'

'And what about the woman we fished out of the sea. What's happened to her? Is she all right?'

'Yeah, she's fine,' Greg replied, casually, as if it were quite normal to rescue people from drowning and rush them back to the mainland. 'The ambo brought her around pretty quickly. We loaded her into an ambulance at Cannonvale and they took her to the Base Hospital to give her the once over.' He shrugged his shoulders. 'She's probably a bit shook up, but she'll be all right.'

*

Suzi opened her eyes cautiously and then shut them against the strong sunlight. Slowly and with great difficulty, she turned her head away from the glare of the sun and focused her attention on the man by her side. His freckled face bore a wide grin.

'Hi there,' he said, shouting above the sound of the roaring outboard motors. 'How are you? Can you talk?' He motioned to the driver who eased off the throttles and then he repeated the question. 'Are you all right?'

'I… I guess so,' Suzi replied, hesitantly, putting her hand to her brow. 'Where am I? What happened?'

'You fell overboard, and we're taking you back to the mainland.' The man smiled encouragingly. 'Do you remember falling?' When she nodded, he continued. 'Well, some guy and his mate rescued you, and now we're headed back to the resort.' Then as if expecting her next question, he added. 'I'm an ambulance officer. I helped resuscitate you.'

Suzi looked from one man to the other and nodded mutely.

'You're going to be okay,' Greg said, increasing the speed again. 'We'll be in Cannonvale in another ten minutes. There's a local ambulance station there, and they can give you the once over just to make sure everything's okay.' He patted her hand. 'Don't you worry now… everything's going to be all right.'

Suzi closed her eyes and leaned back against the seat as the boat roared towards the mainland. Her mouth still felt as if it were full of seawater and her throat was sore from vomiting the water she had swallowed. She gently massaged her temples with her fingers to ease the throbbing pain, and tried not allow her feeling of insecurity to show. There was probably no reason to be concerned, but she didn't know these men, and they could be taking her anywhere.

As the harsh note of the outboard motors decreased and the boat settled down into the water, she opened her eyes to see that they were approaching a small jetty. A creamy yellow ambulance stood waiting on the road nearby, and, as Greg manoeuvred into the wharf, a man walked towards them. He caught the rope that was thrown to him and secured the craft, and then he helped Suzi onto the timber decking.

Her legs felt extremely wobbly, but she was able to walk to the ambulance with the aid of the man. The officer placed a light blanket around her shoulders, but within minutes she shrugged it off because it was too hot. By the time she had been checked over by the duty doctor in the casualty section of the Base Hospital, her light summer clothes were completely dry. Although he was satisfied that everything was all right, the doctor want her to remain in hospital overnight just to be sure there were no complications.

'I can't do that,' she protested. 'I'm flying back to the UK tomorrow. I have to catch a plane to Brisbane first thing in the morning.'

Reluctantly, the doctor agreed to her request, but he insisted that she should visit a GP when she returned to Britain. Then he prescribed a sedative, and minutes later Suzi walked out of the building to find the ambulance officer waiting for her.

He gestured towards the vehicle.

'I thought I'd wait a while, just in case you didn't have to stay in hospital.' He opened the passenger door. 'Hop in, I'll take you back to Airlie.'

*

Charlize opened the door the instant Suzi knocked. She grasped her friend's hand and drew her inside.

'Oh, Suzi thank God you're all right,' she said. 'I've been worried sick about you. When we arrived back in Shute Harbour we were told that your boat had docked an hour earlier and everyone had gone. When you weren't here, I was afraid something had gone wrong.'

Suzi looked at her friend in amazement. Had no one told her friend that there had been an accident at sea? That she was nearly drowned? That she was brought back to the resort in a powerboat? There seemed to be a serious communication problem. She could well imagine Charlize's concern at not being able to find out where she was.

'I've… I,' Suzi began, and then the enormity of her brush with death flooded back and she started to sob quietly. As Charlize placed an arm around her shoulders, she broke down completely. It was some time before she regained her composure and related her experience. She had just finished telling Charlize how she had hallucinated that Steve Pardoe had rescued her, and how his appearance had seemed like a miracle. Just then, there was knock at the door. It was Lloyd. He gave an audible sigh of relief as he saw Suzi sitting on the side of the bed.

'Are you all right?' he asked, looking at her, extremely concerned. He turned to Charlize. 'I was coming to tell you that I heard there was an accident, and I tracked down the skipper of the sailing boat. He told me what had happened and how a speedboat had whisked Suzi back to the mainland.' He lifted his hands. 'He didn't know whether you'd been detained in hospital or not, but he gave me the phone number of the local ambulance station. so I could make enquiries.'

'The ambulance driver dropped me off here, just a matter of minutes ago,' Suzi said.

'Thank God she's safe and sound now,' Charlize said, clinging to Suzi's hand. 'I think I'd have died if anything had happened to you. I'd have felt I was to blame for bringing you to Australia in the first place.'

'Don't be silly,' Suzi said, with a note of exasperation in her voice. 'I chose to come with you, and that's all there is to it.'

'We need a drink after all that,' Lloyd said, and disappeared, only to return within minutes with a vodka and coke for Charlize and a double brandy for Suzi. Then he arranged to meet them in the bar before dinner. After he had gone, Suzi had a leisurely shower. The liquor had dulled the remaining aches and pains, but now that the tension had been removed, she felt quite exhausted.

'I'll be all right,' she said, in answer to her friend's concern, 'but I'll skip dinner downstairs tonight, and have something sent up here instead. I just want to be alone to sort out some things in my mind.' In response to Charlize's anxious expression, she added, 'Now don't you worry… I'll be okay. You go… Lloyd will be waiting.'

While she waited for the meal to arrive, Suzi thought about her vision of Steve Pardoe. What on earth made her think that he had come to save her? Then she realised that more than likely she had hallucinated under the circumstances.

Chapter Twenty-Two

Steve felt quite annoyed by Greg Chaplin's off-hand attitude to the accident.

'She would have drowned if we hadn't reached her in time,' Steve said.

'She might have, but she didn't. We got her out in time, didn't we? So there's no problem is there?' Greg replied.

Steve stared at the other man for a moment as he tried to come to grips with his reasoning. But Greg was right, of course—there was no problem. It was his own concern for the woman that was the issue, and the man was totally oblivious to that aspect of the situation. However, that did not satisfy his need to know if she was all right.

'Yeah, you're right. I just got a bit carried away. The hospital, is it easy to find?' Steve asked, as casually as he could. 'I'd like to find out if she's okay.'

After Greg had given him directions and said goodbye, Steve went to his room and showered. As he washed the salt water out of his hair, he thought about the ridiculous idea he was harbouring. The odds of the woman being Suzi must be astronomical. He thought about the middle-aged woman who had spoken to her on the boat.

Apparently, the two women had spent nearly two weeks touring the state and were due to fly back to Britain within a few days. Even as he towelled himself dry, Steve wondered whether he should leave things as they were. He had tried to put her out of his mind ever since he left Wales, but now, had they been brought face to face again, even if under almost tragic circumstances?

He was reminded of the previous evening when he had visualized her lovely face in the moonlit waves breaking on the seashore. Had that been an unconscious desire for her, or had it been a premonition of what was to come? He recalled the look on her face as he swam towards her in the water. He wondered—had she recognised him in that instant before she lost consciousness? A half hour later, he reached Proserpine.

As he drove slowly down the main street looking for the signpost to the Base Hospital, an ambulance turned out of the road to his left. It never occurred to him at the time that it could have been the vehicle that had transported Suzi to hospital; after all, every ambulance in Queensland was painted creamy yellow.

When he finally found the casualty ward, the nurse was helpful, but apologetic.

'Doctor Hodge treated her for immersion and shock, but was unable to convince her that she should remain in hospital overnight. She said something about having to catch a flight to England tomorrow.'

'Did she give a local address?'

The nurse looked at the treatment card and shook her head. 'No, nothing all at all, only her name—Suzi Lysle Spencer, and her date of birth.' She glanced at the clock on the wall. 'You've just missed her… she picked up a prescription from the pharmacy and left about ten minutes ago.'

Steve thanked the nurse and walked out to the car park and climbed into his car. So he had been right. It really was his Suzi. He shook his head, almost afraid to believe it. He sighed as the late afternoon sun cast shadows across the cane fields, and drove back to the resort area deep in thought. What now, he wondered. Should he try to find out where she was staying in Airlie Beach? He knew that a lot of tourists were bussed in for the day. Suzi could have been in transit. She might even be staying in Proserpine.

Well, he could soon find out. He found an empty phone booth with an intact telephone directory and began calling all the hotels and motels in the area. None of them had a Suzi Lysle Spencer booked into their establishment. He phoned Kerry, the owner of the sailing boat and asked if he knew where the ticket had been purchased. The man grunted a reply and then dropped the phone onto something hard. A few minutes later he came back on the line.

'I'm not sure, but I think it's the last one that was sold. The receptionist at the Airlie Beach Hotel badgered me into letting her sell one more ticket.' He let out a lengthy sigh. 'I shouldn't have listened to her; I was already fully booked. There'll be hell let loose when the harbour master finds out.'

The hotel receptionist kept Steve hanging on the line for nearly two minutes and then asked him to wait some more. He hung up and dialled again, but the line was busy. In desperation he jumped into the Toyota and drove down to the hotel.

'I seem to have a trouble getting through to anyone here,' Steve said, when the girl on the desk looked up from her desk to face him. 'You kept me hanging on the line and now… '

'What's the trouble?' a voice said.

Steve turned around to look at the speaker, a burly man with a shock of unruly hair, staring at him.

'I don't remember addressing you. I want some information from this young lady.'

'What do you want to know?'

The receptionist stared at the man with a resigned look on her face, but said nothing.

Steve took a deep breath and then asked,

'Is there a Suzi Lysle Spencer staying in the hotel?'

'Who wants to know?' The burly man positioned himself in front of the desk.

'I do, she's a friend, and I was told she might be here.'

The man grabbed the register from in front of the girl. He flipped through the pages and then threw it back on the desk. 'You're wasting your time… and ours,' he said. 'She's not here.'

'Thanks for nothing,' Steven said bitterly. 'You sure run a great hotel.'

'If you don't like it, get lost. We don't need troublemakers around here.'

Rather than get into a slanging match or worse, Steve walked outside. *Best forget it* , he told himself; *it's not worth fighting over* . But he was no closer to knowing whether Suzi was still in the area or on her way back to Brisbane.

He phoned his parents that evening and told them he would be back in a couple of days. Norah told him Kirsty and Joey's bodies had already been released and the funeral was scheduled for tomorrow, but she urged him not to hurry home.

'Nobody will be upset if you're not here. The people who count know you were on the way to Queensland to install some pumps when the accident occurred. They won't expect you to drop everything and return.'

When he paid his account the next morning, he asked if the manager at the Airlie Beach Hotel was usually that rude. Then he repeated the man's words.

'Was he a big burly fellow?' When Steve nodded, he continued. 'Ah, that's the publican's brother. He's a bit of a pest. When he's tanked up he's likely to say anything to anyone.'

'But…'

'Oh, he'll be gone by now. He comes around, scrounges some money for booze and then heads off again. Strange sort of fellow. Harmless enough really, but rather intimidating.' The man laughed. 'The staff know better than to argue with him when he's drunk. That's Airlie Beach for you. Full of odd characters.'

'Very odd if you ask me.'

'It's a pity you didn't think to tell me about it when you came back,' the manager said. 'My sister-in-law was on the desk last night, and I could have rung her for you.' He lifted the phone. 'I'll give them a bell now, if you like… see what they know.'

Steve watched as the man spoke to someone at the hotel and nodded.

'She was there. Apparently she was sharing a twin room with a woman called Bronwyn-Smythe. That's why her name wasn't on the register,' he explained. 'But they've gone. They booked out early this morning.'

Steve thanked the man, made his way outside and climbed into the

Toyota. He was still shaking his head in disbelief as he turned onto the highway and headed south towards Brisbane. Why hadn't he thought to go back later? Well, it was too late now. *There must be a reason why I didn't find her in time* . Then he consoled himself with the thought that nothing happens without a reason. He tuned into a local radio station to help pass the time and caught the tail end of the news.

The announcer gave a brief weather summary and then chuckled.

'Now we've got the delightful Dolores with the day's astrological forecast.'

The woman made some indiscernible remark about rude disc jockeys and launched into her daily predictions in a broad nasal twang. Her last words were:

'Don't forget, you can't deny your destiny. Everything is written in the stars.'

Her final words were to roll around in Steve's his mind for the next hour. Was everything written in the stars? Had Suzi's brush with death been preordained? Had he been meant to be on hand to save her? And if so—were their lives inexplicably entwined?

He pushed on for the rest of the day and made Rockhampton just before the sun set. The next day he handed the car keys back at the airport hire desk and boarded a plane for Auckland.

*

Lloyd brought Charlize back to the room a couple of hours later, and stayed long enough to assure himself that Suzi was all right before leaving. She felt a bit guilty about the situation, because she knew they would have preferred to spend the night together, but Charlize soon put her mind at rest.

'Don't be silly. Do you think I'd leave you alone after what you've gone through?' She picked up the electric kettle. 'Do you want tea or coffee?'

As she sipped her tea, Suzi spoke about her lucky escape.

'I'm still wondering if it really was Steve who rescued me, or if that was just my imagination,' she said, thoughtfully. 'The ambulance man said that as far as he knew the person who pulled me out of the water was taken back to the sailing boat. I wonder if I can find out what happened to him afterwards?'

'We'd have made enquires for you if we'd known, but it's bit late now.' Charlize looked at her wristwatch. 'I don't think we'll get much help phoning around at this time of night.'

'You're probably right.' Suzi yawned noisily. 'Let's get some sleep. It's an early start in the morning.'

Lloyd fussed over Charlize as they checked in their luggage at Proserpine airport. It was quite obvious that he was upset that Charlize was leaving. They clung together until the last moment, and then she broke from his embrace and ran across the tarmac to the waiting plane.

'Are you all right?' Suzi asked, as her friend slid into the seat beside her and dabbed her eyes with a tissue.

'Yes,' she sniffed. 'I'll be all right.'

By the time their plane landed at Brisbane airport, Charlize had regained her composure. She told Suzi that Lloyd had promised to keep in touch, and they had already made tentative plans for the future. Neither of them saw their relationship as a holiday romance. 'He's made me promise to phone him when I get home,' she said, brightly, 'and he hinted that he might be able to arrange some time off in a few weeks and pop over to the UK.'

After they had checked in their luggage at the Qantas desk, the two women bought some duty free Australian wine and a few more souvenirs. Then it was time to board the plane for the long flight back to Britain.

*

The brilliant blue skies of Queensland were but a memory as the aircraft descended through the grey clouds and taxied to the terminal at Heathrow. They were back home.

'Well, here we are safe and sound,' Suzi said, as they struggled through the crowded concourse. She flashed Charlize a smile. 'I enjoyed it immensely—it's been great fun.'

'Yes, it's been a wonderful experience, and I'm so glad you were able to come with me.'

They threw their bags into the back of the Alfa Romeo and headed out onto the M25 and west to Wales. Three hours later, Suzi turned the key in the front door and shivered. The place felt like a refrigerator in comparison to the heat she'd been in for two weeks. She should have arranged for Mark to switch on the heating for her. She phoned the Stow Restaurant to say that she was back, and Mark said he wanted to call in after he had finished work.

'No, Mark, I'm not good company right now. The flight was tiring, and I need to catch up on my sleep. Let me rest, and I'll see you tomorrow, okay?'

As she slipped in between the sheets, Suzi recalled the night she and Steve Pardoe had made love in this very room; in this very bed. She stared at the ceiling and wondered why she had not made the effort to find out it if he had been on the powerboat. That thought would be with her for the rest of her life. But what if it had been him? What would she have done she had found him? Would she have professed her love for him and expected him to reciprocate?

Then she reminded herself that he lived and worked in New Zealand and she could think of no reason why he should have been on the Whitsunday Coast in the middle of summer. It seemed unlikely— and yet it could have been possible. But surely, if it had been Steve, he would have checked to see if she was all right? After all he was a very caring person. Maybe he had tried to find her and had been unsuccessful. The questions kept flooding her mind—but no answers came.

'I'll never know for sure, I suppose,' she murmured into her pillow. As she fell asleep, Suzi remembered her grandmother's creed that everything happened for a reason and nothing was accidental. So if it had been Steve who rescued her, it was meant to happen.

*

Mark greeted her with open arms when she walked into the restaurant the next morning, and embraced her for a long time.

'It's great to have you back,' he said, holding her hands as if to stop her ever leaving again. 'I've missed you more than I could have imagined.' He looked her up and down. 'You haven't got much of a tan.'

'I don't tan, I burn. I had to keep covered most of the time. But you should see Charlize—she's as brown as a nut.' Then she laughed softly. 'And hey, you'll never guess what happened... she's fallen in love.'

'Charlize in love? I don't believe it,' Mark said, incredulously. 'She's the last of the great bachelor girls.'

'Well, someone has finally got under her skin.' Over the next ten minutes Suzi filled him in on all the details of Charlize's romance with Lloyd. 'They seem irresistibly drawn to each other. It's quite incredible.' She sighed. 'I'm so happy for her.'

It only took a few days to settle back into the job. Narelle had managed very well in her absence, but was happy to relinquish the role of hostess. Everything seemed as it had always been, but there was one thing that caused her real concern, and that was Mark's obsession with horse racing. He spent all his spare time between the end of the luncheon period until it was time to prepare for the evening meal, hunched over the table by the window, studying the racing section of the newspaper and making copious notes.

When she questioned him, he just smiled.

'It'll pay off, you'll see.'

*

Mark had recouped some of his losses two days before Suzi returned from Australia, but he needed a good win to put him in front again. At last he appeared to have found the horse to change his luck. Golden Shadow fitted the picture perfectly. The horse won comfortably, but its price had shortened as the race time neared and so he didn't win as much as he expected.

'Oh, well,' he muttered, pocketing the money and walking out of the betting shop. 'At least I've proved I can pick winners, so there's no limit to how much I can win.'

Two days later another horse fulfilled all the requirements, and once again he slipped out to place a bet. Like Golden Shadow, it won easily, but this time the dividend was far greater. Now he had a sizeable bank to play with, and he was determined to push his luck and reap the rewards of his efforts.

As soon as everything was back to normal, Mark suggested a day out. He bowed to Suzi's wishes to spend the day poking around country lanes and visiting some of the picturesque places nearby. Inasmuch as she enjoyed the holiday in Australia, she had disliked the harshness of the land and the excessive heat. Now all she wanted to do was revel in the sight of gently rolling hills and the lush green fields of her native Wales.

They headed north along the road that wound through the Wye Valley, turning off into the side roads that took their fancy, until they found a delightful little pub that served a good lunch. When they returned home mid-evening, Suzi was tempted to invite him to stay for evening meal, but then thought better of it, and gently eased him out through the door again.

Why do I feel threatened by him? she mused, as she watched him drive away. It was not as if he had caused her any problems, and so far he hadn't said anything about getting engaged. If only she could be like Charlize. Her friend was still floating on air and singing Lloyd's praises to everyone and anyone who would listen.

'I'll give her a call,' she murmured picking up the phone, but the number was engaged. A few minutes later she picked it up again and hesitated, finger poised over the automatic redial button. Then she replaced the receiver and nodded an answer to her silent question. 'Yes, I'll pop over and see her instead.'

Chapter Twenty-Three

Charlize opened the door and looked at Suzi in amazement. 'What on earth...?' she began. 'I've been trying to ring you.'

'Well, I've been trying to ring you as well, but your phone was engaged so I decided to pop over instead.' She dropped down onto the sofa. 'So what's new? You seem rather excited about something.'

'I've just been talking to Lloyd.'

'That's nice.'

'Better than that, he's on his way over. He was calling from Auckland airport to say his flight has been delayed.'

'But...'

'He rang a couple of hours ago to say that he'd manage to arrange some time off and he'd be on the first available plane.' Charlize gave a little giggle. 'Apparently his partners didn't mind him taking a couple of weeks off at short notice.

'I didn't know he was a partner.'

'Neither did I until a few days ago. He didn't say anything while we were in Queensland, because he was concerned that I'd think he was just trying impress me.' She gave another little giggle. 'He said he didn't want to skite.'

'Skite? What do you mean skite?'

'Oh, it's one of those funny expressions they use in that part of the world. It means to boast, swank, or show-off. Anyway it turns out that he's quite wealthy, has a luxury apartment overlooking Auckland harbour, and a batch, whatever that is, somewhere up north.'

Suzi shook her head.

'Well, how about you then? So what are you going to do, now?'

'Oh, just wait and see what happens when he gets here.'

As she drove home Suzi thought about her friend's revelation. She had known Charlize for many years, and this was the first time she could ever recall her being excited about a man. Normally she treated most of them with disdain, as if they were not worthy of her attention. The occasional one that managed to capture her interest usually did not stay around for long, and very few made it to the bedroom, so Lloyd had to be extra special.

Then she thought of Steve. Would it possible to find out if he had been on the Whitsunday Coast the day she fell off the boat? Airlie Beach was only a small resort town and there were only a handful of places that offered accommodation. But whom could she approach to find out? And was it important? Yes, it was, she decided, but there were still too many unanswered questions surrounding the whole episode. She hesitated; maybe it would be better to leave it alone.

The morning mail contained a letter from Mr Duncan, the solicitor. In stiff legal terms it stated that Steve Pardoe was against the proposal to use Caxton Manor as a restaurant and venue for receptions. He would not consider allowing it to be mortgaged but he would consider selling his share of the property.

So much for that, thought Suzi. Then she continued to read. The solicitor stated that there were no objections to her occupying the building. The letter stated:

Mr Pardoe has informed me that he is conscious of the need to protect the property, and has agreed to your wish to reside at Caxton Manor until such time as everything has been finalised. Well, that's something at least, she mused.

Suzi dropped the letter back onto the table and stared into space. It was quite evident that Steve had very little interest in the building itself, or in its heritage. She found it hard to understand such an attitude, but then she reminded herself that he lived on the opposite side of the world, where values were different, and ancient buildings were hard to come by. Caxton Manor had no charm as far as he was concerned—it was just another old building.

She showed the letter to Mark.

'Well that seems pretty straightforward, doesn't it? His eyes lit up as he looked at her. 'If you move in we could use the conservatory whenever we need to cater for something special.'

'But that wouldn't be right,' Suzi protested. 'I can't pretend it's mine and do just what I like as soon as I move into the place.'

Apparently unwilling to upset her, Mark hesitated before speaking.

'No, of course not, but surely there would be nothing against your hiring a room to the Stow Restaurant occasionally. If you tell Pardoe that you're willing to share the profits he'll probably agree. It would achieve two things. Firstly, it could provide an income from the place and secondly it would prove that your idea was feasible.'

'That's brilliant, Mark. I'll give Duncan a call straight away.'

'What will you do with the bungalow?'

'I'll put it on the market eventually, of course. But I can't do that until I know exactly what's happening about Caxton Manor, or I could find myself without a permanent home. The bungalow should fetch a good price... enough to sort out all my financial problems.' She sighed. 'It would be nice to be free of debt.'

As winter gave way to spring the tourist numbers began to increase and the restaurant trade reacted accordingly. It was too early to predict whether the catering side of the business would follow suit, so Suzi maintained her stance and refused to consider leasing a bigger property.

'We might get it wrong. It's too risky,' she said, the last time they discussed the matter. 'We could bite off more than we can chew and lose everything.'

*

Eventually, as Suzi made plans to move into Caxton Manor, Mark began to wonder whether it had been a good idea to suggest it in the first place. If he had realised that she was prepared to sell her bungalow eventually, he would have offered to let her share his flat. It would have made things a lot easier for him in the long run, and one thing could lead to another if they were living together under the same roof.

If only he could raise enough money himself to buy the New Zealander's share. As half owner he could take up residence and from that point onward he would be in the driving seat. But in the meantime, he had to concentrate on picking another winner.

'Hello all,' Gary Hyland announced animatedly. He had recently returned from an extended holiday in America and looked more prosperous and tanned than usual. He clapped Mark on the back. 'So, how's it going? Are you still betting?'

'Yes, but I'm not doing as well as I'd like to, I'm afraid.'

'Hang in there, you'll be okay.'

'Yeah, I need a break.' He explained the situation to his friend. 'I want to come up with the cash before Suzi gets settled into the manor on her own.'

'Yeah, fine, but don't be in a rush. If you try too hard you'll make mistakes.' He glanced at the clock on the wall. 'Look, I must go. I might slip in later in the week and see how you're doing, okay?'

*

Steve scanned the faces on the other side of the barrier when he walked into the main concourse and gave a sigh of relief when he saw his father. He had dreaded the thought of returning to an empty house.

'How are you son?' Vince said grasping his hand. 'Is everything under control?'

'I'm okay, but how about you and Norah?'

'We're coping… just. The funeral went off without a hitch, thank goodness.' He sniffed noisily.

'Did you…?'

'It's all right, I made a point of talking to the Ruawhane clan. I said that we couldn't notify you in time to come home. I said you sent your condolences… you know all the usual stuff. They were okay about it.'

'Thanks Vince.'

As they drove home, Steve filled in some of the missing gaps of his dealings with Tony Randall and their former employee, Nick Bolte. Then he spoke about his visit to the Proserpine mill and his conversation with the engineer in charge. He concluded by saying, 'Nick's definitely interested in looking after things for us in North

Queensland.'

'And you reckon that Randall's promised to talk to some of his colleagues at the other mills?'

'Yes, and he's a pretty genuine bloke. All the mills stick together… it's a tight community.'

Vince brought the car to a halt outside the house and turned to Steve. 'Now are you going to be okay?'

Steve shrugged his shoulders.

'You mean about Kirsty? Yeah, I guess so. I've had time to think about things, and although I feel badly about the way she died, I believe she did the right thing in going. We may not have liked the idea of her taking up with Joey Ruawhane, but it's what she wanted.'

'Yes, but she'd still be alive if…' Vince stopped, as Steve laid a hand on his arm.

'Yes, alive, but not happy. I couldn't provide what she wanted, nor could you or Norah.' Steve hesitated before continuing. 'I know it sounds a bit callous, but she had some time with the man she really loved, even if it killed her in the end.'

Vince just looked at him for a moment and then stepped out of the car. 'Come on, Norah's waiting for you.'

Tears welled up in Norah's eyes as he kissed her cheek.

'It's so good to have you home, Steve.' She held him close for a few minutes and then broke away. 'I'll make some coffee.' The atmosphere at the evening meal was rather subdued, and it wasn't until they had settled into the lounge that it improved. Both Norah and Vince were keen to hear of Steve's experiences in Queensland, and when he finished relating the episode at Airlie Beach they looked at each other in amazement.

'And you think it really was the woman who is associated with the inheritance?'

'Yes, I do. Crazy isn't it?' Then he told them about the conversation he'd had with the woman on the boat. 'I keep wondering what would have happened if we'd met up again.'

'It's probably better that you didn't,' Norah remarked quietly. 'You've enough to cope with at the moment without adding another problem.' When Vince went to the bathroom, she laid a hand on Steve's arm. 'This woman is more to you than just the other claimant , isn't she?'

'What makes you think th…?' He stopped when he saw the look on his mother's face. 'How do you know?'

'Call it woman's intuition or whatever, but I think she's important to you. Am I right?'

'Yes, and no. I'll tell you about it later,' he said, as Vince came back into the room.

As soon as he finished work the next day, Steve drove out to the cemetery where Kirsty had been laid to rest. The two mounds of earth were heaped high with flowers and bouquets, and someone had placed a small cross on each grave. He stood looking at them for a long moment and then bowed his head in prayer. Unsure of what he should say, he wondered what Kirsty would have wanted to hear. Thoughts whirled around in his head until they took form. There was nothing to forgive and nothing to ask forgiveness for, either. They had both made mistakes, but they had shared a common bond and loved each other.

As he straightened up Steve became aware of someone behind him. He turned to see a middle-aged Maori woman gazing at him intently.

'You must be Steve Pardoe,' she said, without any preamble. When he nodded his head, she continued. 'I'm Kathy Ruawhane, Joey's mother. I had a feeling you'd be here today.'

'I'm sorry I wasn't at…'

'It's okay, your father explained,' Kathy said, quietly. 'Maybe it was better that you weren't here.' She gestured at the graves. 'They're at peace now.' Then she sniffed noisily. 'They didn't have much time together, but they were very happy for a short while.' A soft breeze tugged at the massed flowers causing some of the petals to fall to the ground. Then as quickly as it had come, it went.

Steve cleared his throat.

'I'm sad that things turned out the way they have, Mrs Ruawhane.

My own relationship with Kirsty was very special, but I know that your son, Joey, had more to offer than I could ever give her. She always felt that she should have been born a Maori, a full blood Maori, not half pakeha.'

'She told me that too.'

'Vince and Norah, and myself as well, we never really understood how important your culture was to her.' He choked back a sob and then spoke of their life together. He recounted his reaction to Kirsty the day Norah brought her home and explained that the little girl was now a part of the family. Steve paused as he recalled Kirsty's efforts to fit into their society. 'My folks should have let her go when she wanted to.' He paused again. 'And I was just as much to blame that she wasn't allowed to leave freely.'

'We all do the wrong thing for what we think are the right reasons,' the woman said.

Steve looked at the woman for a long time without speaking. There seemed nothing to say, and yet there was so much that needed to be said. There was a need to communicate, to bridge the gap that had existed between their respective cultures for so many generations. He reached out tentatively for the woman's hand and then sighed deeply as she clasped it warmly between her own.

'I don't know what more to say.' He stifled another sob. 'I'm pleased that I was finally able to let her go.'

'That must be a load off your shoulders.'

'Yes. Yes it is.' He paused and then added, 'Please extend my sympathy to the rest of your family, Mrs Ruawhane.'

As he drove away from the cemetery, Steve thought about their conversation and the words he had offered as a prayer by the graveside. He had difficulty with the concept that a person never really dies, but that they just move out of their body to inhabit another dimension, and yet he was convinced that Kirsty had heard his words. And not only that she had heard them, but he felt she had forgiven him for his misunderstanding of her.

Joey's mother had been right; it was as if a weight had been lifted off his shoulders. When he returned home that evening, Vince handed him a sealed envelope. Steve read the unfamiliar writing on the front. 'Steven Philip Mathews. What's this about? Why are you giving it to me now?'

Vince pulled a face.

'Because I'd forgotten all about it. And it's all yours, Steve.' He shrugged. 'Sorry. I was going through the desk looking for the bits and pieces concerning Kirsty when I found it.'

'It was amongst your parents' effects,' Norah explained, 'tucked into a portfolio of insurance documents, birth certificates, and things like that.'

Steve gingerly opened the envelope and withdrew the sheets of paper. He glanced at the heading on the letter that was clipped to the top. It bore the name and address of a company of share brokers in London, and confirmed the purchase of a large number of shares in an international oil company. He checked that the figure in the letter matched the number of share certificates and whistled softly.

'Well, better late than never, I suppose.' Steve turned to Vince with a questioning look on his face. 'I wonder why you forgot about them until now.'

Chapter Twenty-Four

Suzi looked up as Mark joined her by the window.

'I've been checking out the cheque book against the bank statement,' she said, as he sat down, 'and I've found something that needs explaining.' She pushed the cheque book across the table. 'Did you make out a cheque to Gary Hyland for a thousand pounds?'

Mark fidgeted with the string of his apron before answering. 'Yes,' he admitted, reluctantly. He was about to continue when Suzi interjected.

'But why? We don't owe him any money. He was paid in full the first week in January.' She glared at the man by her side. 'Would you mind telling me what it's all about?'

'I needed some cash,' Mark explained, diffidently. 'Gary lent me a thousand pounds and I gave him a cheque to cover the loan.'

'But you're not supposed to use that money for private reasons. It doesn't belong to you,' Suzi said, angrily. 'The Stow Restaurant account is intended to finance the running of the restaurant. It's not a personal account for you, or for me.'

'I know, but I needed the money in a hurry and I didn't have time to go to the bank.'

Suzi continued to glare at Mark as he twisted his apron string nervously. She felt more than angry; she was distressed that he should take advantage in this way. She felt betrayed. There was really no need to ask why he had taken the money—that was obvious. Gary had been a regular visitor over the past week or two and they had spent most of their time together discussing racehorses.

'What have you done with the thousand pounds? Lost it on a horse, I suppose?'

'On the contrary,' Mark said, brightening up. 'The horse won and I've put the money back into the account. It'll probably show up in the next statement.'

'Where's the deposit slip?

'Probably in my coat pocket. I'll get it for you.' He returned a few minutes later and laid it on the table. 'There it is, see? No harm done.'

'That's what you think.' When he asked what she meant, Suzi replied, 'Never mind. Just leave me alone.'

She watched him walk away, and wondered why he hadn't said anything to her. Surely he knew that she would pick up the discrepancy sooner or later. She had intended to ask if she could borrow money from the operating account to help defray her moving expenses, but had decided it wasn't fair. It was against the principle of their business arrangement. And now Mark had taken advantage of her and done the very thing she had decided was unethical for herself. She gathered up the papers, stuffed them into the folder, and stormed out of the building.

Tears of anger welled up into her eyes as she drove away from the restaurant. She had been so excited about moving into Caxton Manor that she had expected everything else to fall into place, too. Steve had unexpectedly agreed, in principle anyway, to her proposal to use the conservatory for private parties, and suddenly all those plans were threatened. And now she was having strong doubts about Mark's honesty.

Without making a conscious effort, she headed across the village to where Charlize worked. Her friend looked up as she walked into the office.

'Hi, what brings you here?' Then, as she noted Suzi's grim appearance, she cried out, 'Hey… what's wrong?' She slid out from behind her desk. 'You look like you need a strong coffee.' By the time they had finished a second cup, Suzi had unburdened herself and felt a lot better.

The two women discussed various options, but were no closer to a solution when the young office assistant called out to Charlize, 'Will you take line one? It's personal.'

Charlize picked up the phone identified herself and then gave a little cry of delight. She looked at Suzi and mouthed the word Lloyd.

'Yes, of course. I'll be there as soon as I can.' She replaced the phone and stood up. 'I must go. Lloyd managed to get on an earlier flight, and bussed down from Heathrow to Cardiff. I'll pick him up from there.' She kissed Suzi's cheek. 'I'll check with you soon.'

After Charlize had roared off in the direction of the motorway, Suzi drove back to her house to pick up a few things before going to the manor for her protracted stay. Even though it was only a partial house move, her little bungalow looked as if it had been hit by a cyclone. Black plastic bin liners, suitcases, and several wooden tea chests filled the front room and spilled out into the hall. She just hoped she could get everything packed in time for the small removal van that was booked for a pickup in the morning. Fortunately she didn't have to concern herself about the restaurant because Narelle was prepared to cover the lunchtime trade.

*

She dropped her coat on the nearest piece of furniture and looked around. A wave of nostalgia swept over her as she recalled some of the events that had taken place there. Inasmuch as she mourned the death of her mother, the bungalow had provided the means to pursue the long-standing dream to have her own restaurant. Of course, it had been very much her mother's place. She couldn't remember much about the house in Lampeter, where she spent her formative years, but the memory of the main roads in Lampeter had stuck in her mind all those years. They were exceptionally wide—wide enough, so she was told, to allow a trio of horses pulling a cart to turn around in the road.

Her father had been living there at the time. He had gone to Scotland to work on one of the first oilrigs to be commissioned off the Scottish coast. And had never returned. Annabelle had kept up the pretence of their marriage for some years. On the few occasions she had asked about her father, Annabelle had little to say except that he had walked out their lives, and she had no idea where he was.

Suzi had proved later that her mother's allegations were false. Her father had continued to support them even though the marriage had ceased to exist many years earlier. Her eventual enquires revealed that he had been killed in an oilrig explosion off Aberdeen and was buried on the northeast coast of Scotland. The cause of the explosion was a simple enough mix-up. A piece of paper had been lost. Crucially, however, that piece of paper had borne a warning to overnight staff not to use one of two gas pumps from which a pressure relief valve had been removed for overhaul.

It was used in error, and as a result a valve blew and the situation became increasingly dire. Many men died from the effects of carbon monoxide poisoning as they waited for a helicopter that never came. Then came a series of underwater explosions which blew apart the oil and gas lines from the neighbouring platforms. It appeared to coincide with the time her mother sold the house in Lampeter and moved to Wales.

She often wondered about her father. It was not hard to imagine why he had found life with her mother so hard to bear. Her own relationship with Annabelle had always been difficult and fraught with upsets. Fortunately, time had eased the pain and now she was able to accept that her mother must have been slightly psychotic.

As she waited, she traced her fingers over the sofa and wondered if she should keep some of the furniture. But then she considered that it probably would not suit Caxton Manor, which was full of period furniture anyway. The small removal van arrived on time and by mid-morning all the items she needed to take with her had been transferred to Caxton Manor. It had all been so easy. She wandered around the magnificent house, and wondered why she felt so depleted over the temporary move there. She would feel better when her few personal belongings were in place—it would feel more like home to her, and she felt she would soon become used to the change-over.

Mark had promised to call in after lunch, and in the meantime there was plenty to do. Suzi had just finished placing all her toiletries in the upstairs bathroom when the front doorbell rang. She opened the door to find Charlize and Lloyd smiling broadly. Lloyd pulled a bottle of Champagne and three glasses from behind his back and held them aloft.

'We've brought our own glasses, knowing you wouldn't have unpacked yet.'

Charlize kissed her cheek.

'We couldn't miss the opportunity to toast your new house,' she said, as she walked inside and gazed around. 'It's bigger than I remember it, or is there something missing?' Then she shook her head. 'It's probably my imagination.'

'We'd better open this bottle before we do anything else,' Lloyd said, moving towards the drawing room. 'There's nothing worse than lukewarm Champagne.'

After they had finished the bottle Suzi showed them all over the house, and by the time they returned to the ground floor it was nearly one o'clock.

'Let's go down to that little pub near the main road for lunch,' Charlize suggested. 'We'll help you unpack when we come back.'

Suzi was more than game, and really thankful that she did not have to prepare a meal. Lloyd said something to the publican as the two women made their way to a cosy corner table. The man waited until they had settled down and then passed them a menu, while Lloyd stood next to Charlize's chair.

When the waitress came to take their order she placed a freshly cut vase of flowers on the table and smiled as though she was privy to something secret. Minutes later the publican placed a stand containing a silver bucket of ice next to Lloyd, then he returned bearing a bottle of Champagne.

'There we are sir. I hope it's to your satisfaction.'

'A second bottle of Champagne?' Suzi looked from one to the other. 'What are we celebrating this time?'

Charlize squeezed Lloyd's hand as he coloured slightly. 'Go on, you tell her.'

'We're going to be married,' he said.

'And I'm going to emigrate to New Zealand,' Charlize added, excitedly.

'Well, I don't know what to say,' Suzi said, slowly, 'other than congratulations, of course.' She looked from one to the other and then back at Charlize's radiant face and smiled. 'I must say I've never seen you so happy in all the years I've known you.'

When she questioned them about their plans, Lloyd said his firm might employ Charlize as a freelance PR officer.

'Unless I can find something else,' Charlize added.

Lloyd had thought of just about everything. They would be married in New Zealand, and live in his apartment on the north shore until they found a suitable house to buy. He had already made enquiries about her applying for citizenship and made it clear that he had friends who could smooth the way and iron out any hitches.

'We have an old boy network down there, too,' he said.

'But, Charlize, you can't just up and leave everything?' Suzi grasped her friend's hand.

'There's nothing to hold me here, Suzi, and I won't regret leaving the cold weather behind. And as for my job, well, it's just a job.' She squeezed Suzi's fingers. 'You're the only one I don't want to leave. I'll miss you for sure.'

'But what about your family?'

'What family? Father is currently courting his third wife, and he won't leave California for any reason. Mother is content to stay where she is, in Spain, especially now that she's found herself a toy boy. And Geoffrey? Well, I haven't seen my dear kid brother for nearly ten years and I suppose he couldn't care less whether I'm here or thousands of miles away.'

Suzi gave a little sigh.

'Well, I'm going to miss you. I'll be lost without you, to be honest.'

Lloyd coughed discreetly.

'Look, we haven't finished the Champagne.' He pulled the almost empty bottle out of the ice bucket and dribbled some wine into each glass. 'Here's to whatever,' he said, raising his glass. Then he looked at his fiancée. 'We were going to help her settle in, remember?'

'Yes, come on.' Charlize stood up. 'Keep busy… that's the best course of action.'

By the time they had returned to the manor and sorted everything out, and stocked the refrigerators and the kitchen with a delivery they all felt exhausted. By now, Charlize had organised Suzi's bedroom and sorted out her wardrobe as well, casting aside anything she thought unattractive or inappropriate. Mark had called in, but left ten minutes later when he saw he was rather in the way.

They were sitting around the table in the kitchen when Lloyd glanced at his watch. 'I want to make a quick call.' He turned to Suzi. 'Can I use your phone?'

'Of course.'

He was back in a few minutes.

'Right, that's settled. Now, let's think about dinner. I saw a nice little place on the way here. It's called Stew Restaurant or something like that, and I thought we could…' He stopped with raised brows as Charlize gave a hearty chortle.

'The Stow Restaurant, you mean. That's Suzi's place, and it's not an appropriate choice.'

'We'll go to our favourite haunt. We're well known at the Forge Inn, and their food is as good as what we serve,' Suzi said, climbing to her feet. 'There's one condition… I'm paying.'

The proprietor greeted them by name and fussed over Charlize when he was told of her forthcoming marriage. When Lloyd began asking questions about the old staging inn, Suzi was reminded of her evening there with Steve. It all seemed so long ago. She forced her mind back to the present and steered the conversation back to New Zealand.

*

Suzi drove back to the manor in a pensive mood after they had said goodnight. It was quite obvious that Charlize and Lloyd were not only very much in love, but they were also well matched. Although she was pleased they had found each other, her happiness was tainted by the knowledge that she was losing her best friend and confidante. *Maybe I could pack up and go to New Zealand too*, she mused. *What's to keep me here? Maybe I could find Steve Pardoe, maybe I could...* She gave a bitter laugh. 'Maybe I could be a bit more practical, too.'

She slipped into a pair of cotton pyjamas and sat on the side of the bed. There were strange sounds all around her. She listened carefully, but it was no more than the old house creaking as it settled at the end of the day. Her thoughts slipped back to the time when she had stayed there overnight with her mother when she was a small child. The same sort of sounds had really frightened her then. They had been guests of Uncle Bart at the time, and he had insisted they should stay with him until her mother found a suitable home in Cardiff.

Unable to sleep, she made her way over to the window and peered out onto the silent garden. A lone fox stood in the centre of the lawn, and within seconds another appeared, slipping through the hedge like a wraith. The first one waited until the new arrival sniffed its tail and then cavorted across the grass. Suzi gave a little cry of delight as a third one appeared from nowhere. They began tumbling around, then chasing each other around the lawn, but in two minutes, they had gone. Suzi wanted to see more of their antics, but there was no sign of them anywhere; they had melted away like shadows in the night, and all was still and quiet again in the now deserted garden.

After she had climbed back into bed, her thoughts returned to her brush with death on the Whitsunday Coast. She vividly recalled floating in the pale green waters and staring up at the sunlit surface and seeing something strange. When she finally fell asleep, her dreams were full of strange men trying to rescue her from drowning in the sea. As each one reached out to catch hold of her, Suzi looked into their faces, and then eluded their grasp when she did not recognise the person. All the while she sank deeper and deeper into the murky depths. Then, just as her lungs felt as if they would burst, a hand pulled her clear of the water. At that moment the old house creaked again and snapped her awake.

Distressed by the dream, Suzi slipped into a dressing gown and made her way down to the kitchen for a cup of hot chocolate. She laced it with a generous measure of whiskey and crawled back into bed. It was only minutes later that she snuggled down under the covers again, and fell asleep.

Everything seemed different in the morning light. The sunshine added an extra dimension to her joy as she began to rearrange the house. She looked out of the front window just as the gardener arrived. He seemed rather surprised to see her, but expressed his satisfaction that she had moved into the place, albeit temporarily.

'It's not good to leave an old house like this empty,' he said, knowingly. 'They deteriorate quickly if they're not lived in.' When the lawnmower coughed to a stop she called out to him. 'Would you like a cup of tea?' He smiled and gave a thumbs-up sign. As she handed him the mug, Suzi made what she thought was an off-hand comment about some overgrown shrubs. The elderly man looked at her over the top of his mug.

'I've only been asked to cut the grass.'

'Well, can you tidy the place a bit?'

'Aye, just tell me what you want done.'

The man, who asked to be called Aub, seemed pleased to be offered the opportunity to restore the gardens to something like their former glory. He also agreed to do some odd jobs in the house as well.

*

Mark seemed more than pleased to see her when she turned up at the restaurant the following day. He had evidently given some thought to her comments about misusing the business account, and, although he did not exactly apologise, he was subdued.

'Charlize and Lloyd are getting married, soon, Mark,' Suzi said, and waited for his reaction.

His mouth dropped open with surprise.

'I thought you were just having me on when you said she'd fallen in love, but... but married? Wow. It's hard to believe. Pretty fast wasn't it?'

He twiddled with the ladle he was holding. 'How do you feel about it?'

'I'm happy for her, but not for myself… to be honest, I'll miss her dreadfully.'

'Will you go to New Zealand for the wedding?'

Suzi shook her head.

'I don't think so. It's so far away.'

'I'm sure we can work something out if you want to go.'

'It'll be in the middle of our busiest time. I doubt if Narelle would be able to cope with the pressure, and I rather fancy she wouldn't even want to try. No, I'd rather stay here and make sure everything's under control.' Then she turned her full attention on Mark, and her voice was unmistakably sharp. 'I want to know… are you going to continue with this betting business?'

Mark looked taken aback and hesitated before answering.

'I know it doesn't sound very practical, but Gary's done very well out of it, and I'm nearly five thousand pounds in front at the moment.'

'Then why don't you quit and concentrate on finding some other means to augment your income?' Suzi looked fixedly into his eyes. 'Spending hours poring over bits of paper is not the best way to make money in my opinion. You could put that effort into promoting the Stow Restaurant. We could try some mailshots, aimed at the commercial sector to attract them to the place.'

'Yes, you could be right,' Mark agreed, reluctantly. 'We'll talk about it this afternoon, if that's all right by you.'

*

Gary breezed in after lunch to regale Mark with stories of his latest female conquests. The two men laughed and joked about his exploits until Suzi poked her head into the kitchen to ask if Mark was ready to discuss the mailshot. Gary did not take her broad hint and go, but settled himself even more comfortably on a stool and unfolded the latest racing newspaper.

'DewLine is the one to watch,' he said, tapping the paper. 'She won't win this one, but she should win on her next outing.'

'I thought she looked a certainty today,' Mark said, quietly. 'I hope you're wrong, because I've backed her with nearly everything I have… five thousand pounds.'

'Well, I'm sorry, Mark,' Gary said, climbing to his feet with a superior look on his face. 'But I think you've had it. You'll lose your money, for sure.'

Mark's colour sudden drained from his ruddy complexion, but he seemed to pull himself together. As soon as Gary left, he made two cups of coffee and carried them into the dining room. He looked around for Suzi. But she was nowhere to be seen. A note propped against the vase on the table contained her message:

Maybe you can find time to talk about more important matters than horses tomorrow.

Chapter Twenty-Five

Oh, and... DewLine has dropped out of contention as the field enters the final furlong and... The race commentator's words continued even though Mark had stopped listening. His face suddenly flushed as the blood rushed to his head, pounding against his skull to suddenly give him the king of all headaches. He sank down onto a stool and stared at the squawking transistor radio in disbelief—five thousand pounds—lost in a matter of minutes.

'Oh, my God,' he murmured, trying to console himself with the thought that it did not really matter. After all, he had accumulated the money by winning other races, but he felt cheated. It had taken weeks of carefully selected bets to build up the bank and now it was gone— five thousand pounds, just about everything he had. All gone.

Gary had claimed the horse wasn't ready. Better to wait until its next outing, he had said, and reinforced his argument by pointing to the odds. They were far too high for a racehorse of that calibre. The bookies knew it couldn't win, and that was why the price had drifted out to double figures. Unfortunately Mark was unaware of that fact when he placed the bet. Five thousand pounds: the words tumbled around his head over and over again.

He was still reeling from the loss when Suzi arrived half an hour later to prepare for the dinner guests. She acknowledged his greeting, but refused to be drawn into conversation. An uneasy silence permeated the place until the first guests arrived, but it was very plain that she was still angry with him.

'Shall we have a drink after work?' he asked, almost sheepishly.

'No, I've made other arrangements,' she replied, frostily.

When Gary poked his head into the kitchen the following day, Mark was busy preparing for the evening meal. He paused, meat chopper in hand, and was about to say something, but his friend spoke first.

'I was half tempted to place something on DewLine after all, but changed my mind when I saw which way the market was going. It looked good on paper, but that's all, and...' As soon as he saw the anguished expression on Mark's face, he stopped. 'I warned you, Mark, didn't I? Too late was I? Don't tell me you backed it heavily.'

'I put my bank on it. I'm all but wiped out now.'

'Aw... don't worry, you'll pick it up again.' Gary perched on the nearest stool. 'I've lost everything two or three times in the past. It's nothing to worry about. We all make mistakes.'

Mark vetoed Gary's suggestion to slip across the road for a drink, because there was still a lot of preparation to do and he didn't want to antagonise Suzi again. If she came in early and found him in the pub with Gary, it would certainly not go down well.

The atmosphere between himself and Suzi remained cool. She explained that there was a lot of tidying and cleaning to do at the manor, and she wanted to make sure it was done properly. She arranged for Narelle to take care of the luncheon guests two days later so that she could drive Charlize to the airport. When she returned, her eyes were red and puffy and she kept to herself for the remainder of the day.

Mark had been surprised when Charlize decided to accompany Lloyd back to New Zealand. She had quit her job, sold her car, and somehow or other managed to extricate herself from a lease—and just packed her bags, and gone. Suzi had been left in a state of shock for the best part of a week, and was still trying to come to terms with her loss. However, she had steadfastly refused any but the most superficial comfort from Mark. It was as if she did not trust him any more.

Determined not to give up his quest to make money backing the horses, Mark continued to trawl through the racing section of the newspapers. However, most of the likely winners were either being rested or in training for events later in the season, so he was in a bit of a quandary. When DewLine was listed as a starter in another race three weeks later, he looked for something to beat it again. The horse he picked did not fully satisfy the criteria, but he placed his bet anyway. His choice hung in at the last moment. But—it was beaten by the horse he should have backed—DewLine.

'Well, that's it, I'm broke,' he muttered, switching off the radio. 'Everything's gone wrong.'

However, Gary's earlier successes still goaded him on, driving him back to his notes yet again. The next likely winner came a week later, but he had no spare money because he had just paid to have some work done on his car, so he had to bypass the bet. Mark wondered if he could raise a bank loan, but they had already financed the purchase of the car and besides, it would take too long. He looked enviously at the joint account again, but his relationship with Suzi was still strained, and he dared not risk her wrath at this stage.

He was tempted to phone his father to ask for a loan, but Ben would have wanted to know why he wanted the money, and would have refused his request out of hand. Then he remembered that Gary had given him the name of a person who would lend money on a short-term basis. He dug out the slip of paper and rang the number.

'Why don't you come over and we'll talk about it,' the man said, in almost genteel tones. 'I'm sure Gary Hyland wouldn't have given you my name if he didn't know you well enough, but I like to meet the people I do business with.' He gave Mark an address. 'About four o'clock? Will that be suitable?'

Jonathan Wilcox lived in a luxurious house overlooking the River Severn. He explained that he conducted most of his business from home since the advent of computer networking. After he had questioned Mark about his relationship with Gary, and his connection with the Stow Restaurant, he enquired why he wanted to borrow a thousand pounds.

Mark hesitated and then decided that it would probably be better to tell the truth.

'Gary has shared his winning formula with me, and I'm in an awkward situation at the moment, what with heavy repair bills for the car, and so on.'

'I'll need to satisfy myself that your credentials are bona fide,' Jonathan Wilcox said, in a restrained tone of voice. 'I'm an investor, and so I must be sure my investment is not only secure, but will return me a dividend.' He stood up and shook Mark's hand. 'Ring me in a few days.'

When Mark phoned, the man's secretary took his particulars and said that she would inform Mr Wilcox of his call. She phoned back about an hour later and said that the money, five hundred pounds, would be deposited in his bank account. Then she gave him particulars about how he should repay the loan.

Mark spent even more time than usual checking and rechecking his figures to ensure he had picked a winning horse. He listened to the race with bated breath, and gave a sigh of relief when it galloped home clear of the field. After he had repaid the loan, Mark had more than enough to invest in his next choice. Once again he took a great deal of effort to ensure that his horse was the right one.

'You little beauty,' Mark yelled, as his choice scattered the field and romped home. Attracted by his exuberant shout, Suzi poked her head around the kitchen door. Unable to contain his excitement, Mark blurted out. 'That's another one home and hosed.'

'I'm not one bit interested,' she said, curtly. 'I think you're being very foolish.'

His next two choices were not so lucky, and once again he found himself without sufficient funds to bet. Once again he phoned Jonathan Wilcox. His secretary repeated her previous message when he phoned to enquire if he could obtain another loan. An hour later she returned his call. 'The money has been deposited in your bank account.'

The horse lost, so he borrowed more money to try to recuperate his losses.

'Oh, my God,' he groaned, as the next horse was pipped on the post. 'What do I do now?'

He knew that he dared not ask Suzi if he could use some of their capital to service the loan, and he was equally averse to contacting his father. For two days he sweated it out, wondering what to do. Then on the third day, two burly well-dressed men walked into restaurant.

'Are you Mark Brinstead?' one of them asked, ignoring Suzi's polite greeting. When he said yes, the man continued. 'Mr Wilcox said to remind you that he hasn't received his dividend yet.'

Mark swallowed hard and then croaked, 'I can explain.'

The man seemed not to hear him, but just rocked gently on the balls of his feet. Punching his balled fist into his hand, he gazed around the dining room. 'Nice place you've got here.' The smile on his face was hard and cold. 'Mr Wilcox doesn't like to be kept waiting. Do we make ourselves clear?'

After they went, Suzi demanded to know what they wanted. 'Who's this Mr Wilcox? And what's all this about a dividend?'

Mark looked at her for a long time without speaking. Then he muttered something about it being nothing to worry about, and went back into the kitchen. It was only the opportune arrival of a delivery van that stopped Suzi questioning him further. By the time he had stacked the food away, she was gone. He sank down onto a chair and buried his thumping head in his hands.

'Oh, my God, what am I going to do now?'

*

'It's for you, Steve,' Norah said, handing him the telephone. 'Someone with a lovely Scots accent.'

That can only be one person, Steve thought.

'Hello, Jenny, it's nice to hear your voice,' he said, when she had identified herself. 'Where are you?'

'I'm sharing a flat at Greylynne with a girlfriend,' she replied. 'I wanted to settle in before I phoned you.' She paused as if waiting for Steve to speak, and then continued. 'I wasn't sure if it was the right thing to do, because you hadn't replied to my letter.'

'I'm sorry about that,' Steve said. 'I meant to write, but what with one thing and another I never got around to it.' He paused and then continued. 'Kirsty's death was a great shock and it's taken some time for us all to pick up the pieces. I've needed a while to get over it.' Then he told her about his trip to North Queensland, and the freak accident that he was convinced had brought him into a brief contact with Suzi again. 'It was rather odd that our lives should overlap like that.'

'And now?'

'I don't know. I'm thinking of buying a place of my own somewhere, but it's just a thought at the moment.'

'Has anyone else staked a claim to your heart?'

Steve stared into the middle distance for a long moment before answering. 'What do you mean? Am I free? Do I want to get involved with you?' As he hesitated the memory of their previous encounter flooded back. Her sexuality had overshadowed everything else, and his response to her implicit invitation had caused him a great deal of anxiety. Did he want to form a relationship on that basis? Finally, he broke the silence. 'Let's have a drink together and we can take things from there, okay?'

When they met two days later, Steve felt his pulse quicken. The sensuality that Jenny projected seemed to permeate the space around her and reach out to everyone in the room. Other men eyed her appreciatively as she walked to the bar where they had agreed to meet.

She kissed his cheek.

'Hi, there,' she breathed seductively.

'Hello, Jenny,' he said, returning her kiss. 'You're looking very well.' He led the way to a quiet corner of the room. 'How's the new job? Have you settled in okay?'

'Yes, it's great, better than I expected, actually.' Then she told him that she had run into an old school friend from Invercargill shortly after arriving at Auckland, and had been invited to share a flat. 'It's quite roomy.' She looked up at him from under her eyelashes. 'We've worked out a system so that we don't surprise one another at a... in a delicate situation.'

By the time they had finished their second drink, they had shared most of their news and the conversation was flagging. Jenny grasped his hand.

'I was hoping,' she began, and then stopped as she felt Steve stiffen.

'Jenny, I don't feel as if I'm ready to become involved with anyone at the moment. Kirsty's death has had a profound effect on me, far more than I expected, and I need to time to reassess my feelings.' He paused for a moment and then gave a little laugh. 'You're very attractive and the thought of tumbling you into bed is very appealing, but...'

'But?'

'I've had my fair share of playing around, and I don't want to start a relationship based on sex.'

'I was hoping it would go further than that,' Jenny said, softly.

Steve stared into his empty glass for a long minute before answering.

'I don't feel as if I could make that type of commitment. I'd enjoy a physical relationship with you, but like I've already said, it's not what I'm looking for right now.'

'Oh.' She looked at her empty glass. 'Shall we have another?' When he shook his head she picked up her bag and climbed to her feet, and then forced a smile on her face. 'Take care, now.'

Steve watched her walk away and wondered why he had been so definite about things. After all she was more than an attractive young woman; she was a very sensual person, and he could have enjoyed an intimate relationship with her. Maybe he should have taken her out a few times before saying no. Then he laughed softly as he thought of something: 'Stick your finger in the honeypot, and you'll keep going back for more.'

He related the encounter to Norah when he returned home.

'I think you were wise,' she said, quietly. 'You might have had trouble extricating yourself later on.' Then she changed the subject. 'What are you going to do with your shares? Are you going to hang on to them or sell them?'

'I'm not sure, but I'll probably unload a few. I'm thinking of buying a place of my own. I would have done it years ago if hadn't been for Kirsty. I always felt that it was easier to stay here, where you and Vince could help keep on an eye on her as well, especially if I needed to be away.'

'Have you any idea where you'd like to go?'

'Oh, somewhere on this side of the harbour… not too far away. I'll have a look around the estate agents. I bumped into a chap I went to college with the other day by the name of Bridgestone. He's into property development in a big way, and I've arranged to meet him in a day or two to have a look at some property his company has an interest in.'

'Have I met him?' Norah asked.

'Yes, he came to one or two barbecues around that time. You'd have remembered him—tall, good-looking fellow with a mane of blond hair.'

'Yes, I seem to recall one of Kirsty's girlfriends going gaga over one of your college friends.'

'Lloyd was the original playboy.' Steve chuckled. 'No girl was safe while he was around, but apparently he's had a change of heart.' He chuckled again. 'He's getting married to someone he met while he was in Queensland. According to him she's the greatest thing since sliced bread. She must be something very special for him to give up his philandering ways.'

'And what are you going to do about that place in Wales?'

'I've agreed to let the Suzi Spencer live there until it's sold,' Steve replied. 'Apparently she's still hoping to find enough money to buy my share. She wants to turn it into a venue for receptions or conferences.'

'It's been dragging on for a long time now, hasn't it?'

'Yes, far too long.' Steve suddenly realised that the whole situation had caused him a lot of unnecessary concern; it had been like a millstone around his neck. 'I'll get on to my solicitor and get it straightened out one way or the other.' He stood up and stretched. 'I'll give him a bell first thing in the morning—it's time it was settled.'

Chapter Twenty-Six

Suzi stormed into the house, threw the car keys onto the table by the front door, and made her way into the sitting room. She poured herself a generous measure of whiskey and then dropped down onto the sofa. Why were those men threatening Mark? And who was this Wilcox? She guessed that he must have lent Mark money and now wanted it back.

Anger now replaced fear as she thought about what had happened. *I wonder if it's got anything to do with his gambling. It must be,* she thought. *After all, he's already abused my trust by taking money from the restaurant account without telling me.* The other question that required an answer now seemed far more important. Had he jeopardized the restaurant by using it as collateral in some underhand way to borrow money?

Those men had hinted that something would happen to the place if Mark did not pay what he owed this Mr Wilcox. And anything to do with the restaurant included her, so she was being threatened too.

'I should have put a stop to his gambling right from the start,' she muttered, and then gave a bitter little laugh. She sounded like an irate wife. Just as well she hadn't said yes to his marriage proposal—that wasn't the sort of life she wanted.

In an effort to calm her mind, Suzi wandered over to the window and gazed at the blaze of spring colour that bordered the driveway. Aub had managed to coax the garden back to life in just a few short weeks by clearing away the debris and planting quick flowering annuals. It looked as pretty as a picture. The buzz of the telephone cut into her thoughts. It was Mark.

'Suzi, I'm sorry I didn't have a chance to explain things this afternoon.' He sounded as if he was on the verge of tears. 'I need to talk to you about the situation. Can I come over to see you before I start evening preparations?'

'Okay, but your explanation had better be good.'

Mark arrived half an hour later with an abject look on his face. He followed Suzi into the sitting room and waited to be told to sit down. Without any preamble, he explained that he had borrowed the money from Wilcox on the understanding that he would repay the capital plus interest within a stipulated time. Then he went on to say that his period of grace had expired.

'He let me borrow more when I convinced him that I could repay the money…' Mark stopped as Suzi injected.

'So you continued to borrow in the hope that you would back another winner?'

'Yes,' Mark replied, with a sob in his voice. 'But when I lost three races a row, it snowballed.' He spread his hands in a gesture of hopelessness. 'I can't lay my hands on that sort of money at short notice.'

'How much?'

'Five and a half thousand pounds.'

Suzi stared at him in disbelief.

'How did you allow yourself to get into such a predicament?' She tried to hide her disgust as she questioned him about the arrangements he had made to repay the loan, and what percentage he was charged.

'That's exorbitant,' she said, when he quoted the rate of interest. 'Why on earth did you agree to that figure?'

'There wasn't any choice,' Mark replied. 'After all he held all the aces.'

'When were you expected to pay what's owing?'

Mark grimaced. 'It's already days overdue. Like I said, I've exhausted my goodwill,' he groaned softly. 'And now he's demanding his money.'

'And his thugs will smash up the restaurant if you don't pay?'

'I don't know, I…' He lapsed into silence.

'Well?' Suzi's question seemed to jolt Mark.

'I don't know.' He grimaced again. 'Yes, I suppose so. That's how they work isn't it? By intimidation.'

'What about your father; can't he help you?'

'Dad hasn't got that sort of money lying around.' He went on to explain that Ben did not have access to any more than a few hundred pounds at the most. He might sell some shares to get the cash, but it could be weeks before he received a cheque from the brokers. 'By that time the interest would have doubled.'

'What about Gary? He started you on this stupid idea. Have you phoned him?'

'I've left a message on his answerphone, but I think he's on the Italian Riviera.'

'Then phone his mobile.' Suzi almost spat the words.

'He doesn't take it with him.'

Suzi felt sick inside as she considered what might happen if the money was not repaid quickly. These men might start by smashing up the place, but then they might physically assault them too. So she was in as much danger as Mark unless he paid what was owed. Anyway it didn't matter what happened now—it was the end of her dream—the end of the restaurant and everything they had worked for over the past two years.

Without saying another word, she crossed over to the bureau and pulled out her cheque book. It was fortunate that she had not made arrangements to channel the money from the sale of her house into any other account as yet, so there was more than enough to cover the debt. She signed a blank cheque, tore it out, and handed it to him.

'When you find out exactly what you owe you can write in the amount,' she said, in a strained voice. 'Phone the man, tell him you have the money, and get down to the bank first thing in the morning.' She closed the cheque book. 'Don't bother to thank me. I'm doing it for my own safety. I don't want to be disfigured or crippled for life.' She stood up. 'Now get out.'

Mark climbed wearily to his feet and mumbled a reply. He stopped at the doorway. 'Sorry, Suzi. Really I am.'

As he climbed into the car, she called out,

'I've arranged for Narelle look after things tonight. I'll expect you to phone me in the morning as soon as you've settled everything.'

After he had gone, Suzi stood gazing absentmindedly at the wheel tracks on the gravel drive, and her mind slipped back to the day she had chanced upon Steve Pardoe in the house. There had been tyre marks on the drive that day too. It had been a day to remember in so many ways—she had just learned that she was not the sole heir to Caxton Manor, and had unwittingly found the man she wanted more than anything else in the world.

The joy of moving into Caxton Manor had been tarnished by the knowledge that she would never own it outright, and that it would probably be sold to settle the inheritance. Everything seemed to have gone wrong lately. She should never have become romantically involved with Mark in the first place. He had assumed she was prepared to consider marriage at some future date, but thank goodness she had rebuffed his sexual advances. And to top it off, her best friend had migrated to New Zealand.

A tear formed and slipped down her cheek. She felt so forlorn—there was no one she could turn to, no one to share her pain, no one to offer a word of advice. If Judith Brinstead hadn't moved to Cornwall things might be different, but of course it wouldn't be wise to embroil her in the problems her brother had created. Neither Ben nor Jane would understand and, even if they did, their sympathies would lie with Mark; that was only natural. Her only true friend and confidante, Charlize, was thousands of miles away in New Zealand.

'I'll give her a ring,' Suzi said, crossing over to the phone. But as she picked up the instrument, she remembered the time difference and realised she would have to wait until evening.

When she finally got through to Charlize, all she could do was cry. It was some minutes before she was able to explain what had happened to upset her so much. There was a moment of silence on the other end of the phone as she finished speaking.

'I wish there was something I could do for you,' Charlize said, 'I really do. I feel so helpless, here on the other side of the world. I don't even know what to suggest.'

They were still talking when the front doorbell rang.

'There's someone at the door,' Suzi said. 'I'll phone you back as soon as I work something out.'

She opened the front door to find Narelle standing on the doorstep.

'I'm sorry to bother you,' the woman began, hesitantly. 'but I need to talk to you. I was going to ring, but I felt it would be better to talk to you in person.' She paused as Suzi's brow creased with a puzzled look. 'If it's not convenient, then I'll...'

'No, it's all right, Narelle, come in.'

The woman began by saying that it was probably none of her business, but she had become concerned about certain things, and felt she should say something. She told Suzi that everyone at the restaurant was conscious of an underlying current of discontent between her and Mark, and she had become quite disturbed about the situation. Apparently a number of their regular customers had commented about it too. Then she went on to list the number of complaints she had received that evening about the meals.

'It was as if he didn't care what he served up,' she complained. 'I seemed to spend half the night apologising.' She tried to force a smile on her face. 'And we're all concerned about you, too.'

'About me?'

'Yes, you came back from your holiday full of life, and then a couple of weeks later it just seemed to drain away. We thought it had something to do with your friend going to New Zealand, but maybe it's something deeper.' Narelle twisted her hands nervously. 'Like I said, it's probably none of my business, but we're very fond of you, and we don't like to see you unhappy.'

Suzi bit her bottom lip as the other woman looked at her anxiously.

'I appreciate your concern, Narelle, and I acknowledge that there is a problem, but I hope it'll be resolved within the next day or two. I can't explain things at this stage, but it'll be sorted out one way or another.' She clasped the woman's hand. 'Thank you for your consideration, I really do appreciate it.'

'I haven't told anyone I was coming to see you,' Narelle said, climbing to her feet, 'and I won't say anything to the rest of the staff.'

After the woman had gone, Suzi poured herself a whiskey and sank down on to the sofa. As she climbed the stairs to bed, she thought about Charlize's last words. 'Why don't you come down for a visit?'

'That wouldn't solve anything,' she murmured. It would be unwise just to walk away from the problem. Anyway she couldn't trust Mark to take care of things in her absence, and it wouldn't look good if she left the house empty. No, she would have to stay and sort everything out before she could even consider her friend's offer.

She woke half a dozen times during the night and on two occasions found she had been crying in her dreams. The morning light came as a blessed relief. Dragging herself out of bed, she showered, dressed, and hurriedly put on her make-up. Unable to eat because of the fear that gnawed away at her insides, she forced down a cup of coffee and then drove to the restaurant. The sense of foreboding increased as she opened the door. There was nothing amiss, although the burglar alarm had not been activated.

She checked the phone for messages, but there were none. Then she walked through to the kitchen and surveyed the room. Everything had been cleaned and put away as normal. Suzi ran her fingers over the workbench as she considered what to do.

'I don't know that I want to be involved with this place any more,' she murmured, 'now that everything's turned sour.'

The ringing telephone caught her attention. It was Mark.

'I'm at the bank,' he said, in strangled voice. 'But there seems to be a problem.'

'Don't bother to try and explain things,' Suzi said, angrily. 'Just wait there for me.'

The bank clerk had queried the cheque because the amount had not been filled in when Mark presented it. He was not happy with Mark's explanation that it had been agreed that he was to fill in the amount himself, and that he had omitted to do this in his hurry. The clerk had refused to carry out the transaction until he was certain that everything was in order.

It took the best part of half an hour to sort everything out and transfer the money. Suzi was shaking with rage when she emerged from the bank.

'Why didn't you fill in the amount as soon as you knew what it was?' she demanded. 'If you ever put me through anything like that again, I'll...' She left the threat hanging in the air. As Mark attempted to say something, she cut him short. 'I'll see you back at the restaurant.'

When Mark arrived he answered a telephone call, but, while he was talking, he cast furtive glances in her direction and nodded his head. As he put the phone down, Suzi gestured to the phone.

'Have you sorted it all out?'

Mark hesitated. 'Yes, and no. Wilcox claims that I still owe him five hundred pounds.'

'How much more is he going to demand?' Suzi's voice was almost a shriek. Unable to take any more, she turned on her heel and hurried out of the building.

She drove her down the road to her own bank, where, with trembling fingers, she made out a withdrawal slip for another five hundred pounds. Barely able to hold back her tears she headed back to the restaurant. As she turned the corner, Suzi saw two men climb out of a car and push open the door.

Chapter Twenty-Seven

Charlize put the phone down and sighed—if only there was something she could do to help Suzi. For a brief moment she thought about making a quick trip back to see how she could help her, but realised it was impractical under the circumstances, and probably would achieve nothing. And by the time she arrived there, Suzi would probably have it all sorted out.

She gave another little sigh. It was strange how things seem to happen so unexpectedly; in some ways it seemed almost too good to be true. Who would have thought she would be living in a luxurious house overlooking Auckland harbour while she was waiting to get married? Only a few months ago she would have rejected the idea out of hand.

Any qualms she may have had about marrying Lloyd and settling in New Zealand had disappeared without trace. He was all she had hoped to find in a man, and their love for each other became stronger by the day. Lloyd's parents had insisted that she stay with them until the wedding day so that they could get to know each other better. Meanwhile he had taken the opportunity to have his home redecorated.

'Two more days to go,' she murmured, stretching luxuriously as she gazed out onto the sweeping expanse of lawn and beyond it onto the city of sails. She was tempted to phone him at work just to say hello, but resisted the urge. 'I don't want his receptionist to think I'm checking up on him.'

However within minutes he called her. 'Charlize, my darling,' Lloyd crooned into the mouthpiece. 'I've arranged to meet an old friend of mine who's looking for a house in the bay area. I thought you might like to come along for the run so that I can show you a bit more of our beautiful country. We'll all have a spot of lunch together afterwards in a nice little place that specialises in seafood.'

'That sounds great. I'll let your mother know I'm going out.'

Half an hour later, he pulled up outside the house and tooted the horn. As they headed north, Charlize told him about Suzi's phone call. He said nothing, but made the acceptable clucking noises one makes when sympathetic to another's problems.

'I don't regret leaving Britain for one moment,' she said, casting a glance at the man by her side, 'but I do miss Suzi. We've been such good friends for so many years, and now, when she needs me most, I'm on the other side of the world.' She sighed. 'Isn't it strange? Everything has turned out so wonderfully for me, and yet it all seems to have gone pear shaped for her.'

'Do you think she'll be able to sort it out all right?'

'I hope so,' Charlize replied, 'but it sounds as if she's at the end of her tether with Mark.'

Half an hour later they pulled into a parking spot outside an office that bore the legend: Wisecombe and Spencer Real Estate Agents and Valuators. As they did so, another vehicle stopped on the opposite side of the street and the driver tooted.

'Hello, Steve, nice to see you again.' Lloyd climbed out of his Mercedes as Steve walked towards him. While they shook hands Charlize alighted on the other side of the vehicle. 'Say hello to my future wife,' he said, placing a hand under her elbow.

'Hello, Charlize, pleased to meet you,' Steve said, and when they shook hands he had a strong feeling that he had seen her somewhere else before.

Lloyd grinned widely.

'Your eyes are popping out, Steve,' he said, laughingly.

'Yes, well you told me that your fiancée was beautiful, but I think you understated the obvious.' Then he turned back to Charlize. 'I found it hard to believe that Lloyd was contemplating marriage, but now I can understand why.'

'How very kind of you,' Charlize said. 'I think Lloyd and I are two of a kind, although we were both surprised at how quickly it all happened.'

She squeezed her fiancé's fingers. 'But it's the best decision I've ever made.'

'Lloyd said you met in North Queensland, but it's quite obvious you're not from that part of the world. Your accent is Welsh, unless I'm mistaken.'

Charlize looked at him in a peculiar way and was about to say something when Lloyd glanced pointedly at his wristwatch. 'Sorry to rush you, Steve, but I have to keep my eye on the time.'

'Yes, of course.'

'Come on, I'll introduce you to Harry and you can tell him what you're looking for.' He turned to Charlize. 'Do you want to wait in the car or come with us?'

'I'll be all right waiting here for you.'

Before Lloyd said goodbye, he invited Steve to visit when they returned from their honeymoon, and then left the two men discussing the available houses in the area.

'Steve seems a nice guy.'

'Yes he is,' Lloyd agreed, 'he's a genuine sort. We went through college together, but we weren't really close. Then a couple of years ago we met at a barbecue and sort of renewed our friendship. Although we don't see a lot of each other we have a fair bit more in common.'

'Is he married?'

'No, he was going to marry, but apparently his girlfriend suddenly walked out on him and went to live with an ex-boyfriend, some chap who had just been released from prison. Not long after that, they were both killed in a car accident.'

'Oh, how awful. How did Steve take it?'

'I think he was more upset than he's prepared to admit.'

'Did this Steve visit Britain recently?'

'He might have done.' Lloyd was just about to elaborate when the car phone rang. 'Hold on,' he murmured, picking it up and identifying himself.

While he talked confidentially to the other person, Charlize began tying up some loose ends in her mind. Although she knew that Suzi shared the inheritance of Caxton Manor with a man called Steve, and that he lived in New Zealand, she couldn't remember his surname. Charlize knew that Suzi was a bit cut up because the man had a girlfriend back home, but more than that she didn't know. She kept wondering about it; could this be some incredible coincidence? She shrugged and dismissed it, but then realised that stranger things happen every day of the week. Anyway, the facts should be easy enough to check out if she set her mind to it.

Lloyd headed towards the coast and, by the time he had looked over the proposed development area and talked to a couple of the principal parties, it was nearly midday. 'What a pity,' he said. 'The seafood restaurant is closed. Never mind, we'll have a quick sandwich at that café over there.'

Charlize was just about to tell him of her thoughts, when the phone rang again.

'Blast.'

'It's okay, answer it,' she said, as he grimaced. 'It could be important. Someone might be going to offer you a million dollar deal.' By the time he ended the call they were on the outskirts of their destination, so rather than resurrect the conversation Charlize decided to leave it be for the moment. It could wait until another day. At her suggestion Lloyd dropped her off at a taxi rank and headed back to his office.

When she returned to his parents' place, she tried to call Suzi to see what had transpired since the previous day. The restaurant phone remained unanswered, so she dialled the number at Caxton Manor, but there was no response there either. Unable to get through to her friend's mobile as well, she sent a text message. There was nothing more she could do now, but wait for a reply.

As she packed for their honeymoon, she had to make a concerted effort to dismiss the unbelievable idea that had taken hold of her mind.

She and Lloyd had discussed various places, and she felt happy that they had finally decided to spend the week in Wellington. It was one of

Lloyd's favourite places and he hinted that he might like to live there one day. Charlize had been intrigued to learn that many couples chose to exchange vows in a public park. The idea appealed to her, because it was a far better atmosphere than a stuffy register office, and less restrictive than a church. Lloyd had explored the possibility of a church wedding, but had run up against a brick wall. Saturdays were all booked for over two months.

They had finally opted for an open-air wedding in the park, even though the weather was usually unpredictable at this time of year. The day dawned fine and sunny, although it was quite cool. The sun stayed out long enough for the photos to be taken, and then everyone rushed back to the stretch limos to be whisked off to a luncheon at a nearby hotel. Charlize was glad that the celebrations had been kept to the minimum, but she would have liked her best friend to have been there to share her joy. The fact that Suzie hadn't made contact was a major concern, because she had promised to phone and wish her well.

The toasts were kept to a minimum, but it was obvious that Lloyd's parents were delighted to see their eldest son married at last. She formed an instant rapport with his sister, Beryl, and was amazed to learn that his younger brother already had three children and his wife was expecting a fourth. *I hope Lloyd has no plans to emulate Derek's efforts,* she thought.

It was late afternoon when they flew out of Auckland, and within hours they had booked into the Wellington hotel. As the porter closed the door behind him, Lloyd gathered Charlize into his arms. 'Well, Mrs Bridgestone?'

'Very well thank you, Mr Bridgestone,' she replied, loosening his tie.

He looked across at the king-size bed. 'I wonder if the springs or whatever they put in those things are up to standard.'

'We should check it out,' Charlize said, as she continued to undo his shirt buttons. 'I think they'll hold our dinner back for us.'

*

As he said goodbye to Lloyd, Steve promised to keep in touch and wished them well for their wedding day. His friend had explained that guests were restricted to immediate family out of deference to Charlize, because she didn't know anyone in the country.

Harry Wisecombe didn't have anything that looked remotely interesting on the books, but assured Steve that things could change in the near future.

'I'll get in touch with you immediately I find anything that might be suitable,' he promised. As far as Steve was concerned, it had been a complete waste of time, but, he reasoned, it had given him a chance to look over the area.

On the way back to Auckland he tried to think where had seen Charlize, but it eluded him. Unable to concentrate clearly he pulled off the main road and found a small café and ordered some coffee. As he spooned sugar into the cup he began to put the pieces together in his mind.

Lloyd had only given him sketchy details about how he and Charlize had met, but—he had mentioned the name Suzi. When he recalled his conversation with the woman on the sailing boat, it all fell into place. She had told him that Suzi was holidaying with a friend from Wales who had been smitten by a New Zealander. She also mentioned that the girl had said they were sharing a room at the hotel in Airlie Beach. Although he hadn't been successful when he tried to trace her, a subsequent enquiry revealed that the room had been booked in the name Charlotte Bronwyn-Smythe. So, was that Charlotte the friend whom Suzi called Charlize?

In his mind's eye Steve re-enacted the scene as the woman toppled over the side of the boat and disappeared beneath the waves. He recalled thinking he had seen a flash of recognition on her face as he reached out for her, and his own feelings as the ambulance officer turned her head towards him when he began resuscitation. He had made every effort to locate her but neither the skipper of the sailing boat, nor the powerboat operator, nor the nurse in the casualty department at the Base Hospital had been able to help.

Steve took another sip of coffee and then smiled as he suddenly remembered that he might have seen a photograph of Charlize in Suzi's house. 'That's got to be it,' he muttered, cursing himself for not having made the connection when Lloyd said the two women were from Wales.

He gave a laugh and banged the table hard with his fist. 'Yes, that's it,' he exclaimed loudly. Conscious of his outburst, he glanced around the room. It seemed that everyone including the proprietor was staring at him. 'Sorry folks,' he apologised, 'but I've just realised something important.' When their faces relaxed, he smiled.

He paid the bill and left soon afterwards. As he continued driving towards Auckland he allowed the thoughts to surface again. It was quite obvious that until today Charlize did not know that he and Lloyd were friends. So where did he go from here? Should he try to find out what had happened back at Airlie Beach? Did Suzi have any idea that he was the one who rescued her? And if she had, did she try to find him? Moreover, did she want to? That was the big question. He gave a hollow laugh at the incredible turn of possible events. Suzi's best friend had come to New Zealand to get married to someone he had known for years? Well, no matter what the truth of it was, there was nothing he could do about it right now. He would leave things as they were—for the moment—and then at some opportune moment perhaps he could broach the subject with Charlize when he visited them at a future date. He just had to be patient.

*

Steve was still in a pensive mood when he drove into the factory yard. He had been unsettled ever since he had returned from Australia. Nothing in particular had gone wrong, but on the other hand everything seemed insignificant—as if he were waiting for something to happen. He felt that he had done the right thing in refusing Jenny's invitation to form a relationship, even though he still had a niggling desire to bed her. However, he had also convinced himself that he didn't want to consider a relationship with anyone at all right now.

Vince looked up as he walked into the office.

'See anything you liked?'

'No, but there's no great hurry,' Steve said, picking up a drawing of a new pump design. 'Are we ready to move on this?' When his father nodded he carried the drawing across to his desk and checked the figures.

Steve wondered how things were going with Caxton Manor, and decided it was high time that he really did something about settling the whole business once and for all. I'll ring my solicitor first thing tomorrow, he thought. Then he remembered tomorrow was Saturday; it would have to wait until Monday.

*

One of the men half turned in her direction as Suzi walked into the restaurant. He paused for a brief moment and then picked up a chair and swung it at the nearest hanging lamp. As the fitting shattered he threw the chair across the room. When he picked up another, Suzi lunged at him.

'Stop,' she screamed.

His companion stepped in front of her and held up his hand as if to strike her in the face.

'Leave it be lady, or you'll be next.' Then he called to the other man. 'That'll do, Bernie.' He jerked a thumb at Mark. 'He said you'd gone to get the rest of the money.'

Suzi nodded her head dumbly and fumbled for her purse.

'Yes, I did.' But before she could open the clasp the man snatched it out of her hand and removed the money. He rifled through the wad of notes before stuffing them into his jacket and then pushed her out of the way. When Mark protested, the man shoved him against Suzi, knocking her off balance. She tried to save herself by clutching at a nearby table, but it gave way and she fell heavily to the floor.

One of the men poked Mark in the chest.

'Don't do anything stupid like going to the police.' His voice was thick with menace. 'If you do we'll come back and sort you out quick smart.'

As the door closed behind them, Mark rushed to Suzi's side.

Almost at once he saw that one arm was twisted awkwardly beneath her body. She moaned as he tried to turn her over and then she lost consciousness. He eased her back onto the floor and dialled the emergency number.

*

The siren whined into silence as the ambulance ground to a halt outside the restaurant. The officer questioned Mark about what had happened, and gave him an odd look when he explained that Suzi had stumbled and fallen. Although the man made no comment about the smashed lamp, Mark knew he had noticed the debris on the floor and the broken chair against the wall. The two ambulance officers eased Suzi onto a stretcher and loaded it into the back of the vehicle. Minutes later it roared off towards the hospital.

Mark's stomach turned over as he watched the ambulance disappear around the corner. He slammed the door shut and climbed into his car, then hurried back to the restaurant, and hastily posted a note on the front door: 'Closed due to illness.' Then he rang Narelle.

'Suzi's had an accident,' he blurted out, when the woman answered. 'Can you ring the other girls and tell them we'll be closed for the rest of the day.'

'What happened?'

'I haven't got time to tell you at the moment,' he replied, testily. 'I've got to get to the hospital. I'll let you know as soon as I can.'

It seemed that every car and every traffic light conspired to make the journey to the hospital as awkward as possible. When he finally found a parking spot, Mark hurried into the building, identified himself, and asked about Suzi. The nurse directed him to a nearby waiting room.

'Someone will see you directly,' she said, in an officious tone of voice.

Chapter Twenty-Eight

The light appeared to come from a long way away and seemed to bore right through her eye to the very recesses of her brain. Suzi made a half-hearted attempt block it out by lifting her arm, but the pain was so severe that she almost passed out. As the light was extinguished, she focused on the face of the man hovering over her. He raised his hand.

'Can you see my fingers?' When she whispered yes, he nodded. 'Okay, it's probably nothing more than concussion.' Then he called to an aid. 'Take this woman down to X-ray.'

It was quite some time before Suzi found herself tucked up in bed with her arm in plaster. The X-ray had pinpointed two fractures of the left forearm, but fortunately there was no damage to her skull or backbone, even though she was conscious of a back pain. As she recalled what had happened at the restaurant, she saw Mark hesitantly approaching the bedside.

'How are you feeling Suzi?' He spoke in a subdued voice. 'The doctor says you're going to be all right.' Then he added, 'Thank goodness.'

'I don't know that I want to talk to you, Mark.'

'Is there anything I can do? Can I get you anything?'

Suzi looked at him in silence for a long time before answering. She didn't want him anywhere near her at the moment, but if she was to remain in hospital for more than a night she had to rely on his help. With great restraint, she asked him to contact Narelle.

Mark pulled out his mobile phone and was about to punch in the woman's telephone number when a nurse grabbed his arm.

'Can't you read? There are signs all over the hospital telling people to switch off their mobiles.' She glared at him. 'Turn it off immediately.'

'Sorry, I forgot. I'll go outside and ring her.' He was back within minutes. 'She's on her way.' He fidgeted with his car keys, and then said,

'I'll get back to the restaurant and tidy things up.' When she waved her hand dismissively, he added, 'I'll pop in later, okay.'

Suzi watched him walk away with a sense of relief. She closed her eyes needing to blot out her surroundings while she considered what to do next.

Narelle arrived fifteen minutes later.

'Oh dear, what happened,' she cried grasping Suzi's free hand. 'Mark told me you had an accident. Did it happen on the way to work?'

'It's a bit complicated, I'm afraid. I'll explain it all to you later, if you don't mind.'

'Of course. What do you want me to do?'

'I need some things from home. Can you get them for me?' She explained where to find what she wanted. 'My keys are in my handbag and that's at the restaurant. Mark should be there, but if he's not you'll have to phone him and tell him to open up for you.'

'But I can't tell…'

'Don't worry, he'll give you no trouble.'

Narelle made a list of the things Suzi wanted from Caxton Manor and then painstakingly wrote down her instructions about resetting the burglar alarm. She gave a deep sigh and stood up. 'I thought something was terribly wrong as soon as…' She stopped and sighed again. 'I'll be back as soon as I can, dear.'

After the woman had gone Suzi leaned back against the pillow and closed her eyes again. She would probably be incapacitated for several weeks, even if the plaster was removed before then. So any thought of running the restaurant was out of the question. As things stood at the moment, she had no desire to go near the place at all. Narelle could take over as hostess in the short term, but she could not be expected to do it for more than a week or two at the most. So the only long-term solution was to hire someone until she was fit enough to resume the role.

Tears welled up into her eyes as she realised that someone who should have known better had compromised all she had worked for.

Mark's actions of the past few weeks had whittled away her respect for him, and now their business relationship was under threat too. 'I just don't trust him any more,' she murmured. Then she asked herself if she would ever feel comfortable working with him again. 'Probably not,' she murmured, as she closed her eyes.

Unfortunately they both had too much invested in the restaurant just to close it up and walk away, and neither could continue to operate without the help of other. If she bought Mark's share of the business she would have to employ another chef, and that would be a problem, because it was his style of cooking which attracted people. And she might end up with someone like Gary, who had trouble keeping his hands off the staff. The real stumbling block was her lack of finance. She was solvent, but only just, since sorting out Mark's gambling debt.

She had just drifted off to sleep when she heard a discreet cough. She opened her eyes to see Narelle peering at her from the bottom of the bed.

'Hello dear. Are you feeling any better?'

'Not really. I feel pretty rotten,' Suzi replied. 'My head is still fuzzy and every joint and muscle aches.'

'I managed to find all you need.' She placed an overnight bag on the chair beside the bed, and then gave a little nervous laugh. 'I hope I've locked up the place securely.'

'I'm sure it'll be fine.'

'I asked Mark what happened and he said that you'd surprised a burglar.' She shook her head knowingly. 'You were lucky he came in just at the right time and frightened the man away.'

Suzi smiled wanly, but made no comment. At least Mark had had the presence of mind to think of a likely reason to explain the damage to the restaurant. It made sense to blame the injuries on a non-existent burglar, because the police would be unlikely to investigate.

'How are you going to manage in that big house by yourself?' Narelle asked, interrupting her train of thought. 'You won't be able to look after yourself with a broken arm.'

'I have a woman in to do the cleaning,' Suzi replied, 'and maybe she'll be able to do a bit extra.'

'Well, if she can't manage, my sister, Eileen could probably help you out,' Narelle said. 'She's on her own now and she's always looking for something to do.' She looked enquiringly at Suzi. 'Shall I ask her to come and see you?'

'I'll think about it, and let you know.'

After Narelle left, Suzi drifted off to sleep again until the evening meal was being served. As it was cleared away, Mark arrived.

'Hello, Suzi, how are you now?' His voice was ragged. 'I thought I'd better come and tell you what's happened.' He explained that he had contacted the police and told them that they had surprised a burglar. 'They didn't bother to come near the place,' he muttered. 'They seemed to lose interest when I told them the guy was wearing a motor cycle helmet, and they said there was nothing they could do unless I could identify the person.'

'You went to a lot of trouble to concoct a story.'

'Well, I thought I should have some excuse for the smashed furniture.' He gave a hard bitter laugh. 'I broke the back window to make it look more authentic.'

Suzi stared at him.

'There's no end to your duplicity is there? It's just as well Narelle told me the story you gave the police, otherwise I could have made a complete fool of myself if they had called on me to verify your statement.'

'Sorry, Suzi, but I had to think of something quickly.' He coughed nervously. 'I phoned Prudential and had a talk to Malcolm Stewart. He'll drop by in the next few days, and fill out all the forms.' He shuffled his feet nervously. 'Did you ask Narelle to take over the hostess job?'

'No, you can do that,' Suzi replied, frostily. 'In fact you can take care of all the arrangements. It was your stupidity that got us into this mess.' She was tempted to close her eyes to shut him out. 'I'm too tired to be bothered with you now, Mark.'

'Sorry, Suzi,' Mark murmured, 'I really am.'

'Please don't come here to see me again. I'll phone you when I get out, and then we can discuss what we are going to do.' As he turned to go she called out, 'You had better find someone to drive my car back to Caxton Manor.'

'Okay.' He hesitated and then reached into his pocket. 'I nearly forgot. I found your mobile on the floor. It must have fallen out of your handbag.'

After he had gone she looked furtively towards the door to see there was no one around, and then turned it on. The battery was low, but it had recorded three messages, all from Charlize. She opened the first one. 'Where r u. Please ring.' The other two messages were of a similar nature. Charlize had apparently rung the restaurant, left a message on the answerphone at Caxton Manor, and then started sending text messages.

Suzi switched if off and sighed. In all the upheaval she had completely forgotten that Charlize and Lloyd were about to be married. About to be married? No, they would be on their honeymoon now, she reminded herself.

The next time a nurse came into the room she enquired if it was all right to send an urgent message to her friend in New Zealand. The young woman shook her head, but offered to take the mobile phone outside the building and do it for her.

'Thanks, you're a sweetie,' Suzi said. She keyed in the words: 'I'm okay. Will phone soon,' and handed it to the young woman. 'Just press "Send".'

*

Mark walked out to his car and threw himself behind the wheel. He remained sitting there for a long time thinking about what he should do. Suzi had made it quite obvious that she wanted as little to do with him as possible, and under the circumstances he couldn't blame her. She had every right to be upset. He had to admit she was right—he had been stupid, and of course there was no way she would consider marriage now. He started the car and drove back to the Stow Restaurant.

'It's not too bad,' he said, aloud as he surveyed the damage. Most of it could be repaired in time to open for lunch tomorrow, he surmised. And there shouldn't be any problems about insurance—Malcolm should be able to take care of that situation.

He sat down on the nearest chair and sighed. What should he do now? Mark was convinced that Suzi would want to end the partnership, and once again he felt she was justified. He knew that he could probably operate all right without her, but she would be hard to replace. Maybe Judith could step in temporarily; she had worked in a restaurant to augment her income some years ago. But the long-term situation had to be addressed. Where would he get the money to buy Suzi out?

Rather than explore all his options right now, he began clearing up the mess. He picked up all the broken glass, vacuumed the floor and replaced the light fitting before rearranging the tables. Finally, he dumped the broken chair out at the back of the building. Then he did a quick check to see if he had covered everything. As he closed the front door, a feeling of abject sadness swept over him, threatening to drain all his remaining energy. That evening he rang his father.

'How much money do you need?' Ben asked cautiously. 'And why does Suzi want to sell out? I thought you two were thinking of getting married. What's happened to that idea?'

Mark tried to explain that he and Suzi had not been seeing eye to eye lately, and they felt it would be better to terminate the partnership. When his father questioned him further, Mark blamed the break-up on Suzi's trip to Australia, even though he knew he was lying. Then he reminded Ben that Charlize had recently migrated to New Zealand and suggested that Suzi might like to do the same. After he had repeated the whole story to his mother, he asked Judith if she could help him out in the restaurant for a few weeks.

She hesitated for a minute, and then agreed, but reluctantly. Then she spoke to someone else in the room before resuming their conversation.

'Dad just said to tell you he'll come to see you next weekend,' Judith said. 'And if it's okay with you, I'll wait until I can get a lift up. It'll be easier than travelling by bus.'

'What about Jonathan? Will he mind if you take off for a couple of weeks?'

'He'll be all right. Don't worry.'

After he hung up Mark breathed a sigh of relief. He was well aware that Ben was bitterly opposed to gambling in any form, and he had found it hard to lie to his father, but he did not want to incur the man's anger at this stage of things. He felt confident that they would be able to work something out, even if it meant making his father the major partner. Now all he had to do was tell Suzi of his decision and see how she felt about the idea.

He had just walked into the restaurant the next day when the phone rang.

'The doctor said I could go home,' Suzi said, brusquely, when he answered. 'Did you manage to get my car back to Caxton Manor?' When Mark said he had, she continued. 'Narelle's sister, Eileen, has agreed to move in for a while. You might like to pick her up to save her getting a taxi.'

'How are you getting home?'

'That's been taken care of,' Suzi said, curtly. When he said there was something he needed to discuss with her, she added. 'Yes, and there are quite a few things I wish to discuss with you, but they can wait until later.'

*

Narelle watched her closely as she terminated the call.

'Are you all right?' she asked, in a concerned voice.

When Suzi replied that everything was under control, the woman started the car and swung away from the hospital. She didn't say anything more until they pulled up outside Caxton Manor. 'I'm glad Eileen agreed to help out.'

'Yes, it was very kind of her.' Suzi forced a laugh. 'After what I've been through lately I'm sure I'd have managed. I've lost my best friend and fallen off a boat and nearly drowned, so I dare say I'll survive this as well.'

Mark arrived with Narelle's sister moments after they arrived. He said hello and then mumbled something about the need to get back to the restaurant to start preparations for dinner. After he had gone, Suzi showed Eileen where everything was, and then the three women had a cup of tea in the drawing room. While they were talking, Suzi's mobile bleeped; it was a message from Charlize.

The text message contained a Wellington phone number along with the words: 'Good news u r still alive. Ring soon.'

Suzi waited until eight o'clock that evening and then rang the number.

*

Charlize eased herself away from the sleeping figure by her side and stretched languidly. She smiled as Lloyd stirred, made a little mewling sound and then nestled into her again. She was just about to kiss his cheek when the phone rang.

'Yes?' When she recognised her friend's voice she sat up bolt upright and almost shouted into the mouthpiece. 'Suzi! Where are you? What's happening?' The questions tripped off her tongue one after the other.

Lloyd eased himself up on one elbow and looked at her enquiringly as she talked. Then he climbed out of bed and went to the bathroom, and by the time he returned Charlize was sitting up clasping her knees.

'Do you want to tell me what's happened?'

'Oh, Lloyd, you can't imagine the mess she's in.' Charlize heaved a sigh as she related their conversation and concluded by saying that she had invited Suzi to visit them for a while. 'She's going to think about it.'

'That's a good idea. We won't have enough room for her, but I'm sure Mother would be only too happy to put her up for a few weeks.'

'Good, I'll tell her that next time we talk.'

'Right. Now we'd better think about making a move. They won't wait for us just because we're newlyweds. The weather forecast is good, so the crossing should be pleasant and the trip up the fjord to Picton should be absolutely stunning.'

219

*

Mark phoned the next day to say that Malcolm Stewart had called and had promised to process the claim as soon as he could. He also said that the police had not contacted him again, and he didn't think that they were too concerned about the incident. Then he asked when he could visit her.

Suzi hesitated. She was unwilling to have anything to do with him right now. However, the situation had to be addressed and the sooner it was done the better.

'I suppose you could call this afternoon if you wish.'

Straight afterwards, Suzi rang Jeff Bates, the solicitor who had acted on her behalf when they had formed the partnership. He was astounded to learn that she wished to terminate the agreement, but readily agreed to sort it out as quickly as possible. She made it quite clear that she expected Mark to buy her share of the business.

'There is also the question of my personal involvement in the operation,' she explained. 'I feel that I should be recompensed for the goodwill I have generated since we took over the restaurant.'

'I'm sure we covered the possibility of one party buying out the other,' Jeff assured her. 'And as for the other aspect, I'll have a look at the terms of agreement you both signed at the time.'

As she put the phone down, Eileen tapped on the study door.

'There's a man at the door who wishes to speak to you in person,' she said, 'but I told him you were not receiving visitors.' She handed Suzi the man's business card. 'He asked me to give you this.'

Suzi almost laughed at the woman's terminology—not receiving visitors. It was as if she had already established herself as guardian of the lady of the manor. She smiled at the older woman. 'It's okay, you can show him in.'

'I wonder what this is all about?' she murmured, as she glanced at the name on the card.

Chapter Twenty-Nine

Steve spent the next few weekends looking at houses, but nothing seemed to suit. When he came home and expressed his frustration, Norah chided him.

'Don't be so impatient. It's not as if you're in any great rush.'

'No, I suppose not. It's just so time consuming and I want it all sorted out as soon as possible.' Steve pulled a beer out of the refrigerator and flipped off the top. 'I saw a nice place today, but the agent said someone has already put a deposit on it.'

'There'll be others.' Norah watched him drain the bottle and reach for another. 'You've given Vince the itch now. He wants to start looking for something smaller.'

'We could go around together.' Steve grinned at her. 'That's not a bad idea really, you could check out the kitchen and storage space for me.'

'Why?'

'What suits me might not suit a woman. I don't want to buy something that will need extensive alterations somewhere along the line.'

'Who do you intend sharing it with?' Norah asked. 'You're not dating anyone at the moment, let alone getting serious enough to contemplate anything permanent.' She gave him a quizzical look. 'Is there someone waiting in the wings, or are you taking a long-term view of things?' Then she leaned closer, and whispered. 'Or is it Suzi Lysle Spencer?'

'That's most unlikely under the circumstances. I don't have any contact with her, and I have no one in mind at the moment.' Then he shrugged and smiled. 'You never know what's around the corner. To be honest, I don't want to buy something with a poor kitchen layout, or not enough storage space, and find out I've made a mistake after I've moved in.'

'How's your friend, Lloyd, coping with married life?' Norah asked, changing the subject.

'Very well apparently,' Steve replied. 'He phoned me the other day to invite me over for a drink. He said they're getting on like a house on fire.' He laughed. 'Of course it's early days yet, but he's beginning to talk like a married man already.'

'Let's hope it continues that way.' Norah picked up the discarded beer bottle. 'Don't fill yourself up with booze… tea will be ready soon.'

Steve walked out onto the patio. He felt strangely reluctant to take up Lloyd's offer because he didn't feel ready to face any close friend of Suzi, and by now he had firmly convinced himself that Lloyd's new wife was Suzi's friend. Moreover, she and Lloyd would have put two and two together by now. They would know he had saved Suzi's life while they were all staying at Airlie Beach, and that he was the other claimant to Caxton Manor. He hadn't told Lloyd that he had tried to find Suzi that day, so they might have assumed that he wasn't overly concerned about her whereabouts one way or the other. The other side of the coin was just as likely. If Suzi knew all the facts and still hadn't bothered to contact him, then that indicated she didn't care too much about his feelings and didn't want to know.

Maybe that's why I don't want to visit. Charlize might tell me something I don't want to hear, he thought. Maybe Suzi had recognised him, but didn't want him to know she had. He smiled at the way these thoughts were racing through his head, and then began to wonder why he still hadn't heard any more from his solicitor. It was time the situation in Wales was sorted out now. Initially, he had been quite excited about the inheritance, but it had not taken long for his enthusiasm to wear off. He had not objected when Suzi asked to occupy the house until things were sorted out, but of course that would not resolve the long-term problem.

If he had known originally that there was someone else involved, he may not have made a claim on the property in the first place. The old house meant nothing to him personally, and even if he had inherited it outright, he would have sold it to the highest bidder. After all, he could well afford to forget about Caxton Manor altogether now—it meant nothing to him, especially since the portfolio of shares bequeathed by his deceased father had enriched him considerably. It all meant he was not overly concerned about the outcome of the inheritance. He took another pull on the bottle and sighed as his mind went back to his time with Suzi. He recalled their time together, and in particular the feeling of oneness he had experienced with her. It had far exceeded anything he had ever felt with any other woman.

'I was sure she felt the same way,' he murmured, and then chided himself yet again for acting like a lovesick schoolboy. He reasoned that he was meant to meet Suzi; he was convinced that it was meant to happen—that somehow or other it had been preordained.

*

He brought up the subject of the inheritance with his father a few nights later, and mentioned his idea of going to Britain to straighten things out. Vince lowered his newspaper before speaking.

'You don't have to ask me if you want time off, son. You just go, okay? A break away will do you good.' He peered anxiously at his adopted son. 'You should have spent more time in Queensland—there was no reason to rush home. You could have had a week or two in Brisbane or on the Gold Coast.'

'I wasn't in the mood,' Steve said, 'what with Kirsty's death and all.'

'Fair enough. In any case you can always go back if you feel like it.' He gave a snorting laugh. 'We'll write the expenses off as a business trip—just say you're checking on the pumping equipment.'

'Yes, maybe. In the meantime I'll sort out this inheritance business. It's dragging on too long.'

The two men discussed the current workload, and decided that unless there was some unforeseen problem Steve could leave immediately. The next morning he booked the flight and then rang Duncan personally and asked him to set up a meeting with Suzi. He made it absolutely clear that the situation had to be resolved now. However his attempts to speak to her personally were unsuccessful.

*

Suzi shook the man's hand and motioned him to a chair as Eileen closed the door after her.

'What can I do for you, Mr Gillam,' she asked, glancing at the card again. 'Have you come to tempt me with more suitable premises for the restaurant? If you have, I'm sorry to inform you that we are not contemplating a move.'

'On the contrary, Ms Spencer,' the man replied. 'I am making enquiries on behalf of an international company looking for suitable property to rent in this area. I can lease this beautiful place for you at a very attractive rate.'

'Why do you think I would want to rent out the manor?'

'I had no idea whether you wanted to or not, but I became aware of the property, and decided it would be worth enquiring.' Mr Gillam adjusted his glasses as he waited for Suzi's comment. When she remained silent, he continued. 'I've been asked to find something large and imposing with a nice garden. The company wants a place that has the potential to entertain guests as well conduct its business in this part of the UK.'

'How much?'

'Oh… thousands a month, but I can't name a figure right now. That would have to be considered, and satisfactory to both parties… you and the company.' He paused when she raised her eyebrows. 'We could probably write in a maintenance clause as well, so that you wouldn't have to concern yourself about its upkeep. You would simply pocket the money. You would have no expenses at all.'

Suzi toyed with the man's card as the thoughts raced through her mind. Could this be the opportunity she was looking for? Then she almost laughed aloud. An opportunity to do what? She had no plans to go anywhere, and there were still a lot of issues to be resolved before she could even consider the offer. And of course there was Steve Pardoe. Would he be agreeable to the proposition? She pushed the thoughts from her mind as the man coughed politely.

'I'm not in a position to give you an answer one way or the other at the moment, Mr Gillam,' she said, climbing to her feet. 'First of all, I need time to think about it, and then I'll have to talk to my solicitor, but thank you for your offer.' She shook his hand. 'I'll call you if I want to discuss it further.'

After the man had gone, Suzi phoned to make an appointment to see Mr Duncan.

'Ah, Ms Spencer, yes, ah I was just about to call you. I've had a phone call from Mr Pardoe, in Auckland, New Zealand. He asked me to set up a meeting within the next few days to discuss the outstanding business of the inheritance.'

'That's why I'm ringing you,' Suzi said, trying to keep the excitement out of her voice. She outlined the letting agent's proposal, and asked the solicitor to find out the legalities of such a proposition. Then she agreed to be available for the meeting with Steve.

A wave of apprehension replaced the initial excitement she had felt at learning of his imminent arrival. On one hand she wanted to see him again, and on the other hand she did not want to risk a rebuff if he was not interested in her. Then she thought about the Stow Restaurant and her business relationship with Mark. It seemed as if everything was conspiring to keep her guessing about her future.

'What do I really want to do?' she murmured. The dream of operating her own restaurant had been realised, but that was about to come to an end. Her other cherished dream concerned Caxton Manor. She had longed to live in the house from the day Uncle Bart had first shown her over the premises as a young girl, and of course she had realised that too. Was there no other dream to fulfil?

Over the past few days she'd time to think about things more clearly. She had become uncomfortably aware that her idea to use the property as a convention centre and reception venue had not been well thought out. The income generated by the occasional function probably would have been insufficient to cover its upkeep. And of course, it was beyond her financial means to use it as a private dwelling—it was far too big for that, anyway. There seemed to be no alternative but to sell the place, particularly because Steve had indicated that he was not interested in keeping it under any circumstances.

I'll wait and see what he says about things, she thought. Then she picked up the phone and called Mark.

'I want to settle things as quickly as possible. I've instructed my solicitor to proceed with the termination of our contract, so you know why I need to see you.'

'Yes, of course, Suzi. I can make it tomorrow afternoon, if that's all right.'

As she replaced the phone she thought about their conversation. He had sounded rather upbeat. He seemed to be managing quite well without her. Narelle was still coping as hostess, and he was employing one of the casual waitresses, who had bookkeeping experience, to take care of the accounts and banking. The young woman had queried a few things with her from time to time, but seemed to have everything under control.

She wondered if he had already made arrangements to buy her share of the business. Had Ben agreed to provide the finance? Mark had casually mentioned that Judith might be able to help out for a while, so it was obvious that the whole family was involved now. Then she wondered what storyline he had concocted to explain her actions.

The following afternoon she watched him climb out of his car and stride purposefully towards the manor. He seemed to exude confidence. It was not the Mark she had known for the past few weeks. Eileen brought him into the drawing room and gave Suzi a look that she interpreted as 'just call if you need help'.

'My solicitor has already discussed things with your man,' he said, after he had asked after her welfare. 'You'll be pleased to know that I've been able to find someone to take over your share of the business. However I can't agree with your solicitor's claim for loss of potential income.'

'And what about the inconvenience caused by the injuries I sustained during the attack on my person while I was extracting you from your mess?' she asked, curtly. 'Or doesn't that matter any more?'

'Yes, of course it does, but...'

'I was told that I could sue you to recover damages.' As Suzi paused, Mark looked down at his hands. 'When can I expect your solicitor to have documents ready to sign?'

'I'll have to inform him of this new development.'

'And then?'

'It shouldn't take too long. I'll ask him to give it top priority.'

'I suppose your father has put up some or all of the money you need?' When Mark didn't respond she added. 'More fool he. I suggest you keep him keep him away from me lest I tell him the truth.' She looked at him meaningfully. 'You know what I mean.'

Once again, Mark agreed. Suzi knew that he would not have access to the extra money she had demanded, but she was prepared to agree to a down payment and the rest of the money over a stipulated period. The threat of legal action had made him shudder; he would not want his duplicity uncovered. The police, the insurance company, and ultimately his moneylender would learn the facts and they could all cause him a great deal of trouble.

'That's it then.' Suzi stood up. 'I'll tell my solicitor that we are in agreement, and that he should expect to hear from your solicitor soon.'

'Yes, of course.'

As he drove away, Suzi felt quite light-headed. It was not her nature to threaten people, but she consoled herself with the thought that he already had a guilty conscience about the way he had deceived her. Now, she was only making it clearer to him, but it didn't make her feel any better about things. It was a hollow victory. She was staring pensively out through the window when Eileen came into the room.

'Are you all right, dear?'

'Not really. I have just arranged to sell my share of the Stow Restaurant, and I feel as if a part of me has been cut away. Do you know what I mean?'

'Yes, I felt that way when Norman died.' Eileen hesitated and then continued. 'Narelle said that you might use this place as a convention centre, but if you've sold your share of the restaurant you won't be going ahead with that idea.'

'No.'

'Do you mind if I ask what are you going to do now.' She stopped and looked at Suzi expectantly. 'Narelle intimated that there might be the opportunity of this becoming a permanent position.'

'Oh, I'm sorry, but that's out of the question. I couldn't afford to live here and, even if I did, I wouldn't want to employ live-in staff.'

'I thought it was too good to be true. I've only been here a few weeks, but I love this old house. Edgar and I have some interesting conversations.'

'Edgar? Who's Edgar?'

'Oh, didn't you know you had a resident ghost?' Eileen chuckled. 'Edgar used to live in the old cottage that stood here long before this house was built. He's a lovely old fellow—knows all the family history and loves to talk about it.'

'A ghost? Uncle Bart never mentioned a ghost… and I've never seen one.'

'Edgar says your mind is always too full of everyday things to pay any attention to him. And he said your uncle just ignored his presence.'

Suzi laughed softly.

'I suppose I should pay more attention next time I hear strange bumps in the night.' Then she became serious. 'You're welcome to stay until I've had the plaster taken off my arm and can fend for myself, but I can't make any promises beyond that point.'

As Eileen left the room, Suzi thought about the meeting with Steve in two days' time. What would he say when he found out that she was no longer associated with the Stow Restaurant and that she no longer wished to use the manor for receptions? Then she recalled her conversation with Frederick Gillam, and wondered if his offer could solve all their problems.

'That's about the only positive thing to come out of the mess,' she murmured. 'I just hope that Steve will be amenable. I've had enough drama.'

Chapter Thirty

Steve gazed up at the sky as he walked out of the concourse at Cardiff airport. The sun was a pale orb behind the thin covering of clouds and the weather was decidedly chilly, far colder than on his previous visit. He slipped behind the wheel of the hired car and headed towards the M4.

The thoughts that had swirled around his head since leaving Auckland came back again. There was no logical reason for him to come back to Wales; he could have dealt with the matter on the phone. So what lay behind his decision to come here? And even more importantly why hadn't Suzi contacted him? Surely, they could have worked something out? Even if he accepted reverse charge calls, the bill would have been cheaper than a business class airfare.

There seemed to be no rational answer, and he was loathe to admit that he wanted to see her again. He had never had a problem like this with any other woman. As far as he could ascertain, neither of them had considered the possibility of ever meeting again, and he had certainly not contemplated a return trip to the UK. He wondered whether things would have turned out differently had they known their common link with Caxton Manor when they first met. It was impossible to speculate about what might have happened.

Then he thought about Kirsty, but he had been able to put her tragic death behind him and move forward. He felt no need to cling to the memory of what they had shared. So why couldn't he do the same with Suzi?

The memory of her popped up at the most unusual times; it was as if she continued to demand recognition. Maybe that was why he had rejected the opportunity to have an affair with Jenny MacTavish—maybe he felt that Suzi's existence would overshadow their relationship too.

Kirsty had evidently sensed the bond they had forged, and on one occasion she had accused him of whispering Suzi's name in his sleep. Of course there was only one answer—the memory of their closeness must have been lurking in his unconscious mind all the time.

He was still thinking of the ramifications of the situation as he turned into the street that ran past the Stow Restaurant. There was no sign of a yellow Honda in her parking place, so he decided not to stop and say hello. After he had booked into the hotel, he phoned Mr Duncan to confirm the appointment.

'Ah yes, Mr Pardoe. I've contacted Ms Spencer and she has agreed to the meeting.' He confirmed the arranged time, made an obtuse remark about the weather, and then said goodbye.

'Pompous old codger,' Steve muttered. 'Thank goodness I won't have to do any further business with him after tomorrow.'

The combined effect of the jet lag and lack of sleep forced him to bed for a couple of hours, and it was nearly time for dinner when he climbed groggily to his feet.

He resisted the urge to phone the Stow Restaurant and make a reservation. If Suzi was not willing to communicate by letter or phone, then confronting her in person might cause an embarrassing situation. He left the hotel and wandered down the road until the softly lit interior of the Asian Curry Link drew him inside. As he viewed the extensive menu he thought of Kirsty. She probably would have ordered one of everything and gone back for seconds. The last thing he did before climbing into bed was to ring home.

The next morning dawned grey and overcast, but by the time Steve had finished breakfast the sun was breaking through. There were still a few hours to fill in until the appointment with the solicitor, so he decided to drive around the area for a while. Something drew him towards Caxton Manor. When he saw that the front gates were open he drove into the grounds. He parked the car under a huge copper beech tree, climbed out of vehicle, and stretched.

The garden looks nice, he thought; somebody must be taking care of it now. The neatly trimmed lawns were edged with a variety of spring flowers in various stages of bloom. Forgetting that Suzi had taken up residence, Steve continued to walk around the property. It was only when he noticed a car parked in an outbuilding that he remembered it was now her home, even if temporary. Suddenly he felt like an intruder. Unwilling to confront her under these circumstances he made his way back to the car and was just about to unlock the vehicle when someone addressed him.

'Can I help you?' The woman's voice was crisp and demanding.

Steve turned to find a middle-aged woman with a displeased look on her face.

'Er... no,' he began, and then stopped. 'I was just having a look around, that's all.'

'This is a private dwelling. It's not open to tourists.' Eileen's abrupt tone of voice made it clear she was not prepared to accept any excuses.

'I appreciate that, but...' He stopped as the woman continued to glare at him. He had no idea who she was, but apparently she was not going to tolerate uninvited visitors.

'I'll thank you to leave immediately.' Her manner was curt and dismissive.

With a nod of his head, Steve climbed into the car and drove away.

*

Eileen watched him go and then returned to the house. When she entered the kitchen, Suzi was filling the kettle to make a cup of coffee.

'The nerve of some people,' Eileen said, clipped tones. 'I found some man wandering around the garden as if he owned the place. I told him it's not a public domain and sent him packing.'

Suzi paused, one hand on the tap.

'Did he say what he wanted?'

'Just having a look at the place, that's what he said.' Eileen sniffed. 'Sounded like an Australian. I don't know how they behave at home, but they seem to think they can do what they like over here.'

'What did he look like?' Eileen described the man in detail, and Suzi laughed softly. 'Actually, he does own the place, well half of it anyway.' Embarrassed, Eileen coloured deeply. 'Never mind, I'll tell him you were just mindful of my welfare.'

By now, Suzi was uncomfortably aware of how fast her pulse was racing, just like it had every time she met Steve on his first visit to Britain. This annoyed her, but there was little she could do to stop it.

I wonder why he came to the house, Suzi mused, as she dressed for their appointment. Maybe he wanted to talk to me before meeting formally at Duncan's office. Then perhaps he had second thoughts about it when Eileen had confronted him. Had he changed his mind again? Would he oppose Gillam's offer? Was he going to demand some form of recompense for the time she had used the building as a private dwelling? The questions tumbled over each other in her mind.

As she parked outside the solicitor's offices, Suzi recalled the day she had breezed into the place, confident that everything was legally hers, only to be told that someone else had made a claim on the estate. It had started a chain of events that she could not have imagined in her wildest dreams. So much had happened since that day and now, as she locked the car, she wondered whether or not she was in for another shock.

Steve stood up as the receptionist announced her arrival. She was acutely aware of his stare as she returned Mr Duncan's greeting and shook the man's hand. She turned to Steve.

'Hello, Steve,' she said, a trifle abruptly, suddenly feeling threatened by his intense scrutiny.

It took him some moments to realise that she had draped a coat over her shoulders instead of inserting her arms in the sleeves, but it did not completely conceal the sling and plaster cast.

'What happened to your arm?' he asked, ignoring her greeting.

'I had an accident at the restaurant,' she said, in an off-hand manner, as if it were of little consequence.

'At the Stow Restaurant?'

'Yes!'

'When I phoned the restaurant I was informed in no uncertain terms that you were no longer associated with the business.'

'Well, I...'

As she hesitated, Steve continued. 'And when I phoned Caxton Manor I was told that you were unavailable to take any calls.' He glared at her. 'It seems the only way I was going to reach you was here, with Mr... Mr Duncan.'

'But that's...'

'And this morning I was ordered out the gardens.'

Suzi stared at him in amazement. How could things have reached this stage? How could those few slips of the tongue be misconstrued? How had he managed to reach the wrong person on both occasions? She was just about to remonstrate with him when Duncan cleared his throat noisily in an attempt to overcome the awkward situation that had arisen, and bring the matter in hand to their attention.

He shuffled the sheaf of papers noisily.

'Ah yes, now, Mr Pardoe,' he began and then looked hurriedly at Suzi. 'And you too, Ms Spencer. I've checked out the offer made and it seems in order.'

An awkward silence encapsulated them as the solicitor outlined the proposal that he had received from the letting agents. He explained that there was no legal barrier to the acceptance of the offer, provided they both agreed to sign the necessary documents. He concluded that it was very attractive offer.

Steve questioned him at length about the lease, whether it was renewable, and what would happen if the company decided to terminate the lease earlier than the contract specified. There were all kinds of questions that he put carefully to the solicitor. And finally, he asked whether it would be more practical to sell the property.

As he spoke, Suzi watched him closely. This was a side of him she had not seen before. His manner was totally professional, business-like, and almost coldly clinical. He had seemed vulnerable and subdued when they first met, although he had given the impression that he was in control of his life, but now he seemed to be taking it a step further. She glanced down at her hands as he caught her gaze, but then felt her eyes drawn back to his face.

He is an extremely attractive man, she thought. He carries himself well... but there's a wariness about him, as if he's holding something back. She wondered if he felt threatened by what he perceived as her deliberate attempt to avoid him when he phoned. Or maybe he was upset because he had felt the need to come back to Wales to settle things personally; maybe he just did not want to show his feelings, or perhaps he even resented being with her in that situation. She was still trying to fathom her thoughts, which oscillated between anger and disappointment, when Duncan called her by name.

'Ah, Ms Spencer, er... it would appear that Mr Pardoe is satisfied with the arrangement and is willing to sign the lease.' He rubbed his hands together. 'Now it just depends on you.'

Suzi looked at Steve and then back to the solicitor. It all seemed so easy. Just sign a piece of paper and say goodbye to a dream. For a moment, she was inclined to dispute the agreement, to argue that she was losing her inherent home, as well as a lifelong ambition. However, she knew that it had little bearing on the need to settle things. Reluctantly, she nodded her head.

'Yes, of course. It all seems satisfactory.'

'Ah yes. Good,' Duncan said, with a sigh of relief. 'I'll have the papers drawn up as quickly as possible.' He looked at Steve, 'I believe you have already booked your return flight to New Zealand.'

'Yes, I thought I made it perfectly clear that I wanted this matter finalised by the end of the week.' Steve glowered at the old man. 'I have no desire to remain in the country any longer than necessary.'

'Ah no, of course not.' The solicitor clambered to his feet and stretched out his hand. 'Well, I'll have the documents ready to sign within the next forty-eight hours.'

After Suzi left the room, she lingered outside the door for a few minutes, but when Steve did not emerge from the building within a reasonable period, she climbed into her car, wondering why he had not taken the opportunity to discuss things. Surely there was no reason to ignore her. All the doubts and fears about his lack of interest in her resurfaced as she unwittingly drove towards the Stow Restaurant.

Mark seemed taken aback as she pushed open the kitchen door and peered around. He greeted her warily.

'How's the arm?'

'Oh, it's coming along all right,' Suzi responded, unsure why she had bothered at all to call into the restaurant. Maybe she needed to have one last look before she lost this part of her dream as well.

'We can complete everything on Wednesday,' Mark said, looking awkward. 'Dad's arranged for the transfer of the money, and has signed all the necessary papers.' He fiddled with the apron string. 'Judith will be here soon. Will you wait to say hello?'

'No, I don't think so,' she replied, indecisively. 'I might drop in another day.' She glanced around the dining room, noting the paintings on the wall and the furnishings she had so carefully selected, and sighed. The whole place bore the imprint of her personality, and now it was no longer hers. Mark watched her in silence. She turned to him and held out her hand. 'Goodbye Mark, I hope it all goes well for you.'

'Thank you, Suzi.' Mark's voice caught as he spoke. 'Maybe...' He left the sentence unfinished as if he understood the shake of her head as she walked out through the door.

She slid in behind the wheel of the Honda, grasped it with both hands and tried to blink back the tears that filled her eyes. What had she done to lose everything that was dear to her? The restaurant was gone. Soon she would have to move out of Caxton Manor, and it seemed that she had lost any chance with Steve Pardoe as well.

'What's to become of me now?' she murmured, wistfully. 'Where do I go from here?'

Chapter Thirty-One

As they made to leave Mr Duncan's office, Steve stood aside for Suzi to pass through the doorway first, but then he turned back when the solicitor called out for him to confirm the name of his hotel. Although he hurried, by the time he reached the reception area, she was nowhere in sight. He rushed outside only to see the tail end of her car disappearing around the corner.

'Oh, well, if that's how she wants to behave, so be it,' he muttered angrily. 'That's three out of three. At least she could have had the decency to pass the time of day.'

The rest of the day Steve spent wandering around Cardiff, feeling quite at a loss as to why Suzi had not wanted to talk to him. He was most disturbed that he had allowed this to affect him so deeply. At one point he even considered telephoning her to remind her that he had saved her life when she fell off the boat. But he changed his mind; if she didn't know it was he who had saved her, she would wonder what he was on about.

'Not worth the hassle,' he murmured. He reasoned that she must know what had happened, because he was convinced that Lloyd would have discussed their conversation with his wife. And he was sure Charlize would have told her what he said. Evidently, she doesn't feel the same way about things now.

After a restless night at the hotel, he checked with the receptionist several times during the morning, but there was no message from Duncan. Unwilling to idle away another day in Cardiff, Steve caught an early train to London, and wandered around the city. A chance cancellation at the Windmill Theatre provided the opportunity to see the world-famous play *The Mousetrap*. He enjoyed the show and returned to Wales that evening in a better frame of mind.

237

It was late the next morning before he received word from Duncan that the documents were ready to sign. When he enquired if Suzi would attend at the same time, the man said she had asked for an appointment later in the day. Steve breathed a sigh of relief, because he had no desire for a repeat of the atmosphere of the previous meeting.

Duncan thanked him profusely as he left, and assured Steve that he would be only too willing to represent him in any further negotiations. When he returned to the hotel, Steve checked to see if there were any phone messages for him and felt relieved that there were none. Although he desperately wanted to clear the air with Suzi, he had convinced himself that she would not want to listen to what he had to say. In the end he decided to apply his golden rule to the situation.

'What's finished, is finished,' he muttered, but he felt saddened that it had turned out the way it had. Then he asked himself why he had expected her to have any feelings for him. Maybe she had seen their time together as just one of those things that happened when a man and woman are thrown together by circumstances; circumstances that generate passion.

He had plenty of time to spare before the flight departed so he spent some time in the comfortable lounge. As he sat sipping a coffee, he still felt the need to tell Suzi why he had decided to travel to Britain rather than act through his solicitor in Auckland, and he wondered if he should write to her. And then there was another matter. He was convinced that Lloyd, through Charlize, had relayed his version of the events that had taken place in Queensland. But more importantly, he needed to salve his own conscience.

After buying a writing pad and stamped envelope in the concourse he settled down under an ornamental palm. His thoughts flowed once he set pen to paper. He wrote about his peculiar relationship with Kirsty and how he had tried to cope with the trauma of her untimely death. He mentioned about how he had wrestled with the idea of forgetting about Caxton Manor and even considered signing his half of the inheritance over to her. He closed by saying how much he regretted not having declared his feelings for her, and that he wanted her to know that even though their time together had been brief, she still occupied a very special place in his heart.

He read the letter a couple of times, unsure whether to sign and seal the envelope or tear it up. For what seemed an interminable age he sat, pen poised, in agonising indecision. Then he looked up to see an elderly woman on the next seat watching closely. She reached over and touched his arm lightly.

'Send it anyway,' she urged him. 'If nothing comes of it, you have lost nothing, but you will have been true to yourself.'

Her earnest look convinced Steve that she was right.

'Okay,' he said, with a smile. 'I'll take your advice.'

As he posted the letter, Steve felt a sense of achievement. Whether Suzi responded or not wouldn't matter now; he had declared his love, and that was enough.

The return flight was far more enjoyable, and he stepped off the plane with a great feeling of contentment. It did not matter what happened to Caxton Manor in the future, because he had hinted to Duncan that if there were any disagreement about the current arrangement, he would deed his half share over to Suzi Lysle Spencer. As far as he was concerned, he could consign it all to the past, or even treat it as if it had never happened.

*

Suzi had difficulty seeing through her tears as she drove away from the Stow Restaurant. She almost stumbled into the manor as Eileen opened the door and went straight to her room without saying a word. It took some time for her to regain her composure, and, when she finally came downstairs, Eileen had a cup of tea waiting for her.

'Are you all right, dear?' the woman asked, in a concerned voice.

'I'll be okay,' Suzi replied. 'I've just had a bit of a shock, that's all.'

'Would you like to talk about it? Sometimes it's better to get it out of your system.'

Over the next half hour Eileen coaxed Suzi to unburden herself. She made no comment as she listened to the story of love found and lost again. She listened sympathetically at how disappointed Suzi had been over not being able to turn Caxton Manor into a reception venue, and finally, she listened patiently to the distressing story of the loss of the restaurant. As she came to the end of her narrative, Suzi burst into tears again.

'I've got nothing now,' she sobbed. 'I've signed the manor away. The restaurant's gone. My dearest friend is thousands of miles away in New Zealand and I have no one to turn to.'

'How long before you have to vacate the premises?' Eileen asked.

'I've agreed to move out at the end of the month.' Suzi dabbed her eyes dry. 'It's just as well that I still have my little bungalow to go back to, but that is leased out for a year. I'll have to work out what to put into storage and what to sell.' She grasped the older woman's hand. 'But there's good news for you. The company who are leasing this building have agreed to consider you as live-in housekeeper, if you want the job.' She pulled a business card from her handbag. 'Here it is. Give them a ring now and see what they offer.'

Eileen came back from the phone with a broad smile on her face, and related her conversation with the personnel officer. The company had agreed to her status in the house, the rooms she could occupy, and a monthly wage. It was a wonderful opportunity, but she lamented the fact that it had come about at Suzi's expense.

'If things had gone the way you had planned, I'd be still be in a bedsit,' she said, quietly. 'And now I've got a lovely home. And you've got nothing.'

'It doesn't matter,' Suzi said, in a brave attempt to be cheerful. 'I can always start again, but you deserve a break after all the hard knocks you've suffered.' She kissed the woman's cheek. 'I'm happy for you.'

*

After Suzi had signed the lease documents, Duncan shook her hand warmly and repeated the promise he had made to Steve. When she returned home, Eileen said she had arranged for some large cardboard

packing cases to be collected from a nearby industrial estate. She had
begun to clear out one of the outhouses and suggested that Suzi's
things could be stored there until she had found another place for them.

'There's no need to spend money on storage if you don't have to,' she
said, firmly. 'And if you want anything in a hurry, I can find it for you.'

That evening Suzi phoned Charlize and related the events of the past
few days.

'Where are you going to live?'

'I'll find somewhere, don't worry. Between everything, I've got
enough money for that now.'

'It's a pity you've leased your house. If you'd known that Mark was
going to buy your share of the business…' She stopped short of
completing the sentence.

'Yes, I know, but it's easy to be wise in hindsight, isn't it?'

'Well, the first thing you should do is come over for a visit,' Charlize
said, in a voice that brooked no argument. 'Lloyd's mother has two
or three spare rooms and said she'd be happy to put you up for a few
weeks.'

'I'll think about it, okay?'

'No, don't think about it, ring up and book a flight now.'

The sound of footsteps crunching on the gravel driveway preceded
the deep chime of the front doorbell. Suzi said a hurried goodbye
to her friend and hung up. The postman needed her signature for a
registered package. After he had gone, she made some coffee and
carried it out into the garden. She had only just sat down on a bench
when she heard the sound of Aub's old Granada chugging up the drive.
Seeing her there, he parked it under the copper beech and sauntered
over to where she sat.

'Looks as if I'm just in time for a cuppa.' His face crinkled into a grin
as he gestured at the mug in her hand. Then he put out a restraining
hand. 'No, no, I'm teasing. I can wait until you've finished.'

'Nonsense. I'll get it for you now, because I've something to tell you.'
When she returned with his coffee, Suzi handed him Gillam's business

card and explained that she was vacating the manor within a few weeks. 'They'll need someone to look after the garden, so it might pay you to give him a ring.'

By the time she had answered Aub's queries about the new tenants, and tried to parry his questions about her plans, she was close to tears again. It seemed that whenever she talked about her situation she became overwhelmed with emotion. Rather than continue the conversation, she made an excuse to let him get on with the work, but the negative thoughts would not go away. Now, Charlize's suggestion to visit her seemed more attractive by the minute. Yes, she decided, I'll go as soon as I feel good enough to travel.

Suzi walked back into the house and picked up the bundle of mail that she had dumped on the hall table. She found a comfortable chair in the study and sifted through it. One letter stood out from all the others. The envelope bore the imprint of Heathrow Airport, and was simply addressed: Suzi Lysle Spencer, Caxton Manor. She tore it open with trembling fingers, and read the first few words aloud.

My dearest Suzi,

I am not sure whether I should be writing this letter. It seems as though things couldn't get any worse than they are right now, so it might be better if I get everything off my chest.

Her eyes filled with tears as she continued to read. Twice the letter slipped from her fingers as she stopped to consider what was written there. By the time she reached the last paragraph, it was quite obvious many of her own thoughts had been echoed here. The final words leapt out from the page:

I don't know why I felt so threatened, or why we were so hostile to each other at Mr Duncan's office. It is hard to accept that there may be a reason behind it all, but they say that nothing happens by chance. I wonder why things can't be more straightforward.

More tears sprang to her eyes as she read the bottom line.

No matter what happens, I will always remember you as someone I could have loved for a lifetime with the whole of my being.

Suzi bit her bottom lip as she recalled her nonchalant replies to his questions, and his reaction to her terse words. Why had she been so off-hand with him? He had every reason to be upset. She had eventually realised he had been the man who saved her life, and she had not even thanked him for pulling her out of the pale green waters of the Whitsunday Passage. But at least now she knew that he had made every effort to find her afterwards.

Still clutching the letter in her hand, she wandered into a secluded part of the garden and dropped down onto a bench seat. Her thoughts swung from one extreme to the other as she considered what to do. Maybe Charlize had the right idea; maybe she could move to New Zealand, and open a restaurant there, and… and… invite more heartache? No—she shook her head at the thought.

She was still staring into space when Eileen found her an hour later. The woman had seen the crumpled envelope on the floor of the study and had gone looking for her.

'Are you all right, dear?' she asked, softly. When she saw Suzi's tearstained face and swollen eyes, she pointed to the letter in her hand. 'I hope it's not bad news.'

'Good… and bad,' Suzi replied with a deep sigh.

Once again, Eileen coaxed her to share her feelings, and when Suzi had finished, she advised her to let things settle in her mind before making a decision about her future.

'Only fools and the dead don't change their minds,' she counselled. 'It's an enormous decision to make, so don't be in too much of a hurry. Wait until you can think more clearly about things. You have to be quite certain in your mind about such important matters.' She grasped Suzi's hand. 'Come on, I'll make a pot of tea then we can get on with the packing. Keep busy—that's the best idea. It'll take your mind off things.'

*

The following weeks sped by as Suzi prepared to move out of Caxton Manor. Everything she wanted to retain had been packed away, and the most of the excess furniture was up for auction. Daily trips to the physiotherapist had helped rebuild the muscles in her arm, and now it felt quite normal. She had given a great deal of thought to Charlize's invitation, and finally decided the time was right to take a holiday in New Zealand. There was no reason not to go.

When Suzi phoned Charlize, she squealed with delight.

'That's the best news you've given me for a long time. You'll love it here. The people are so friendly. I'll get Lloyd to fix things up with his mother so that you'll have somewhere to stay. You'll love her, she's ever so nice.'

'It's okay, you don't have to keep selling the place to me, I'm practically on my way. I moving out on the Thursday before Easter, so I'll book into a hotel for the night before the flight on the following day.'

'That's great, but it's a pity things turned out the way they have with Steve Pardoe,' Charlize said, sadly. 'He's a really nice guy, and Lloyd thinks…'

'And Lloyd thinks what?'

'He thinks the guy is crazy not to drag you over here.' Over the next few minutes Charlize related what had happened when Steve finally dropped in to say hello and wish them well. When she had finished, Suzi gasped.

'The letter he wrote to me before he left the country echoes what you've just told me. Now I know why he was so abrupt when we met.' She groaned softly. 'He'd taken the trouble to fly over here to settle everything, and I didn't even bother to invite him to dinner, nor ask where he was staying. I did nothing.'

'Well, it's not the end of the world,' Charlize said, in an effort tried to console her. 'He's here in Auckland, and Lloyd will be only too happy to act as an intermediary.'

'Okay, I hear you. Expect me some time over Easter.'

One week later she said goodbye to Eileen and climbed into the Honda. She forced herself not to look back as she drove out through the front gates, but her eyes still brimmed with tears.

Chapter Thirty-Two

Steve came home to find his father tucked up in bed with a bad dose of influenza. Norah had finally convinced him that it was better to stay home rather than infect the rest of his workforce, but now she was having second thoughts.

'Talk about a pain in the you-know-what,' she complained. Then she shrugged. 'He hardly ever gets sick, so I suppose it's to be expected.' She shoved Steve towards the bedroom. 'Go and talk to him, tell him the factory won't grind to a halt because neither of you is there.'

Vince brightened up as Steve came into the room. 'How'd it go, son? Everything okay now?' He didn't wait for a reply before continuing. 'Now those pumps. Burt seems to think there's a big problem so you'd better slip down there straight away and sort it out.'

'Okay, I'll take care of it.'

Within a few days Steve felt as if he had never been away. He soon found out why the equipment wasn't working a hundred percent and rectified the problem. By the time everything was running smoothly again, Vince had recovered enough to return to work—much to Norah's relief.

The three of them were sitting around the table a few nights later discussing Steve's trip to Wales, when Norah brought up the subject of houses. She and Vince had finally chosen a smaller place, but there were only two bedrooms.

'That means no spare room.' Steve looked from one to the other. 'I get the hint. You mean it's time I found a place for myself.' He grinned. 'Okay. Now that I've straightened out the mess in Britain, solved the pump problem, and had time to recover from my jetlag, I suppose I should start looking.'

'Well, it doesn't look too bright does it?' Vince said, looking over the top of his wineglass. 'I mean the managing director of Voxlin living at home with his parents. It's not very impressive, is it?'

'Managing director?'

'Yes, it's about time I took a back seat and let you run the show. You've proved time and again that you do a better job than I can now.' He reached across the table. 'Congratulations son, you've made the big time.'

'And you deserve it,' Norah added.

The rest of the workforce was equally surprised by Vince's decision, but they were unanimous in adding their congratulations. It was decided to close the workshop an hour earlier than usual the following Friday and celebrate at the nearest pub. Most of the staff were married, so after a few drinks they made their excuses and left. Vince bought one more round, and then declared the party over.

The next morning Steve took a taxi to town and picked up his car, and then he spent the afternoon looking at houses that were being advertised for sale. The rest of the weekend he spent driving around the bay area, still looking, but finding nothing he fancied. He approached Harry Wisecombe to see what he might have, but he had nothing to offer.

'I'll let you know the moment something special comes on the market. I know the kind of place you're looking for,' he said, as Steve bade him goodbye.

When the remaining pumps were dispatched to North Queensland, both Steve and his father gave a sigh of relief. It had been touch and go whether they would meet the deadline. Nick Bolte had promised to phone when they arrived and keep them up to date with the installation, so they were both dismayed when the man's daughter rang a few days later.

'Dad's been rushed to hospital,' she said. 'He went fishing this morning, jumped in the water to untangle his line from the propeller, and landed on a jellyfish.'

'How bad is he?'

'The doctor says he'll be all right, but it's a bit scary. It was just pure luck that a friend was close by and took him to hospital before any irreparable damage was done.' Her voice faded for a moment. 'He'll be upset that he's let you down.'

'It's okay. Don't you worry, and tell Nick we'll take care of it.'

Vince turned to Steve. 'Looks like a job for the managing director,' he joked. Then he became serious. 'Sorry son, but you're the only one who can do it. We can't rely on casual workers at this stage.'

'That's okay. Nick was going to do the Babinda job first, but he didn't explain why. Never mind, I'll sort it out when I get there. I'd better book a flight to Brisbane now.'

'When will you leave?'

'Easter Saturday is as good a time as any.'

The next few days were spent checking that everything had been dispatched and arrived safely. Steve packed a selection of tools and tossed in his own hard hat for good measure. A punctured rear tyre nearly caused him to miss the plane. As Vince roared up the departure terminal and stopped with a squeal of tyres Steve jumped out of the car. He yanked a bag from the back seat, banged the car roof and ran into the building. The stewardess looked pointedly at her watch as he raced up the walkway and into the waiting aircraft.

'Another minute and you'd have been left at the gate,' she remarked dryly. She pointed to the nearest seat. 'Sit there until we've taken off.'

As she spoke, the aircraft moved away from the loading area and headed towards the runway. Ten minutes later they were airborne.

*

Suzi's flight was delayed because one of the pilots had to be replaced at the last moment, but the passengers were assured that the lost time would be made up before the plane reached New Zealand. The captain had been right, and they touched down at Auckland within minutes of the scheduled time. Charlize waved frantically as Suzi walked into the reception hall. The two women clung to each other for a long time as they embraced.

'It's so lovely to see you again,' Charlize sniffed. 'You wouldn't believe how much I've missed you.'

'But you've got Lloyd.'

'Yes, but I've still missed you. Come on, let's go.' She picked up one of Suzi's bags and led the way out of the terminal. 'Lloyd is nearly as excited as I am about it all. His parents are visiting friends at Cormandel Peninsula over the weekend so you can stay with us until they return.'

The two women were just about to cross the road when a car pulled up outside the departure terminal with a squeal of tyres. A man jumped out, pulled a bag from the back seat, slapped a hand on the car roof and ran into the building. Suzi stared at the running figure and then grabbed Charlize's arm.

'I swear that man looked like Steve Pardoe.'

'What man? Where?'

'Never mind, he's gone now,' she said, as the man disappeared into the crowd of people thronging the concourse. 'It was probably my imagination.'

The two women spent the first day catching up on each other's news. Charlize arranged a party for the following evening to introduce Suzi to her new circle of friends. She confided that she had also invited Steve, reasoning that if they met on neutral ground it would be better for them both.

And now, as they gathered in the lounge, Suzi looked in vain for Steve. The disappointment was almost crushing. Then Lloyd appeared at her side.

'I've just had a phone call from Steve's mother to say he's been called to an urgent job in Australia. Apparently their representative in North Queensland has been rushed to hospital and Steve was the only person who could supervise the installation of their pumps.' He clasped Suzi's hand. 'I'm so sorry to disappoint you, Suzi. His mother apologised for not phoning sooner, but she forgot.'

'When did he go?'

'Saturday.'

'Then it really was Steve I saw at the airport.' She sniffed softly, as Charlize joined them. 'Why do things keep going pear shape?'

'He might be back before you leave.'

'Don't count on it,' Suzi said bitterly. Then she turned to her friend. 'Sorry Charlize, I don't want to spoil your party.' She looked meaningfully at the collection of bottles on a nearby table. 'Let's get hammered and forget about it all.'

She almost tiptoed out into the kitchen the next morning. Charlize laughed at her woebegone expression.

'You did nothing out of the way, so there's no harm done.' She put her arm around Suzi. 'What will you do now that Steve's out of the picture?' When Suzi hesitated, she continued. 'I had hoped to spend more time with you, but my workload has suddenly increased, and I'm afraid the next few weeks will be critical to the success of my work here. I am so sorry, Suzi.'

'That's okay, I'll take off and have a look around by myself, and then I'll make up my own mind about the place.'

Lloyd returned from a round of golf just before lunch and suggested that they should take advantage of the lovely weather to have a look at some of the northern beaches. By the time they returned late that afternoon Suzi understood why Charlize was so enamoured with the country. She was really impressed with the bay area and could well understand why the properties there attracted such high prices.

'Come on,' Lloyd said, the next day. 'I'll take you on a tour of the suburbs on the south side of the harbour.' Suzi enjoyed looking around, but by mid-afternoon the main roads were filling up with holidaymakers returning home after the Easter break. 'Time to head home,' he said, 'and we'll finish off the day by eating out at the bistro this evening—it's a smart place.'

*

The next day Suzi caught the train to Wellington, and had just settled into the window seat when an elderly gentleman sat down next to her. He doffed his hat as he said hello.

'So we're travelling companions.' A smile played around his lips. 'Now if I get too garrulous you just tell me to shut up. I won't be offended.'

'I wouldn't do that,' Suzi said. 'I'm sure you're the perfect gentleman.' When he nodded she glanced at the unusual badge fastened to his coat lapel. 'Are you a returned service man?'

'Yes, I am, and somehow I've managed to outlive most of my contemporaries.'

'That's quite an achievement.'

'I suppose so. Now let me tell you something. When we gather to honour our dead companions we offer a prayer that contains the lines... "Age shall not weary them nor the years condemn..."'

'"And at the going down of the sun, and in the morning, we shall remember them."' Suzi finished the quotation.

'That's very good.' The old man sniffed. 'Unfortunately age wearies those of us that survive.' Then he gestured at the airline label on her carry bag. 'I can see you're not from this part of the world, and you're definitely not Scottish. Irish... perhaps?'

'Welsh.'

'Ah yes, I've read a few books about Wales. *The Stars Look Down* and *How Green is my Valley*. Dreadful times, such suffering and hardship for those poor people.' He paused to allow her to respond and then went on. 'Things have improved in Wales since those days, I should hope.'

'Yes, they have. All the mines have closed, except for one that's kept open for tourists. The economy is bustling, though.'

'Good, now let me tell you all about this beautiful land you're visiting.'

The old man kept up a running commentary as the train made its way through the pleasant green countryside. By the time they reached Wellington, Suzi knew a great deal more about New Zealand than when they had started. He grasped her hand as they prepared to leave the carriage.

'Now, remember what I said, don't fly back to Auckland... catch a bus. Stop off at Taupo and have a look at Rotorua, and visit the hot pools.' He chuckled. 'But don't get up to any tricks in the rivers—they are heated by the geysers, and can harbour some nasty bugs.'

Suzi kissed his cheek and made her way out of the railway station and then she caught a cab to the city centre. She spent the next day strolling around the windy capital.

Chapter Thirty-Three

Nick Bolte forced a grin on his face as Steve approached the hospital bed.

'Sorry about this, mate.' He spread his hands wide. 'I should've known better to jump in the water without looking, but…' He stopped again.

'Never mind. Just get well again.'

'Yeah. I thought I'd be up and about in a few days, but there are complications. Secondary infection or something.'

'Just as well you were rushed here then.'

'Yeah, you're right.' Nick grimaced at the memory. 'You can't imagine the pain. It was horrific. I passed out a couple of times on the way into town. Anyway enough of my problems, so, to put you in the picture, let me tell you what I've done so that you can get on with the job straight away.'

Steve was delighted that everything went according to plan, but it took longer than he had anticipated, so he had to work through the two next weekends. He finally flew down to Brisbane late Tuesday afternoon, two weeks after he had arrived there, and the next day he caught a plane back to Auckland.

Vince met him at the airport.

'You look a bit ragged, son. Everything go all right?

'As well as could be expected, but I had to put in a lot of hours.' He threw his bag on the back seat. 'I'll need a couple of weeks off to recover.'

'How's Nick?' Vince asked, ignoring the hint.

'He's all right. Well, no, he's not all right, but he's on the mend. He showed me his leg.' Steve shuddered. 'It's a terrible mess. He'll be scarred for life.'

'But he's still on side.'

'Yes, he'll be able to check that everything's operating okay. I think we'll do well over there, now that we've got our foot in the door.'

*

After spending a night in Nelson, Suzi continued south to Greymouth and caught the TranzAlpine Express to Christchurch. The travel agency had made arrangements for her to take a tour that started the following day. It included Mount Cook, Queenstown, and Milford Sound.

After dinner one evening she made her way up a gentle slope to a little sanctuary that overlooked the surrounding countryside on one side, and Lake Taupo on the other. The restful environment was in direct contrast to the hustle and bustle of the past few weeks and within a very short time the world and its problems all seemed to fade away.

One by one the events that had caused her so much trouble were gently consigned to the past. A face swam into view. Mark still wore his chef's hat, but she could barely distinguish his features from the line of men who stretched out behind him. Men who had pursued her over years with varying degrees of success—the fiery Italian, Giorgio, the cuddly Andy, the bookish Cedric, and many more.

A wave of sadness engulfed her. Could she have found lasting happiness with any of them? It seemed not. The women who had featured so strongly in her life seemed to materialise against the backdrop to the starlight night—her waspish mother, June, and Judith, and Uncle Bart's half-sister, whose 'old worldliness', had enchanted her as a child. Each had played a role helping her to become the person she was. But who was she? The answer continued to elude her.

A discreet cough behind her brought her back to the present. She looked around to see a member of the staff standing in the doorway. The affable man held up a set of keys.

'We usually lock the doors at night,' he said, quietly.

'Of course.' Suzi climbed to her feet and stretched. 'I've been here for hours.'

'Yes, it has that effect on people, and it'll be open first thing in the morning if you want to return early.'

The images that had been impressed on her mind repeated themselves in vivid dreams that night. It was only when she thought more deeply about the succession of faces in her dreams that she realised two were missing—Charlize and Steve Pardoe. She could understand why her friend could not be consigned to the past because they still enjoyed a close relationship. But Steve? Maybe she hadn't finished with him yet.

As soon as she had finished breakfast the next day, she decided continue with her journey. The bus trip to Rotorua was marred by a nasty road accident, but they were only delayed for a short time. She spent the following day visiting the Maori settlement, talking to some of the older inhabitants, and standing silently in the Kiwi house to catch a glimpse of the shy nocturnal bird. On return to the hotel she took advantage of their spa and lazed away the evening in a small, intimate lounge. The next morning she headed north to Auckland where Charlize welcomed her back with open arms.

'Well, tell me all about it—what you did, who you met, and so on. I wanted to know everything.' She sat down close to Suzi and took her hand. 'I'm taking tomorrow off so that we can spend some time together before you go back home. It's going to come pretty fast, and then you'll be gone.' She shook her head. 'I'll miss you like hell, Suzi Lysle Spencer.'

After stowing Suzi's bags in the boot of her BMW the next morning, Charlize paused before starting the engine. 'At the risk of repealing myself… .'

'I know, I know… if ever I want to come back, Lloyd will use his influence with the right people to help me get started in some kind of business.' She touched Charlize's arm. 'If I had to make a decision right now, I'd cancel my ticket and stay, but I need to think things through first.'

They both shed a few tears as they parted outside the departure gate, and Suzi was still a bit dewy eyed when she boarded the aircraft an hour later. The trip back to England was uneventful and, by the time she had reclaimed the Honda from the long-stay car park, it was mid-morning.

Where to go and what to do? She headed west on the M4 until she came to the turn off for Oxford, and from there she headed west through Gloucester and Hereford. Something was drawing her towards Lampeter.

*

Norah handed Steve a letter when he came home that evening. 'This arrived two days ago.'

He studied the unfamiliar handwriting and grimaced. He turned the envelope over—there was no return address, but it bore an Auckland postmark.

'I wonder who this is from,' he murmured, tearing it open. As he read it, he gave a gasp.

Dear Steve,

I've spent a great deal of time agonising over what I should write. I had been looking forward to seeing you again, but for some reason or other fate kept us apart. I dearly wanted to say I'm sorry that I was so insensitive and inconsiderate when we met in Mr Duncan's office.

Steve felt a lump form in his throat as he continued to read. In many ways the letter seemed to echo the very thoughts and feelings he had also entertained about Suzi. It was as if she had tapped into his mind as she wrote it. The next two pages contained a summary of what had happened over the past few months. She lamented that she had not made a greater effort to find him at Airlie Beach, and then she went on to explain why she had terminated the partnership with Mark. Finally, she mentioned Caxton Manor, and said she was both relieved and pleased that it had not been sold.

Maybe in time I can let it go too, but at the moment it would be too great a wrench.

Once again Steve allowed his mind to slip back to their last meeting, and then he returned to the letter. Suzi's closing paragraph seemed even more poignant.

Both Charlize and Lloyd are urging me to come back to New Zealand soon. Lloyd has promised to make sure there is no problem concerning residence, and

Charlize dearly wants to keep our friendship alive. I feel the same way—we need each other. In the short time I've been here I can understand why she has fallen in love with the country. It really is special.

First, I must return to my roots, because when I am surrounded by things and places that I love, I will be better able to tell whether you mean more to me than anything else in this world. Then, I will consider whether I should come back.

He stared at the last few words took a deep breath and read them again. *I can't just take a chance that you feel the same way about me. So I will wait until I'm sure.*

As he finished the letter, Norah came back into the room.

'Are you all right, Steve?' she asked, anxiously.

'Yes, and no,' he replied, then uncharacteristically handed her the letter. 'I'd like you to read this.'

Norah handed it back to him with a sigh. 'That's the woman you've been waiting for isn't it? What are you going to do about it?'

'I don't know,' he replied hesitantly. 'I'll have to think about it first.'

*

As Suzi drove slowly down the main street of Lampeter she noted that it hadn't changed much. The shops looked the same, the pubs looked the same, and even the groups of students lounging on the pavement looked the same. But of course it was all different now, because she had changed.

It took her only a short time to realise that it had been a mistake to return to the town where she had spent her childhood. She wondered why she felt the need to distance herself from the Stow Restaurant and Caxton Manor. Was she concerned about meeting old friends, or the customers she had cultivated over the years? Did she think the past wouldn't catch up with her in this part of Wales?

The next morning she rang Eileen to say she was on her way back. It was mid-afternoon when she pulled up in front of the manor. The garden was in full bloom and a number of executive-range cars were parked neatly to one side of the building. The receptionist smiled sweetly as she walked into the foyer.

'Can I help you?'

When Suzi explained that she wished to speak to Eileen, the woman stiffened momentarily and said, 'I'll call her for you.'

The middle-aged woman seemed to be delighted to see her again so soon and embraced her for a long time. With her help, Suzi sorted out some of the things she needed for her immediate personal use, then she made a list of what she was going to send for auction. The few pieces of furniture that remained could be stored until she decided what to do about them. Once back at the hotel she was using, Suzi sat quietly and contemplated her future. With so much on her mind, she spent a restless night and was glad to see dawn breaking, and even more pleased to hear the familiar voice of Eileen when she rang her the next morning

'There's a letter here for you. It's postmarked New Zealand, from a Steve Pardoe. Shall I forward it to you?'

'No, I'll come and pick it up.'

Suzi couldn't get there fast enough. She grabbed the blue airmail letter, and ran to the privacy of her car with it. She slit it open hurriedly and scanned the contents. Then she sank back into the car seat and read them again.

Dearest Suzi, it began, and then went on to repeat many of the words and phrases she had used in her letter to him. Steve made it quite clear that he understood why she had reacted so strangely in Duncan's office, and blamed himself for not making a greater effort to sort things out while he was in Britain. He closed with the words.

I really hope you will come back one day and we can have a chance to talk.

That evening she made up her mind to go, and phoned Charlize.

'Expect me by the end of the week. I'll get everything sorted out and I'll let you know when I'll be there.'

'That's wonderful. I'll get Lloyd to see what he can do to hurry things along when you get here.' She was just about to say goodbye when she said, 'What about Steve?'

'I dare say that'll sort itself out one day,' Suzi said. 'I think maybe we've both been given a chance to redeem the past.'

'That's wonderful,' Charlize's voice rose with excitement. 'Would you like Lloyd to drop the hint that you're coming back soon, or do you want to surprise him?'

'What do you think?'

Chapter Thirty-Four

As they sat around, relaxing, Charlize looked at Lloyd and then back at Suzi again.

'So you want to buy a house straight away, Suzi? Why?'

'Because it'll give me a base and make it easier for me to establish credit.'

'She's right,' Lloyd agreed, 'although I'd be inclined to settle for a flat in the city first up, and then look around for a property.'

'No. I don't want to live in the city.' Suzi picked up a map of the northern beaches and tapped it. 'I want a place there. Somewhere reasonably close to the city, but unaffected by the suburban sprawl.'

'Okay. Let's see who can help.' Lloyd punched a name into his mobile phone and waited for an answer. 'Hello Geoff, it's Lloyd Bridgestone. Look, a friend of ours has just arrived from the UK and she's wants something special.' He nodded. 'Yes, that's what I told her. Okay, I'll put her on.' He handed the phone to Suzi. 'Right, you tell him what you're looking for.'

'Well?' Charlize asked, with an engaging smile as Suzi finished talking. 'If he's got anything suitable we might as well take a run up there now.'

The two women spent all afternoon inspecting the available houses, but nothing caught Suzi's fancy. They drove down to a small cove and wandered along the sandy shore until a chilly wind forced them back to the car. As they headed back towards the city, Charlize asked, 'And what about Steve? You didn't tell us if you want us to do something. Lloyd could arrange to bump into him somewhere.'

'No, leave it be. We'll meet at the right place at the right time.'

Two days later Geoff Spencer rang to say they had just listed a new property, and urged Suzi to view it as soon as possible because he expected it to be snapped up. Charlize agreed to run her out to see it the following day, and it was mid-morning before they parked outside Wisecombe and Spencer's offices. Both of the partners were out so the receptionist gave them directions to find the place.

As they left, she called after them, 'There's a house across the road that might suit, so you might as well look at that one as well, while you're there.'

*

Steve was just about to go out that evening when Norah called him to the phone.

'It's Harry Wisecombe.'

The man acknowledged his greeting and then said, 'Look Mr Pardoe, I don't want to sound as if I'm pushing you into anything, but I've got something that should suit you down to the ground. The price is right and the vendor is desperate to sell.' He listed some the salient features of the house, and then urged Steve to act immediately if he was at all interested. 'It won't last long... not at that price.'

'Okay, I'll come up first thing tomorrow.'

'Well, be early, because I'd hate to see you miss out again.'

After he had said goodbye, Steve told his mother what Wisecombe had said, and admitted that after months of inspecting properties, he had come to the conclusion that he would never find what he wanted. But even as he spoke he began to wonder if this could be the right one. On impulse, he rang back and arranged to meet the estate agent outside the property the next day.

A sense of anticipation permeated his whole being as he drove to see the house the next morning, but he could not explain why he felt that way. 'I'll know soon enough,' he murmured, pulling up outside an attractive bungalow that bore the name, 'Rutherglen'.

'Good morning.' Harry Wisecombe shook Steve's hand as he climbed out of car. 'I must warn you I've got a feeling that Geoff is trying to sell this one from under me.' He gestured to the 'For Sale' sign outside a house on the other side of the road. 'I'm pretty sure the couple of women who are looking at that place right now will be over here in minutes.'

'Will that matter?'

'Well, this is a much more attractive property.' He gave a nervous laugh. 'It would be a pity to have it snapped up under your nose, wouldn't it? If you fancy it, of course.'

Steve gave the blue BMW a cursory glance and followed Harry up the garden path. When Harry rang the doorbell, the vendor answered and invited them inside. Almost at the same time, Charlize and Suzi emerged from the other property directly across the road. They checked the estate agent's brochure, and walked over to the house that Steve was already viewing.

The vendor was answering Steve's questions when the front doorbell rang again. He suggested that the estate agent continue to show Steve around the house, and excused himself to answer the door. After a few minutes he returned and looked quizzically at Harry.

'I was unaware that your partner had also arranged for someone to look at my bungalow this morning. Shall I ask them to wait until you're finished? He looked beseechingly at the two men. 'I know it may not be altogether ethical, but I hate turning anyone away.'

'That's okay,' Steve replied, 'but give me first refusal, because I think this is what I've been looking for.'

The man returned to the front door and asked the two women inside. 'Someone else is viewing this bungalow right now,' he said, 'and he's more than just interested in it, but you're welcome to look around.'

'Oh, now I really like this. It's lovely,' Suzi said, as she walked into the kitchen area. 'Lots of bench space, big cupboards… and a great view of the sea. Oh yes, I like it.' As she continued to inspect each room, Suzi became more and more enthusiastic. 'It's ideal. It's exactly what I had in mind. I think I'll make an offer straight away.'

Somehow or other the two parties continued to move around without making contact. Suzi and Charlize walked into the reception hall just as Steve and the estate agent came back into the house from the garage. They both approached the vendor from different angles as he stood in the hallway.

The look on his face was picture of disbelief when they both chorused at the same time:

'This is what I'm looking for.'

The man looked from Steve to Suzi and back again.

'But you can't both have it.'

At that moment Steve caught sight of Suzi. He caught his breath and stood still as though transfixed. Then he moved quickly across the hall.

'Suzi Lysle Spencer,' he exclaimed, with disbelief, as he reached out for her.

'Steve Pardoe. Oh Steve.' Suzi pushed past the vendor and threw herself into his arms.

As they embraced, Charlize gently shoved the two men into the sitting room out of the way.

'Oh, my Suzi,' Steve whispered into her hair. 'I'm never going to let you go again.' He whispered her name again and again before gently tipping her head back to look into her face. The depth of love he saw in her eyes convinced him beyond any doubt that it was right to love her so deeply. Then, as he pressed his lips to hers, Suzi sighed contentedly.

'I knew it would all come right in the end,' she said. 'I just knew.'

Charlize watched from the doorway with the happiest of smiles, and lifted her eyes to the heavens. She gave a naughty wink.

'Well… I don't know who arranged this, but the place is right, the time is right, and Suzi was right. Those two can't deny their destiny—it was written in the stars.'